To Anne

Something Like Happy

Sasha Greene

with best wishes for your own writing!

hi

A division of HarperCollins*Publishers*

www.harpercollins.co.uk

Harper*Impulse* an imprint of
HarperCollins*Publishers*
The News Building
1 London Bridge Street
London SE1 9GF

www.harpercollins.co.uk

This paperback edition 2019

First published in Great Britain in ebook format by
HarperCollins*Publishers* 2019

A catalogue record for this book
is available from the British Library

ISBN: 9780008325015

This novel is entirely a work of fiction.
The names, characters and incidents portrayed in it are
the work of the author's imagination. Any resemblance to
actual persons, living or dead, events or localities is
entirely coincidental.

Set in Birka by Palimpsest Book Production Ltd, Falkirk
Stirlingshire

Printed and bound in Great Britain by
CPI Group (UK) Ltd, Croydon CR0 4YY

To anyone who has thought they would never get through the day, but somehow managed.

You are amazing.

And in memory of all those who couldn't.

Chapter 1

Nick leaned over the grey stone parapet, considering the distance to the road below. It should be enough to kill him. His heart pounded at the thought, but it was the easiest way he could think of. One simple jump, and he'd be gone. And even if he didn't succeed, at the very least he'd be in hospital, which would mean a blessed release from his daily grind and the ache of loneliness that wore him down.

He focused his gaze on the skyline and gripped the rough surface with his shaking hands. Easy peasy. All he had to do was close his eyes and jump. He went through the motions in his imagination. Early tomorrow would do it. Sunday morning was always deserted. He needed just a little more time to gather his courage.

It had to be tomorrow. There was no other choice. No way he could go back into that office on Monday morning.

When Jade saw the figure on the bridge, standing tall in his bright blue jacket, she thought at first he was looking at the scenery. But as she came closer, she saw his eyes were closed. White knuckles gripped on tightly to the edge, and she suddenly knew exactly what was going on.

You have to talk to him.

This wasn't how she had imagined her sunny Saturday panning out. A casual stroll through town, up the hill, look at the view. Definitely not getting involved in the life of someone who was obviously planning to jump.

Really? When you know exactly what this bridge means to you? Do you want to make the same mistake twice? You could do something right for once.

She clenched her fists, fully intending to walk on by, but found her mouth opening. 'I wouldn't lean so far over if I were you.'

A female voice broke into Nick's thoughts. That was definitely a local accent from the sound of it. He felt a surge of irritation hit him and didn't bother turning to look at who was behind him. Jeez, what was wrong with this place? His life was filled with people telling him what to do, and now he couldn't even plan his suicide in peace without someone interfering.

'Go away.' He folded his arms, standing stiffly, ready to wait until she disappeared.

'It'll hurt if you splat on the road.'

Her matter of fact tone and choice of words surprised him, and he swivelled to look at the speaker. A short, waif-like girl stood in front of him. She looked no more than eighteen. Her pale skin clashed horribly with her long dyed jet-black hair, which was gathered up in the worst-kept hairstyle ever. Wait, was that strips of sparkly green in among the black? Her bright red coat combined with her goth-style hair was like nothing he had seen before in his life.

'Go away.' He turned away. 'Leave me in peace.'

'You don't look like you want to be left in peace. You look sad. Sad people normally want cheering up.' It was childlike, how direct she was. And somehow kind of refreshing.

Nick turned again and frowned at her. 'Don't kids of your age have better things to do than harass strangers?'

'Kids?' She folded her arms, squinting at him against the sun. 'I'm twenty-fucking-three, for God's sake.'

The same age as himself. Now that he looked closer at her, he could actually see fine lines at the corner of her eyes. He was willing to give her the twenty-three, although she still looked young for her age.

Nick couldn't help himself. 'Do you always swear so much?'

She shrugged. 'Sometimes.'

This just wasn't how Nick had imagined his day panning out. Here he was, stuck on a bridge, arguing with someone about swear words. It all seemed kind of surreal.

'Anyway,' the girl said, looking as if all this discussion bored her, 'I came to give you my happy list. You look like you need it.' The cold spring wind whipped her hair around her face, and she reached for a handful, tucking it behind her ear.

'Your what?' Nick frowned again. He wasn't quite following. His brain, so focused on what he had been thinking about before she interrupted him, was struggling to catch up.

'A happy list. I wrote it. It's things to do when I feel sad. To cheer me up.' She spoke slowly, as if she was speaking to someone in a foreign language.

'Like a bucket list?' Nick was intrigued.

She blew out her cheeks, obviously considering the idea. 'Kind of, I guess. But a bucket list is things to do before you die. These are things you can do all the time.'

'Anyway.' She made a dismissive gesture with one hand. 'If you want to come with me to the top of the hill, I'll show you the first thing on the list.'

She turned and walked away towards the gravel path that wound up through the scattered tombstones of the Necropolis, leaving him staring after her. His head swivelled back to the drop below. It was a choice between his own dark thoughts and the idea of talking to someone who claimed to have the answer to happiness. It took only a moment before he hurried after her.

Jade crossed her fingers tightly in her pockets as she walked away. Had she said enough to hook him? Or had she been too harsh? A surreptitious glance behind her showed that he was following her, and she breathed a quick sigh of relief. At least she had got him away from the edge. Now all she had to do was work out how to convince him that life was better than the alternative. Yeah. All she had to do was that. Just exactly what had she got herself into here? And how the hell was she going to do it?

Nick caught up with the red coat when she was already halfway up the slope, breathing hard as he came alongside her. He hadn't realised how much he had let himself go over the last six months. He looked at her, expecting another pithy comment, but she just smiled politely at him and continued walking.

He found himself considering a heavily decorated gravestone to his right. The Necropolis. A strange idea really. Rich people, paying vast sums of money to make sure they were remembered when they died. It all looked very impressive, he thought. But did anyone really remember who these people were?

They walked in silence all the way up the winding path, until they came to the top and the girl sat down on the steps of a large stone tomb. Seating himself beside her on the chilly stone, Nick realised that from here they could see pretty much all of Glasgow. In fact, he had never really seen it quite like this. An impressive mix of architecture spread out below him, framed by the curves of the hills beyond. Sunshine glinted off the tiny wind turbines in the distance.

'I'm Nick, by the way.' He offered a hand.

She took it gingerly. 'Jade.' Her hand was cool, but firm.

Nick looked out at the view again. 'So, what's this list you're talking about?' He couldn't help asking. Any chance at happiness was worth a shot.

'Well, this is number one.' She gestured with her hands. 'Go and look at a stunning view.'

She spoke the last words as if she was reciting something she had committed to memory.

'Is that it?' Nick was surprised. 'I'd expected something, well, more dramatic.'

'And you call this not dramatic?' She pointed at the view.

He had to admit that she was right. White fluffy clouds raced along the mountain tops. Below them the busy sounds of the city echoed up, blown to them on the wind. The seagulls whirled, shrieking as they dived among the tops of the mass of buildings below them. The variation in architecture was pretty amazing. Brutal sixties monstrosities combined with elegant Victorian buildings and to their right the squat spires of the cathedral reminded him of the ancient history of the city.

'I take it you're not local then?' It was more of a statement than a question from Jade.

'No.' Nick wondered how she had guessed, but then realised that his accent would mark him out, just as clearly as hers had showed she was Glasgow-raised. 'I'm from Fort William.'

Jade looked at him for a long while, as if considering something. The grey smudges under her eyes stood out in her pale face. 'Tell you what. Meet me next Saturday and I'll tell you the second thing on the list.'

'I thought you were just going to give me the list.' Nick didn't know if he wanted to get involved with what she was suggesting. He didn't know her. This could just be some trick. To get him to –

To get you to what, exactly? His brain gave him a mental slap. *Five minutes ago you were thinking about killing yourself. What have you got to lose?* He found his hands were trembling again and he tucked them under his arms, hoping she hadn't noticed.

He pushed away the part of him whispering that he shouldn't get involved. Making connections when he wasn't going to be around much longer would just be an added complication. But then, if he met this girl next weekend, that meant another week in his job. Living with the snide comments and the subtle bullying. Could he really do that? Was he really strong enough?

'OK,' he found himself saying.

Jade looked him directly in the eyes, a worried frown on her face. 'You promise?'

The sunlight turned her brown eyes into gold-flecked pools that seemed to hypnotise his brain. 'I promise.'

Jade got up, brushing off her hands. 'Great. Ten a.m. Clydebank station. Don't be late.' She started to walk off down the hill.

'Wait,' he called after her. 'You should give me your number.'

She waved a thin hand dismissively, not even bothering to turn. 'No need. I know you'll be there. A promise is a promise.'

As soon as she knew she was out of sight Jade sank down behind a nearby grave stone, making sure she was hidden from his view. Her legs were suddenly wobbly.

Talking to Nick had brought back images that she just didn't want to see again, and they played out in her head like some kind of disjointed horror film. She balled up her fists into her eyes, but tears squeezed slowly out the sides and ran down her arms, chilling her skin as the wind dried them away.

See. This is why I didn't want to get involved.

She needed to, though. For herself and her own sanity. She couldn't go back and change the past, but if she could change the future, help someone else in the same situation, then maybe she could start to trust herself again. Maybe she could learn to sleep at night.

After a long while she lifted her head, staring out across the vast expanse in front of her. She took a deep breath, and then another one. She could be strong. She would be strong. She had Mum. And Dad. And Lily. And, just maybe, with Nick, she had the chance to redeem herself. To try and make things right.

Fumbling for a tissue in her handbag, she rose stiffly and began the slow walk back down the hill and towards home.

The sun was low in the sky by the time she put her keys in the front door. She opened the door to a warmth and a smell of food that made her stomach rumble. Her mother, she found in the kitchen as usual, her head bent over a pan. When she saw Jade she wrapped her in her arms and, ignoring her protests, smoothed back her hair.

'Where have you been all this time?' The question was not demanding, just curious.

'Just around the city.' Jade didn't really want to share what had happened with Nick. 'I went out up to the Necropolis and then I walked home.'

'What, all the way from town?' Her mother stirred the sauce, anxious not to let it burn.

Jade shrugged. 'It's not far, just a few miles.' She noticed the size of the pot. 'What, are we having a party around for dinner again?'

Her mother laughed, pushing back her own short black hair as she did so. 'No. Just meals to put in the freezer. I thought I would make some for you to take to work.'

Jade sighed, torn between love for her mother and an ongoing irritation at how she never listened. 'Mum. You know we get food at work.'

Her mother tutted, stirring the pot again. 'Yes. Chips and burgers and all that rubbish. No wonder you are so pale these days. I'm making you some proper food with vitamins in it.'

Jade was going to complain again but gave up and hugged her instead. 'You're the best, Mum, you know that.' Her mother blushed, unused to such compliments from her daughter.

Jade sat down at the table, ready to sink into the warmth of the kitchen. But she couldn't get the image of the man on the bridge out of her mind.

'What's wrong?' The question intruded into her thoughts, and she looked up, surprised.

'What do you mean?'

Her mother pointed at the table. 'Usually I put crisps out, they're gone in five minutes.'

Jade looked, and yes, there was a blue bowl on the table. She took a handful, savouring the sharp tang of the vinegar. 'My favourite. Thanks Mum.'

She told her mother about Nick.

'Oh, Jade.' The older woman closed her eyes. 'Not the same place. What made you want to go up there?'

Jade reached for her hand, squeezing it tightly. 'I'm fine, Mum, really I am. It's just my way of dealing with it.'

Her mum squeezed back briefly before returning to the stove. 'Well Jade, you know best,' she said, determination in her tone. 'You know I just want you to be happy, that's all.'

There were a few minutes silence, then she turned towards Jade again. 'Go and call your dad in for dinner.'

Jade went next door into the living room. The TV was on, but her dad had fallen asleep on the big black sofa as usual. She hated to disturb him when he was like this. He'd be out at work all night and he needed all the sleep he could get.

She put a hand gently on his shoulder, and he stirred, smiling up at her. 'There's my girl. Must be time for dinner, eh?'

There was very little conversation during dinner, as they sat round the little table in the kitchen. Jade preferred it like this now that there were just three of them. The warmth of the kitchen enclosed them as if the house was hugging them, and while they were here Jade could block out thoughts of what real life was like and just pretend that things would go on like this for ever.

Eventually Jade's dad rose, wiping his mouth. 'Best be off,' he said. 'Taxi fares don't grow on trees.' He wrapped his arms around his wife and kissed her soundly. 'Thanks for the dinner, sweetheart.' She squeezed his bum playfully, while Jade said 'Eew, get a room!' and they all laughed together. It was a ritual that had been played out ever since she could remember, and she couldn't imagine a family dinner without it. She held the image in her mind, savouring the warmth it generated in her thoughts.

Jade helped wash up and then went to her room. She lay on her bed, staring at the ceiling. She suddenly wished she had taken Nick's number. She felt an overwhelming urge just to contact him. She was so curious to find out his story. Who he was, where he came from, the whole works. But no, she would just have to wait until next Saturday. Patience is a virtue, she reminded herself with a little smile. That's what Grandma would have said.

She looked over to where the photos sat on the small white bookcase. Growing up she had always wondered why people had pictures of dead people lying around, but now she knew. Her grandma smiled out from her frame, looking encouraging, as she always had. She must have been a strong woman, thought Jade. Having a Chinese woman as a daughter in law, at a time when the communities barely talked to each other, must have been tough. But then, anyone seeing Jade's parents together couldn't doubt that they were deeply in love; even now, after almost thirty years of marriage. She lay back on her pillows, thinking about all these good things, and let the feelings of warmth and caring wrap around her like a blanket.

Nick lay on his bed, fiddling with his watch. The whole thing today had just seemed surreal. That girl – Jade – appearing out of nowhere, just at the time when he was at his lowest point. He knew his mother would say God had sent her, if he talked to her about it. He wasn't so sure about God as his mother was, although he did sometimes wish it was all that easy. It would be so nice to be certain that all of his life was this way for a reason. But that was one of the problems. He couldn't speak to his parents about this. Didn't want them to worry about him.

Plus, if he was really honest, he was a bit frustrated with them too. He tried to go back home as often as he could, but his parents hadn't been to visit him since the day they'd helped him move here. Sure, they were busy, but couldn't they at least take a couple of days off every now and again? He had even offered to take some days off during the week, but his mother would mutter about mounting costs and bills, and his father would just be vague as usual. It almost seemed like they didn't really care about him now that he was far away.

And Jamie too. His best friend was always happy to see him when he went home but hadn't bothered to come down and visit either. So, the last time Nick had been home was Christmas, and it was hard to keep making an effort when the feelings just weren't returned.

He ran his hands through his hair. It wasn't even a year ago that he had come to Glasgow. So full of hope that the big city would offer a good time and some new friends. Fort William was a great place for the outdoors, but the night life wasn't exactly buzzing, and he had been looking forward to doing a whole host of new things. So where had it all gone so wrong? What had happened in a year to bring him so low? It wasn't anything specific really. More a series of small individual events that had finally driven home to him just how lonely he was. But actually, he could maybe pinpoint a couple of things that had been really pivotal. The walking group was one of them ...

Nick stared at his computer screen. He was going crazy. Six months in Glasgow and he still hadn't made any friends. None of his colleagues were even vaguely into the same things as he was. And that football club had just been full of students.

Scrolling through a web page, he finally found what he wanted. A walking group. It would be great to get out into the mountains again and this one looked very popular. It would be a good chance to meet some people who also liked walking. They had a walk planned this Saturday, so he signed up immediately, full of excitement.

Friday night he checked the weather. Beautiful sunshine. It couldn't be better. The next morning bright and early he strapped on his walking boots, took his rucksack from behind the door where he had packed it the night before and set off to the station.

He had brought his map just in case, although it looked like the organisers were very experienced. That was great. It meant that he could just relax and get to know the people in the group as they walked along. He rubbed his palms together, feeling a small twist of excitement at the thought of getting out into the countryside again.

When he got off the train at Helensburgh it was obvious who he should meet. A group of eight or nine people in outdoor clothes were standing around in the car park, and they were joined by some more people who had been on the train. Most of them looked like they were retired, but there were a couple of people who looked closer to his own age. He summoned his courage and went up to them. He had to start somewhere.

'Hi. My name's Nick.' He held out his hand to one of the younger men, who was dressed in black walking gear.

'Tony,' the man said, grasping Nick's hand firmly. 'And this is Bill.' He indicated the other younger man, who was sporting a very impressive beard above his warm red jacket. 'We're the leaders of the group.'

The other members introduced themselves. They all seemed very friendly and Nick felt his spirits lift. By the time they left the station there must have been at least twenty people with them. They walked up the road and out of the town. The sunshine seemed to be making everyone happy.

Nick found himself chatting to one of the older men, who said that he had joined the group when he retired. Apparently, Tony and Bill had only recently taken over the group after the previous leader had left. 'We're very lucky to have them,' the man said. 'They're both qualified as mountain leaders.'

Nick felt a surge of happiness. He was back doing something he really enjoyed. They stopped for lunch on the top of a hill, sitting on a rocky outcrop of stone, and everybody exclaimed at the view all the way across the river. Some of the less fit people were congratulating themselves about managing the climb.

Nick took out his sandwich. The view was truly spectacular, and he could hear the singing of a skylark. He let out a deep breath, and then breathed in the freshness of the air. He was back where he belonged and days like this were just what he needed.

Glancing over to the west, he could see a front of cloud which looked pretty nasty. He gestured to Tony and Bill, who were sat not far away. 'What do you think about that?' He pointed at the cloud.

Bill looked over at it and shrugged. 'Not an issue. The forecast says we'll be long gone by the time that arrives.'

Nick wasn't sure. He had learned from painful experience that you couldn't take things like that for granted. As the group finished their lunch and started slowly down the far side of the hill, he kept glancing over his shoulder, still worried about the weather. About half the people didn't have waterproof trousers. And a couple of them didn't even have waterproof jackets. If that cloud rained down on them, they would be soaked to the skin in seconds.

And sure enough, an hour later the cloud was upon them, and a few minutes after that it started to rain miserably. The cloud was so thick they could barely see ten metres in front of them. Nick felt for his compass in his pocket, just to reassure himself. If they got into trouble in the mist then they might just need it. And his fancy GPS watch that his parents had given him last Christmas. He had been ecstatic when he had unwrapped it and grateful to his parents – those things were so expensive, and they really couldn't afford it.

Bill and Tony gathered the group around them. 'OK guys, we have to stick together. Keep sight of the person in front of you and check you can still see the person behind. The path is really clear, so we shouldn't have any problems.' They produced ponchos from their bags for the two without coats, which impressed Nick. Clearly these two made sure they planned ahead.

They trudged on, conversation less forthcoming now as they squelched through the mud. Nick had his head down, water dripping off the hood of his coat, and didn't see the fork until he was almost on it. The people ahead of him had taken the right fork, which was the logical direction to turn back towards Helensburgh, but something just niggled at him. He lifted his map case and wiped the drops off it, so he could study it carefully. Yes, that was it. The bridge ...

He hadn't realised that he had stopped walking until he heard a small noise of surprise from the person walking behind him. Ahead the group members that he could see had stopped, obviously wondering what had happened. They came trickling slowly back in twos and threes, looking worried.

Bill came striding over. 'What's up?'

Nick pointed at the map. 'I think we should take the left fork. It leads down to a bridge and we can take this as a short cut.' He indicated a lane on the map. 'The other way will take us at least two hours more than that.'

Bill snorted. 'That would be true if we were there. But we're not.' He pointed at a fork much further back on the map. 'We're here. So we take the right fork here, and the left fork later on.'

Nick felt the colour coming into his face. Of course. He had misread the map. What a stupid thing to do. But ... he studied the map again. He could have sworn that they passed that hill just before the clouds came down. His instincts were screaming at him and he just knew he was right. If it was just him, in his nice warm waterproof mountain gear, he wouldn't have minded. But a couple of the group were starting to shiver, especially since they had stopped, and he felt like he had a responsibility to them.

'Come on, Tony,' he said. 'Back me up on this one. We passed that turn ages ago.'

Tony shook his head, not even bothering to look at the map. 'No, Bill's spot on. Right fork is the way to go.'

Nick felt his face flame red. What should he do now? He was so convinced he was right, but what if he wasn't? Was it worthwhile standing up for, just to get back a couple of hours earlier?

He looked at the group clustered around them. An extra two hours for some of them would make a big difference in this rain.

He grabbed Bill by the arm and steered him away from the watchful eyes. 'Look, you know we passed that fork not long after lunch,' he said, careful to keep his voice lowered so no one else could hear him. He had spoken without thinking, and the last thing he had intended was for this to become a public battle of wills.

Bill looked him up and down scornfully. 'Tell you what, we'll split up the group. You take half of them your way, and we'll go the right way. We□ll meet at the café by the station and see who gets there first. Losers pay the bill.□

Nick felt like he had no other choice but to accept. Now all he had to do was make sure that all the less able people in the group somehow came with him. What had meant to be a fun day out had suddenly turned into a stressful situation, but that was OK. Growing up in the mountains had got him used to dealing with what the weather threw at you. If only dealing with people was so easy.

The group split fairly amicably into two. Nick was happy to see that the two without proper coats were coming with him. Or had Bill and Tony engineered that specially? He didn't want to think about that possibility. Best just to believe the best of people. It was always his approach to life.

During the walk back the clouds cleared, but a stiff wind started up, and Nick was glad when they got to the café and he could have a hot cup of tea. There was no sign of the others though. Not that he should have been surprised. He couldn□t feel elation at the fact he was right. Not when half the group was still out on the mountainside somewhere.

It was almost an hour and a half later when the other half of the group trudged in, looking weary and very muddy. However, some seemed excited by the experience, talking about massive bogs they had been forced to cross and fences that had to be climbed. Bill and Tony just sat in a corner with their coffees, not looking at Nick. He decided he would leave and let them get on with it. It was their group after all. But not before a couple of people gave him hugs and thanks and said they would post their pictures on the group site.

That night he considered the experience. Not great, he thought, but not a disaster. He found himself suddenly looking forward to the next walk. It was a bit of an eclectic group, but they were all very nice. Even Bill and Tony had just made an honest mistake. He reached for his phone. He would just see if anyone had posted any pictures yet.

But for some reason, he couldn't get into the group. He could see it, but he no longer seemed to be a member. He sank back on the couch in bewilderment. It must be Bill and Tony.

A message to the website support returned the information two days later that he had been blocked from the group for 'inappropriate behaviour'. The email that he received gave the impression that he had been lucky not to have been blocked from the entire site, so heinous was the nature of his supposed crimes. When he saw the email, he felt a surge of anger and his hands clenched. He started putting together an angry reply to the site moderator. But then the anger died away, and he felt a wave of sadness wash over him. If they didn't want him, then he would just move on. Find something else to do with his time.

He did have a look for other walking groups online, but there didn't seem to be anything else that was really what he was looking for. His experience with the first one had made him cautious of anything that seemed even vaguely competitive. And as the winter blew in then it didn't really seem to be something that anyone wanted to do anyway.

* * *

The thought of meeting Jade sustained Nick through work all week. When Saturday came he was so desperate not to be late that he took an earlier train and got there twenty-five minutes ahead of time. A bitter wind forced him into a cafe not far from the station, where he kept repeatedly checking his watch, paranoid that he would miss her.

He needn't have worried. At precisely one minute to ten she strolled up, dressed in her usual red coat. There was still no hat, but her hair was tamed into a beautiful long plait that ran half-way down her back. The sparkly green flashed in and out of the braid at surprising intervals.

'Wow, you look half-presentable,' he joked, suddenly feeling nervous. 'Are we going somewhere special?'

Jade gestured in the direction that she wanted them to go and linked her arm through his as they walked, a move that surprised him. She had seemed so remote the day when they first met. Almost alien.

'Lily likes to see my hair like this.' She looked up at him with a smile, touching it with her other hand.

It was the first time he had seen her properly smile, he realised, and he was completely blown away. He knew it was a cliché, but it really did transform her face. She did look better than when they first met, he thought, sneaking a glance at her when she wasn't looking. The dark smudges under her eyes were less prominent, and there was a bit of a glow in her cheeks. Although she could just be wearing makeup. Was that a hint of gloss on her lips?

'So who's Lily?' he asked, suddenly remembering what Jade had said.

Jade smiled again. 'You'll meet her. Today. We're going to see them all.'

'Them?' Nick couldn't help feeling a bit lost. Or was he just distracted by the woman walking along beside him?

She just laughed, squeezed his arm and increased her pace, dragging him across a junction and down a side street. She stopped in front of a large two-storey brick-built building.

'Sunnyside Retirement Home,' Nick read off the sign.

'I started coming here a couple of years ago. It started just as a way to give a bit back to the community. And then I met Lily.'

'She must be someone pretty special.' Nick could see the faint smile that played over her mouth and made his deductions from that. 'I'm looking forward to meeting her.'

'Oh, you will.' Jade took his elbow and steered him through the double doors. 'But I also want you to meet Archie.'

'I think I'm just going to go with it and not ask any more questions.' Nick couldn't help a smile starting on his own face.

A friendly woman dressed in pink hospital scrubs greeted them from behind the reception desk. Nick noticed that she was wearing fluffy pink earrings to match. Despite her clothes the entrance hall looked nothing like a hospital. Two big blue comfy chairs stood ready for anyone who was waiting, and there were modern-looking photos of Glasgow landmarks around the walls. It smelled clean and fresh, and there was no hint of disinfectant.

'Hi Sandra, this is Nick,' Jade said. 'I've brought him along to help out today.'

The woman looked him up and down in an appraising manner, but not unkindly. 'Hope you have big muscles,' she said. 'Clive's just called to say he's got the flu, so we'll be needing someone to push Archie.'

Nick was really starting to wonder what kind of crazy scheme he had got himself in for. 'Just what is it we're supposed to be doing today?'

'Oh yeah, I forgot to tell you.' Jade was unrepentant. 'We're taking a group of these people to the Riverside Museum.'

'And just how are we going to do that?' Nick had a crazy vision of trying to get a big group of wheelchairs onto the train while other passengers cursed the delays they were making.

Jade laughed, her eyes lighting up. 'Just relax and go with the flow. Loosen up. It's all been planned.'

They turned down the corridor into what was obviously some type of lounge. About fifteen people sat around on dark grey sofas and comfy chairs. But, just like the entrance hall, this was no depressing beigey communal living space. Bright pictures decorated the walls, and hand-made cushions were scattered on the sofas. Lovely arrangements of fresh flowers were dotted around, giving off beautiful scents.

'That's Sandra's work,' Jade said, seeing him looking. 'She was a florist before she came here.'

Jade seemed to know everyone, and she introduced him, although Nick quickly lost track of all the names. Two of them she kept for last, though, and Nick knew this must be Lily and Archie.

Archie was sitting in a wheelchair beside Lily, hunched over slightly. He had a massive hooked nose and chin under a large mop of messy white hair, and his face looked like someone who had spent a lot of time outside in his life. He reminded Nick of his grandfather actually. What he could remember of him.

'This is Archie,' Jade made a gesture with her hand, 'and this is Lily.' She smiled at the older woman and gave her a warm hug in greeting. 'They're not married, although you could be forgiven for thinking that.'

'Never have been, and never will be.' Archie's tone was gruff, but looking closer Nick could see his eyes were twinkling.

Nick was surprised to see that Archie was smartly dressed in shirt and tie with a bright red jumper.

Archie must have seen his expression, because the old man reached out and put a hand on Jade's arm. 'Your young man there seems to be surprised that we're all spruced up for today. What did you expect? A group of lolling, drooling imbeciles?' He waved an arm in the air and made a face that was clearly meant to be an imitation of his words.

'Oh hush, Archie.' Lily spoke for the first time. 'Stop with your antics and be kind to the young man. Otherwise they'll leave you here without anyone to push you around. And you know how much you're looking forward to that new tram they've bought recently.'

Nick was just about to say something when a group of other people entered the lounge. Most appeared to be retirement age themselves, and although there were a couple of other people who looked like they were a bit closer to his age, he and Jade were clearly the youngest by far in the room. All the newcomers sat themselves wherever there were free spaces, and a chatter started up in the room as people greeted each other and started catching up.

'What are we waiting for?' Nick wanted to know.

'Keith,' Jade said. 'He drives the minibus.'

'Ah,' Nick said. He perched himself on the edge of a seat, suddenly unsure of himself and feeling very self-conscious.

Lily patted him on the arm. 'So, young man, what do you do with your time?'

He turned towards her, looking at her properly for the first time. Her white hair was elegantly swept up in a carefully sculpted style, and the wrinkles on her face only made her look more beautiful, not less so. He suddenly wondered what she had looked like when she was younger.

'I work as a programmer. For a consultancy. We mainly work for banks.' He realised he didn't sound very forthcoming and hurried to add some more. 'You know, internet security and that sort of thing.'

'Ah.' Lily seemed to absorb this information for a minute. 'Sounds like a very important job.'

Of all the things Nick had heard his job called, important wasn't one of them. He was just a graduate, on the bottom rung of the ladder. 'Sorry? How do you mean?' He couldn't help the question slipping out.

Lily nodded slowly. 'Well, if you're in security, you're keeping people's money safe, isn't that right?'

Nick paused to think about this, rubbing his chin while he did so. 'I guess so. I'd never thought about it like that. But I only started less than a year ago. I'm just a minion for my boss.'

Archie cracked a laugh, startling Nick. 'The minions always do the most important work, lad. Forget the bosses who swan around drinking coffee all day.'

Which was pretty much what his boss did most of the time, Nick reflected. He was saved from having to reply by the arrival of Keith, and shortly after that found himself pushing Archie out of the building and up a steep metal ramp into the slightly faded minibus. Jade and Lily followed slowly, with Lily leaning on Jade's arm. The minibus was full by the time they set off. As they eased away from the kerb someone struck up a version of 'Pack up your troubles', and soon half of the bus was singing, with varying levels of tunefulness. Nick couldn't help grinning. Whatever he had thought he would be doing this morning, this hadn't been it.

Jade, sitting across the aisle from him, leaned over and nudged his arm. 'Not going to join in?' She was smiling again, he noticed, and he wished that she would do it all the time.

Nick shrugged. 'I don't know all the words.'

Jade gave a shrug to match his own and laughed. 'I don't think that really matters for most of the choir.'

A small thread of warmth crept through him. Nick smiled back at her, took a deep breath and opened his mouth to sing.

Chapter 2

It wasn't far to the museum, for which Nick was grateful. He couldn't claim to be a great singer, but he was musical enough that by the time they had done ten verses of 'Tipperary' and been through 'Imagine' at least three times it was starting to wear him down just a little. They got out right in front of the building. The wind had dropped, and the spring sunshine was making the river sparkle. It was pretty warm for the time of year.

Nick had seen the museum from the train a few times, but only from a distance. Up close it was much more impressive. The silver metal exterior gleamed in the sunlight, and the massive glass frontage seemed to be drawing people in towards the entrance doors in the middle.

Jade saw where he was looking. 'Award-winning, apparently.' Her tone made it clear that she was in no way impressed by the grand design.

She looked at her watch. 'Normally everyone goes off and sees what they want to see, and then we get back together for lunch. Everybody? Midday at the café?'

There was a chorus of assent, and everyone started to filter off. Nick looked expectantly at Jade, but she shook her head. 'You're here for Archie. You need to ask him what he wants to see.' She looked at them both. 'Normally we wouldn't let the two of you go off on your own, but ...'

Archie sat himself up straight in the wheelchair. 'This is where you try to tell me I'm classed as a vulnerable adult, eh?'

Jade's face turned pink, and Nick nearly laughed out loud.

'You know that officially the law might say yes, Archie, but practically I don't believe it for a second.' Jade wagged a finger at him. 'So go on, both of you. Get out of my sight before I end up keeping an eye on you both for other reasons.'

Nick took the back of the old man's wheelchair and went to push him inside, but the old man shook his head. 'Take me round for a turn outside the building, lad. I need a bit of fresh air in my lungs.'

Nick gratefully steered him round the side of the building and down towards the river. He too thought that it was a pity to be inside on such a glorious day. Archie stood unsteadily, pulling himself up using the railing, and they both stood in silence for a while, watching the sunlight playing on the water.

'I used to be outside all the time, you know,' Arche said suddenly. 'A mountain guide, I was. There isn't a Munroe in the Highlands that I haven't climbed.'

Nick couldn't work out whether to be impressed for Archie's achievements, or sad at the condition the man was in now.

'Oh, don't be sorry for me, young lad,' Archie said, patting him on the arm. 'I've had a good life. Ninety-two I am now. It's my time to rest.'

'Ninety-two?' Nick could hardly believe it. They stood in silence for a few more minutes, then Archie sat back down in the wheelchair.

'I wanted to be a mountain guide,' Nick found himself saying.

Archie looked up at him. 'Really? What happened?'

'I worked for a friend for a year. When I left school. His dad died about that time and it took the two of us just to keep the family business going. It was one of the best times of my life. But when the recession really hit, he said he had to let me go. I had plans to start up on my own, but all the training and equipment and insurance and everything was just too expensive, and I had to finally admit that it just wasn't going to happen ...' Nick trailed off, then collected himself. 'My parents said I should go to college and get some proper qualifications. So I did something boring and predictable that would always get me a job.'

Archie nodded, as if he understood, but Nick went further, trying to explain why he had sold out on his dreams. 'My parents ... they own a B&B up in Fort William, and barely have enough money to make ends meet themselves. I just didn't want to be a burden on them.'

Archie nodded again, taking everything in. 'Life never works out the way you expect. It's full of surprises. Look at me. I never thought I'd end up in Glasgow. I was sure I'd be killed falling off a cliff or something.'

Nick did have to laugh at that. 'What made you come here?'

'I've got a niece here. With grandkids of her own. The family persuaded me to move down here, and to be honest, I'm not sorry. Glasgow is a great city. Lots going on. And it's great to see more of my family.'

'Yeah.' Nick thought of his parents. 'Family is special.'

They stayed in silence for a few more minutes, the quiet settling around them like a comfortable blanket.

'Fort William!' Archie laughed, as if suddenly remembering something. 'Now there's a good place for walking. I should tell you about the time I went up Ben Nevis and had to rescue a man who got stuck in a snowstorm in his shirt sleeves! Wheel me inside, lad. I want to go and look at this new tram there's been such a hoo-ha about.'

Jade and Lily walked slowly through the front doors of the museum, Lily leaning heavily on her stick and relying on Jade's arm for balance. 'What do you want to see?' Jade asked, as they paused for a second to have a look around.

'I heard they've revamped the shops along that nineteenth century street they have.' Lily gestured with her stick in the general direction. 'Let's go see those.'

They browsed the shops, pointing out things of interest to each other. As they sat for a minute in a dentist's waiting room, just to let Lily have a rest, she nudged Jade gently. 'What about this young man of yours? Where did you find him?'

'He's not my young man.' Jade was quick to defend herself. 'We only met last Saturday. I found him on the bridge.'

'Ah.' Lily's gaze seemed suddenly sharper, but Jade didn't shrink from it. She had already shared a good deal of her history with the older woman and had found more love and acceptance than she could possibly have ever hoped for.

'Yes.' Jade kept her eyes steady. 'I don't think he's very happy. So I brought him here, knowing how you helped me, and I was hoping that you would be able to help him too.'

The older lady pursed her lips. 'I don't help people, you silly muffin.' She slipped an arm around Jade's shoulders and pulled her in for a hug. 'You were the one who helped yourself.' She gave a sigh. 'And Nick has to help himself. All we can do is give him the opportunity.' She chuckled suddenly. 'But I'm mighty curious how he's getting on with that crusty old codger.'

Jade's eyes danced. 'Should we go and see if he's pushed him in the river by now?'

Lily shook her head. 'No, my dear, let's leave them to it. I want to go and see the dressmaker's across the way.'

And, of course, they had to go and sit in the old-fashioned Subway carriage for a bit, even though they had both done it many times before. While they were sitting, waiting for the sound effects that would make them feel that they were rushing through a tunnel, Lily nudged Jade again. 'But tell me, don't you think that he is quite a handsome man?'

'Who, Archie?' Jade said, wilfully misunderstanding.

Lily snorted, poking Jade with her stick. 'As if! You know who I mean.'

Jade considered Nick for a while. Thinking about how she had seen him on the bridge, all pale and tired with his hat jammed down over his ears. Then the transformation she had seen today, wavy brown hair flopped untidily over his forehead as he sang lustily at the top of his voice. And the flash in his bright blue eyes when he had grinned at her.

'Well,' she said reluctantly, 'I guess you could maybe say that. Just a little!' she amended, as the older woman gave a crow of victory. 'And that doesn't mean I'm going to start dating him. I couldn't cope with dating someone like that. It would just be too much to worry about.'

Lily looked at her with a knowing look. 'I hear you. But then again, isn't it worthwhile sometimes taking a chance in life?' She heaved herself off her seat, gathering her stick up in one small feathery hand. 'Now, get me to that café. I'm parched for a cuppa.'

The four of them sat at a square table in the café. Archie abandoned his wheelchair in favour of a proper chair. Three of them had soup, and Nick went for a massive cheese and pickle sandwich. The place was busy, with people chattering all around them. A couple of children ran around the room, laughing as they dashed in and out of the tables. The smell of fresh coffee made it seem warm and cosy.

'I can't believe how much stuff they have crammed in here.' Nick waved his arms around to illustrate his point. Even the café had small displays littered around the edge of the room. 'They have cars stuck up on the walls! And a whole steam train! I don't know why I've never thought to come here before.'

'That new tram looks very spangly,' Jade remarked, knowing Archie had been keen to see it.

Archie sighed happily. 'Ah yes. Brings back a lot of happy memories. Now, I remember the time I jumped off the roof of one, just to avoid the ticket inspector ...' And he was off, waving his arms around as he told them what had happened. Jade didn't mind. All of his stories were interesting ones, and she loved hearing about how things used to be.

'So how did you start doing these trips?' She realised Nick was speaking to her and drew her attention back to him, blushing slightly as she remembered her earlier conversation with Lily.

'You mean how, or why?' Jade wasn't sure exactly what he meant.

Nick had just taken a bite of his sandwich and took a moment to swallow before answering. 'I mean, what got you into it. How did you think about doing this stuff? You know, giving up your free time just to take other people out.'

From the pause in his voice she knew he had almost been going to say old people. She winked at him, just to make him aware that she had caught his almost-mistake, and the back of his neck tinged slightly with pink. Intelligent, though, with Lily and Archie sitting right there. Her eyes twinkled, thinking of how the conversation would have gone if Nick had said the word old. Maybe not though. Lily and Archie were chatting away on the other side of the table, completely engrossed in a discussion about different models of trams.

'My gran died a couple of years ago. I miss her a lot.'

Nick's eyebrows rose. This obviously wasn't what he had been expecting her to say, but Jade carried on. 'I used to mope around the house. It was my mum who got me into this.'

She indicated one of the younger grey-haired helpers, sitting a couple of tables away. 'Connie over there is friends with her. So I started coming down to the home to help out, just to get out of the house. And then I met Lily.'

Lily looked over at the sound of her name. 'What was that, dearie?'

She put emphasis on the dearie, and Jade laughed, knowing it was on purpose. 'I was just telling Nick how much of a burden you are and how I hate taking you out.'

Lily reached over and gave Jade's hand a quick squeeze. 'Gripe away, dearie. I'm used to it. Especially living in the same place as this old codger.'

Archie drew in a breath, pretending to be offended.

'Sorry.' Lily's eyes twinkled. 'I should have said, living in the same place as this fine gentleman.'

'It doesn't make your complaint any better, you know, wrapping it up in such fine words,' Archie grumbled.

Nick lust looked at them all, and then burst out laughing. Creaky laughs, as if they were a little rusty with lack of use, but laughter all the same. And Jade just had to follow suit. She was so happy to be here, and Nick being around just made things better. She suspected he and Archie might be good for each other. If only she could persuade Nick to come back again. If she knew he had someone else keeping an eye on him, then she could leave him alone, happy in the knowledge that he had some kind of support network to keep him going.

They finished their lunch and Jade caught the attention of some of the other helpers, whose nods of agreement showed that they were also ready to go. By the time they were gathered back at the front of the museum it was past one and Keith was waiting with the minibus. The piled in, Jade sitting next to Nick again.

She touched his arm gently. 'Enjoyed yourself?'

Nick turned his face towards hers, and she could see he was grinning again. 'Very much so. Far more than I expected to, actually.'

'Good.' Jade decided to just say what was in her head. 'Because I was hoping you'd come back when we go again in two weeks.' Nick was silent, and Jade wondered if she'd misjudged him. 'Of course, if you'd rather not, then—'

'No!' Nick interrupted her. 'It's just – well – won't that other guy be back next week? I wouldn't want to trample on his patch.'

Jade laughed. 'Oh, we always need people. There's always someone who can't make it each week. And we can only take as many people out as we have helpers. So you'd be very welcome.'

Nick ducked his head, obviously embarrassed and happy at being wanted. And Jade suddenly wondered exactly what he had gone through, to drive him to stand on that bridge and have those kinds of thoughts. Maybe she would get to the bottom of things. And if not, then at least she could try to provide him with some sort of community to love and support him while he was here.

'I'll walk you to the station,' Jade said, when everyone was safely back and they had said their goodbyes.

Nick looked like he was about to protest, but then he seemed to change his mind. 'That would be great. And you really should give me your number too.'

'OK, OK.' Jade pretended to reluctantly give in, smiling at him again. She recited the number, while he typed it into his phone.

'I promise I won't stalk you.' The grin was back. Jade couldn't help smiling again in response.

They walked companionably side by side, not really talking much, through the streets that by now were bustling with people, out for Saturday shopping. Jade stopped at the entrance to the station.

'So, what's the plan for next weekend?' Nick wanted to know. 'You know. The next thing on the list.'

Jade had been lost in thought, wondering about Nick and what his story was. 'Oh. Yeah.' She thought for a minute. If he wouldn't laugh at her, she could take him ...

Screw it, she thought. Nothing to lose. 'Kelvin Hall. Quarter to eleven. Wear something comfortable. Sweatpants or something.'

'Are you going to tell me what we're doing?' Nick looked sideways at her.

'Nope. That's part of the fun.' Jade winked at him.

'Oh.' Nick seemed to suddenly remember something. 'Today was all about the second thing on the list. But you never actually told me what it was.'

Jade smiled. 'Do a kindness for someone else. Feels good, doesn't it?'

Nick didn't reply for a second, then he unexpectedly leaned over suddenly and gave her a quick kiss on the cheek. Before she could say anything, he gave her a little wave and disappeared up the stairs. Jade put a hand to her cheek and stared after him for a minute, unsure of the meaning of what had just happened. Then she turned and walked slowly home.

'You look very thoughtful,' her mother remarked later that evening while they were both sitting in the living room after dinner. 'Something on your mind?'

'Just this guy I met. I took him to see Lily today.'

'Ah.' Her mother, never one for excessive speech, could convey a thousand messages with one word. 'So what is he like, this man?'

Jade considered, the images of Nick flitting through her mind. 'Nice. He seems nice.' She snuggled up on the sofa in her blanket, content just to spend some time alone with her mother tonight. 'Let's watch some of your favourite programme, Mum.'

Her mother's raised eyebrows indicated surprise, but she didn't say anything, just reached for the remote. And as the familiar theme music started, Jade felt a strange feeling of contentment, which was something she hadn't felt for a long time.

Chapter 3

Nick lay on his bed that evening thinking about things. He was starting to wonder about the wisdom of taking a bedsit in the centre of town. He had originally done it because then he wouldn't have to spend any time commuting, especially because they occasionally shifted a working day to match the hours in the US and he would get home really late. But he missed green fields and trees. The constant hum of the traffic was getting him down. Maybe if he took a flat somewhere out of the city like Lenzie or Milngavie? The commute wasn't huge, just half an hour each way. And he could spend the time usefully doing something. Reading. Or watching something on his phone. Or something like that.

But then, the real problem was his job. Well, it wasn't really the job. In fact, he liked it more than he had expected to like an office job. He loved the feeling of solving problems and being master of the web. Of fighting the dark forces of evil with only a few lines of computer code. But the real problem was his colleagues, but mainly his boss. Well, actually, all of them. It was all rolled into a massive knotty problem that he had no idea how to solve.

He supposed he should just try to find another outdoor job, but it was hard. He'd been watching websites for months, and the job he'd interviewed for a couple of weeks back – organising outdoor activities for kids – had been the only one he'd seen for ages that was even remotely close to what he wanted to do, even though the owner of the company hadn't seemed much better than the boss he had now. And having them offer him the job, and then a few days later call them to say they'd changed their minds? That had been a major blow.

If they don't want you, you don't want them. He recited the mantra that his dad had taught him to help him stand up to the bullies at school. The trouble was, it wasn't always true. A job working outdoors with a tosser for a boss was better than the job he had now, where he was stuck in an office and still had a tosser for a boss. And so his thoughts continued circling, his chest growing tight as he felt more and more trapped in his head.

If he stayed in the same type of work that he was doing now then he would probably have to go down to London to find another job, and the thought of that scared him even more than carrying on in his current job. Besides, he didn't like the thought of running away. Even though the blokes in his office all seemed the same, odds were that some of them were as frustrated as he was. If he could only find a way to sort things out ...

'New Year, new start.' Nick jumped as one of his colleagues threw a backpack onto a nearby desk. Nick normally had the office to himself until at least nine. He liked to come in early, before eight if possible. It gave him at least an hour before the office banter started up and he got distracted by people asking him for things. But it seemed that someone had decided to start the new year with a new resolution.

'Yeah.' Nick tried to be enthusiastic, but to be honest he was missing the mountains. And being back home. And there wasn't even any snow in Glasgow to make things look pretty. 'How was your holiday?'

'Oh, you know, the usual. Too much food, too much drink. Family rows. Glad to be back really. How was yours?'

Nick thought of the ten days he had spent at home. The wild waves whipped up in the sea lochs. The perfect sheen of the snow on the hills. The deer spread out on the mountain sides like chocolate sprinkles on a white iced cake.

He suddenly realised the other man was waiting for a reply. 'Oh. Great. It was great.'

Too great, he thought, as he returned his eyes to the screen and back to what he was working on. He had come up with some really good ideas over the holiday for a particularly knotty problem the whole office had been trying to solve. Maybe if he spoke to his boss about it then it might make him more likely to get a good bonus come April. Then he could buy that new amazing winter jacket he had been wanting for ages. If he was really lucky it would be in the summer sales … Then he sobered. Maybe he could just send his parents on holiday. They hadn't been abroad for years.

It wasn't long before the office filled up, loud and noisy with people exchanging their holiday stories. Nick wondered some days how ten people managed to make so much noise. Still, they weren't bad people. They had bought him cake on his birthday. And taken him out for dinner and drinks when he first started. It was just that he struggled to fit in to their casual talk about cars, and golf, and women. And he felt like everyone knew it.

It was no use trying to concentrate on work until everyone had settled down. Time for a cup of tea. He rounded the corner into the breakout area, only to find three of the guys in there, clustered around the noticeboard. One of them took something and pinned it up with satisfaction. 'There we go. How about that.' They stood back to admire the view.

Nick looked at the notice board and frowned. Up at the top was a calendar. But not just any calendar. It was some kind of trade calendar, from God knew what kind of company, because January's picture showed a scantily clad woman bent in a supposedly enticing position over a car bonnet.

Nick sucked in a breath. His mother would have been horrified, and not just because she was a devoted Catholic. He found himself speaking before he thought about the consequences. 'You can't put that up there, for goodness sake.'

Andy, the one who had pinned it up, turned towards him. 'Oh yeah? Why not?'

Nick just shook his head in bewilderment. 'How can you even ask that? That's totally inappropriate for an office environment. What kind of image do you think it gives our company? How do you think women will feel when they look at it?'

Andy folded his arms. 'Tell me, when do we ever get any visitors to this office? And there aren't even any women here.'

'What about Sadie?' Nick couldn't believe his ears.

'Her? She's just part-time admin. She doesn't count.' Andy clearly didn't even see her as a member of staff. Which made Nick angry. Before he knew what he was doing, he had grabbed the calendar off the wall and torn all the pages in half.

He dumped them in the bin, trembling, part with rage and part with fear. 'There you go. That's the only good thing that your calendar is good for.'

Andy grabbed Nick and raised his fist under his nose. 'That was my calendar, you little shit!'

'Gents! Please!' Their boss had pushed himself through the group of people watching at the doorway. 'What is going on here?'

'He put up a calendar with naked women on it.' Nick was still angrily defiant.

'And he ripped it in half and threw it in the bin.' Andy crossed his arms again.

The big boss sighed. 'Andy. Nick is right, unfortunately. A naked calendar is not appropriate for the office.'

Nick didn't like the word unfortunately, but since he was being backed up then he supposed he couldn't complain.

But the man wasn't finished yet. 'But you, Nick. Ripping up other people's property is not an appropriate way to resolve a conflict.' He gave a theatrical sigh. 'Since you're so junior, I'll overlook it this time.'

The man turned on his heel. 'Everyone, back to work! Work doesn't do by itself, you know.'

Andy gave Nick a dirty look and walked off back to his desk. Nick took a deep breath. He almost wished he hadn't said anything in the first place, but as he passed Sadie's desk, he looked at her and saw her mouthing 'thank you' at him. His heart lifted. Maybe he had done the right thing?

It was a week later when Nick finally felt ready to go to his boss with his ideas. This was a real gamechanger. It could make them a lot of money. He'd prepared a presentation to show to him, with details of the potential market and everything. He'd grab him right after their weekly team meeting and ask for some of his time. He could barely contain his excitement when he got in that morning.

'Right, everybody,' the boss said as they sat down in the conference room, around the white-topped table. 'We'll go through the regular business soon, but meanwhile Andy has some exciting new ideas to share with us.'

Andy stood up to the usual claps and hoots of approval, and Nick sat back, curious to know what was coming next. But as the slides displayed on the screen, he felt a sinking feeling in the pit of his stomach. It was his presentation. OK, changed a little bit, but his charts were there. And his ideas. All of his precious ideas.

Nick barely registered the rest of the meeting, so caught up was his mind on how Andy had stolen his work. How had the man done it? And then he suddenly remembered. He had stored all his work on his personal folder on the shared drive. And none of it was password protected. Anyone could have looked at his stuff.

As the others were filing out, he grabbed Andy by the arm. 'I can't believe you did that.'

'Did what?' Andy looked at him innocently.

They were the only two left in the meeting room. Nick kept his voice low. 'That was my presentation. With my ideas.'

Andy looked him and folded his arms. 'Prove it.'

Nick looked at him. 'I have a copy of it in my folder on the shared drive! You stole it from there!'

Andy shrugged. 'Like I said.'

Nick made his way back to his desk, his hands shaking. He clicked into his personal folder. And then blinked. The entire folder where he had stored the presentation, and all the research that had gone into it, was gone. Just deleted. He clicked around for a couple of minutes, thinking maybe he'd been mistaken, that he had maybe stored it somewhere else, but when he looked up and caught sight of Andy smirking at him from the other side of the office then he knew. This was revenge for the calendar.

Nick got up and marched straight into his boss's office. 'Excuse me. Can I have a word?'

The man leaned back in his chair with a friendly smile. 'Sure. What can I do for you?'

Nick closed the door, then sat down in the chair across the desk. 'It's hard to say this, really. But I need to tell you that those ideas, the ones that Andy showed us this morning, they were mine. I came up with them. He took them off me without me knowing.'

His boss was silent for what seemed like a long while, and then he finally spoke. 'Nick. I know you're very new to the team. And all this may seem very new to you, being fresh out of university. But I have to say that we're a team. We work together. There's no point putting someone down just to make yourself look better.' He leaned his arms on the desk, looking very stern. 'And I have to tell you that accusing someone of stealing your ideas is a very serious accusation.'

He waited a while longer, while Nick shifted in his chair, feeling the blood rise to his face. If even his boss didn't believe him, what was he going to do?

Then the older man sighed suddenly and leaned back in his chair. 'Look, Nick. Whatever issues you and Andy have, you need to sort them out. He's a longstanding valued member of this team. The clients trust him. I trust him. And if you can't make this work between you, then maybe you should think about finding another job.'

He held up a hand as Nick started to speak. 'I'm not saying that in a bad way, Nick. I really like your work so far, and I think you have a long and promising career ahead of you. It's just that if you want to get on in this world, you need to learn how to fit in. And become a team player.' He smiled at Nick brightly. 'Now. Is there anything else?'

Nick shook his head, feeling his shoulders slump. 'No. I understand.'

Nick's stomach growled, bringing him back to the present. It was after the presentation fiasco that things had really turned toxic in the office. The subtle bullying. The not-so-subtle comments. It had got to the point where he felt physically sick every time he walked through the office door. That's why he had started applying for new jobs. And had been so elated when he thought he was finally getting away, only to have his dreams dumped in the bin.

He checked his watch. Way past dinner time. At least he felt hungry. That was an improvement, although he still didn't feel like cooking. He jumped up, almost banging his head on the cupboard in his haste. Screw the cooking. He would go and get sushi from that new Japanese place that had just opened around the corner. A reward for completing task two of the happy list. He couldn't wait to find out what was number three.

After dinner he went to sleep and dreamed that Jade smashed her way into his office and punched both Andy and his boss in the face, while Archie ran amok in his wheelchair singing army songs at the top of his voice and running over everyone's toes.

When Nick woke the next day, he realised it was the first time he had slept well in as long as he could remember. He could walk up to the Necropolis again, he thought. Start the happy list over again. And then he would call his mum, he hadn't spoken to her for ages.

Jade eased herself slowly down into the weird half-standing position that the teacher called 'chair pose'. It was a few weeks since she had bothered to come to the yoga class, and she could already feel her thighs complaining at the unaccustomed treatment. She mentally promised them a hot bath when she got home and sneaked a quick look backwards to where Nick was. He caught her looking and gave her a wink. Jade smiled inwardly, glad to know that he wasn't taking it too seriously. She couldn't believe how cool and collected he looked, while her legs were complaining about her five-week break. She sneaked a look at him again, making sure he didn't catch her. Yes, she had to admit that those navy-blue shorts showed off his assets pretty well.

Still, this class was probably the best one she had found so far. A mix of yoga and meditation for beginners, with a teacher who was both incredibly practical and didn't do any of the mystical crap. He was about the furthest thing from a hippie guru that she had ever seen. Short-haired and clad in lycra shorts that she had admired from behind on numerous occasions, he bounced about in front of the class with enthusiasm, and freely admitted his own difficulties in clearing his mind during the meditation exercises. Yes, thought Jade as she twisted herself into another position, hand reaching towards the ceiling, this was about as close to exercise as she was ever going to get. She really should come more often though. She hated to admit it, but she did feel better when she was coming regularly.

Nick sat with his legs crossed and eyes closed as they went into the meditation sequence. He had to admit the yoga had felt really good, but he was a bit sceptical about the meditation. Weren't you supposed to empty your mind? And how on earth were you supposed to do that?

'Right,' the instructor said, 'you're probably all wondering now, what the hell do you do next?'

There were laughs around the room, and Nick couldn't help joining in.

'I want you to focus on your breathing. Just count to yourself as it goes in and out. You're bound to start thinking about something, but just look at those thoughts and say to them "Yeah, whatever."'

There was another round of laughter.

Nick sat up straight and tried to concentrate on the in and out of his breath. He fully expected some stressful thoughts to bubble to the surface, but to his surprise the first thing that came into his mind was his mother, cooking the breakfasts for the guests at the big range like she always did every morning. He couldn't bring himself to greet her in such an offhand way as instructed, so instead sent her a quick hello, and in his mind's eye she lifted one hand to give him a wave in greeting. She had been over the moon when he had called her last Sunday. He sometimes wondered if she was truly happy where she was. Could that be why she had urged him to get out and do something else with his life?

In ... Out ... In ... Out ... With each breath he could feel himself getting more relaxed, and he rolled his shoulders a little, trying to release some of the ever-present tension in them. He could faintly hear the music from the gym next door, and the smell of plastic from the yoga mat that had thankfully looked fairly new and clean when he pulled it from the box in the corner of the room. If he really listened carefully then he could just about make out the sounds of people breathing in and out all around him.

Strangely enough, the next thing that popped into his head was Jade. It was the first time he had seen her with clothes that fit her closely, and he wondered how someone as skinny as her still managed to have such an amazing bum. He'd had plenty of time to admire it from his position just slightly behind her.

He realised he had completely lost his focus on his breathing and started counting again. He was kind of relieved when the instructor called time and they switched back to yoga again.

When the class was finally wrapped up, Jade lay on her mat for a second, feeling happiness and tired muscles in equal measure. Time for a shower, she thought. And then she would take Nick somewhere for lunch. Her stomach agreed with the last thought, and she smiled again.

A shadow fell over her. 'Having happy thoughts?' It was Nick.

She opened her eyes, twisting her head up at him. 'Having thoughts about food.'

He gave her a grin, extending a hand downwards to help her up. 'Great idea. My thoughts exactly.'

They were just rolling up their mats when one of the women from the class came over to them. Stunningly gorgeous was the only way to describe her. She was one of those people whose chestnut-brown hair looked amazing even when it was tied up in a messy ponytail, and her skin was lightly bronzed as if she had never spent a day in Scotland in her life. Jade didn't even want to think about her figure, rounded in all the right places and flat in all of the others.

'Hi. Can I just ask, are you two together?' Her soft, sexy American accent just completed the picture of perfection.

'Yes,' Nick said, at the same time as Jade answered, 'No.'

At the woman's puzzled look, Jade rushed to clarify. 'Oh, we came together, but we're not together, together. We're just friends.'

Were she and Nick really friends? She supposed they were, after a fashion. It would have to do. It was less complicated than the real story.

'Oh, great.' said the woman. She draped an arm round Nick's shoulders. 'Because I think you're stunning. I just wanted to tell you.' She gave Jade a wink. 'How would you feel about going for lunch?'

Nick seemed speechless, and Jade suddenly felt an irrational burst of anger at this person, coming in and interfering in her life and her friendship. As Nick opened his mouth to reply, Jade spoke before she could find out what his answer would be. 'Sorry, but not today. We've got somewhere to be.'

'Oh.' The beauty unwound her arm from Nick's neck, clearly disappointed, and held a card out to Jade. 'Well, honey, if you change your mind, just call me.'

Jade took the card, frowning slightly, as the woman turned away. She looked at Nick. 'Did she ...?'

Nick nodded, obviously struggling not to laugh. 'Just hit on you, yes.'

Jade was still trying to comprehend what had happened. 'So why did she put her arm around you? I thought it was you that she liked.' She shook her head as Nick grinned.

Jade fingered the card. 'Who the hell takes business cards into a yoga class?' She suddenly looked at it in horror. 'Come to think of it, where the hell did she have it stored?'

Nick suddenly lost his battle with laughter and doubled over, gasping as he tried to catch his breath. Jade joined him, laughing so hard that she just had to sink down onto the floor and sit for a couple of minutes. It was only the door opening with the people for the next class that brought them back to their senses.

Nick grabbed her hand, his large one closing around hers, and pulled her up to a standing position, wiping his eyes with his other hand. 'Come on, Miss Stunning. We've got a lunch to eat.'

Chapter 4

As Jade showered, she puzzled over the reaction she'd felt when she thought that the bombshell was coming onto Nick. Did that mean she was attracted to Nick herself? As she had admitted to Lily, she did find him handsome, but he wasn't her usual type. She normally went for bigger, more macho men with muscles and tattoos. Nick was too thin and wiry for her, with not a tattoo in sight. In sight, a wicked corner of her brain reminded her. She shook her head. She would bet a lot that he didn't have one. He just didn't seem like the tattooing type.

No, she said to herself firmly, as she pressed the water button yet another time, it was just that she was afraid of anything messing with their friendship, so soon after they had found each other. Also, of anyone messing with Nick, when he was in such a fragile state. And, she reflected, if she didn't get out of this shower soon, she'd be in danger of losing his friendship from him having to wait for her so long.

They sat in the café with a happy buzz of background conversation washing over them.

Nick was tucking into a full English breakfast. 'So,' he waved his fork in her direction, 'was the third thing on the list, do exercise?'

Jade shook her head, crunching into her toast. 'No. Actually, it was meditate.'

Nick sighed. 'I'm not sure how much meditation I did, really. I did a lot of thinking but can't really say I reached a true meditative state.'

Jade realised he was teasing her, just slightly. 'To be honest, it's not really my thing either. I only started it because some of my Twitter followers suggested it. And I like Peter. He's always funny when he does a class.'

'Wait.' Nick leaned towards her, food momentarily forgotten. 'What do you mean, some of your Twitter followers?'

Jade blushed, realising she would have to tell him. 'I write,' she said, trying to keep her voice casual. 'Not for money. I write short stories and publish them on the internet for people to read.'

Nick raised his eyebrows, obviously impressed. 'What sort of stuff do you write? I mean, what kind of stories?'

'Lots of stuff, really. But I guess mainly science fiction. Or really, what people these days call near future. Things that could happen soon, but not really far in the future. And occasionally some paranormal stuff.'

'So how did the meditation thing come up?'

'Oh.' Jade had gone off on a different train of thought already, and Nick's question dragged her back. 'When I was putting together the happy list. I thought I'd poll people about what made them happy. Twitter is so full of negative people all the time.' She paused, remembering. 'It was great actually. Lots of people just find happiness in simple things. Spending time with their family. Going for a walk with the dog. Anyway, there were a few people who mentioned meditation. So I thought I would try it. And I found the class with Peter, which does make me happy. So I guess it does work.' She smiled as she thought about her favourite suggestion though, from a woman and her vibrator. She wouldn't mention that one to Nick. Not here, at any rate.

'Go on, let's have a look.' Nick's question pulled her out of her thoughts again.

'At what?' Jade looked at him suspiciously.

'At your Twitter profile.' He dug out his phone. 'What's your handle?'

Jade dived for her own phone in her handbag. Doing it this way, with any luck he wouldn't remember it and then wouldn't be able to look it up later. She pulled it up and passed it across to him.

'Wow, more than five thousand followers. I'm impressed.' He scrolled through a few of her tweets. 'Have you ever thought of trying to get published?' He placed the phone back on the table and returned to his breakfast.

Jade retrieved her phone, as if having it back would return the information to the mental box she had opened. She didn't have to tell him the whole story. It was her private life to keep private. Still, she could tell him part of it. The part that didn't hurt that much anymore. 'When I was growing up, I wanted to. I really wanted to write for a living.'

Nick frowned. 'What happened?'

Jade shrugged. 'I went to Glasgow Uni to study English. I was convinced I was going to become the next JK Rowling or Isaac Asimov.' She smiled slightly at the memory.

Nick was clearly listening intently, a piece of sausage left forgotten on his fork half-way to his mouth. She motioned at it and he recovered, did a fake double-take as if he had never seen it before, and ate it.

'Anyway,' Jade went on quickly, 'we had some family problems in my final year and I bombed out of my exams and never went back.'

'Wouldn't they let you re-take them?' Nick was quick in her defence, with indignation in his tone.

Jade twisted a finger through her hair. 'They would have done. But after everything it all just seemed unnecessary, you know.' She waved a hand, trying to sound dismissive.

Nick was silent for a while, as if he was trying to digest what she had said.

'So what do you do for money?' he finally asked.

Jade blinked. She had really been expecting him to ask about the reason she had flaked out of university. Maybe because this was the story she least wanted to tell. But it seemed for whatever reason that he either wasn't interested or sensed her reluctance to go into any more detail.

She relaxed, leaning back in her chair. 'I work at the go-karting centre. Down by the river.'

'No way.' Nick dropped his knife on the floor and hurriedly retrieved it, wiping it on his serviette. 'That's such a cool job. Do they let you drive the cars?'

Jade shrugged. 'It's OK. The guy who runs the place is pretty good. I only work on reception, but sometimes when the mechanics make repairs then they ask us to drive them round for a few laps just to check that things are working properly.'

Nick sighed. 'I don't know why I'm working in an office when I could be doing something like that.' He finished off his last bit of food, placing his knife and fork carefully together.

'I bet I earn half what you do,' Jade pointed out. 'And you don't come home stinking of go-kart fuel.'

'You just had to spoil the fantasy.' Nick sighed again, this time theatrically.

Jade had to laugh at that. 'No job is perfect.'

He rubbed his forehead. 'I don't know ... I loved my job as a mountain guide.'

'So why the hell are you here in Glasgow doing a job that you clearly hate?' She found herself leaning forward, as if to emphasise the point she was making.

Nick looked at her, clearly surprised. 'How do you know that I hate my job? I've never talked about it.'

Jade threw up her hands, wondering if she had to spell everything out. 'Exactly. You never talk about it. Most people who love their jobs, you can't stop them talking about it.'

'I don't hate my job.' He must have realised he sounded unconvincing, because he amended, 'Well, not much.'

'So what's so bad about it?' she found herself asking.

Nick paused, as if wondering which item to pick from a very long list. Or just maybe no one had asked him that question before. He scratched his chin, which was covered in a layer of slightly rugged stubble. 'A combination of things, really. It's a pretty macho environment for starters.'

'Tell me about it.' Jade rolled her eyes. She knew all about that from where she worked. Still, it wasn't like the guys didn't care about the girls ... they just did it in a slightly condescending way. 'I've never heard a guy complain about that before.'

Nick pulled himself up straight, as if this was something that mattered a lot to him. 'We're not all the same, you know.'

Jade suddenly remembered the forgotten half of her breakfast which still lay on her plate and took another bite.

'What is that weird orange stuff anyway?' Nick pointed at her plate.

'It's called sobrasada according to the menu. From Spain apparently.'

He studied her plate, where the sobrasada was smeared on toast with mashed avocado. 'Well, it's the weirdest looking sandwich I've ever seen. I hope it tastes better than it looks.'

'It's amazing.' Jade held out a piece. 'Do you want to try it?'

Nick shook his head, rubbing his stomach. 'I would, but I'm pretty full. I'll have to have a try next time.'

'Oh.' Jade decided it was a perfect opportunity to tease him. 'Does that that mean there will be a next time?' She winked at him.

'Well, what about next week?'

'Next week we're taking the oldies out again. Or have you forgotten your promise?'

'Oh yeah. It's in my diary. I wouldn't have forgotten.' Nick stretched happily, leaning back with his arms tucked behind his head.

Jade slowly crunched her way through the rest of her toast. 'Peter does have a lesson at eight a.m., but that's probably too early for you.'

Nick shook his head. 'Not really. It's only half an hour from my place. How about we go and then have a quick breakfast here before going to pick up the ... oldies, as you call them?' He paused. 'I think I'm going to tell them that you called them that.'

Jade sucked in a breath. 'You wouldn't dare.'

'Never.' Nick smiled, his eyes crinkling at the edges. 'It's our secret.'

And Jade found herself becoming suddenly warm under his gaze. Stop it, she told herself. We're friends, nothing more. You have enough problems to deal with at the moment without taking on someone else's too, remember?

'OK,' she said. 'Yoga, then breakfast, then oldies, as you put it. But that means we might have to wait for the next thing on the list until the weekend after.'

'Can't we do it on the Sunday?'

Jade shook her head. 'Working. You see, another point in the score against my job.'

'You work Sundays?' Nick was surprised.

'Yep, six days a week. And mostly evenings too.'

'Oh, my dreams of go-kart heaven are shattered. I feel for your poor little soul.' He picked up her hand from the table and pressed it against his heart theatrically.

Jade snatched her hand away from his grip, her own heart hammering at the feel of his skin so close to hers. Even through his shirt then she had felt the warmth of his body, and it unsettled her more than she cared to admit. She stood up suddenly, almost knocking her chair over backwards.

'I really need to go.' She grabbed her coat from the chair, wrapping her scarf around her neck right up to her ears, as if she could hide from the world that way. 'I promised to help my mum with some cooking.' It was a lie, but she didn't care. 'Let's pay at the till.'

Nick put his coat on too, seeming to be completely unaware of her inner thoughts, and they wandered back down to the bottom of the hill in silence. The rain fell in a steady drizzle, beading on Nick's hair and making him look like he was grey before his time.

'I'll see you next week then.' Nick leaned in for another quick kiss on her cheek.

'Sure.' Jade found herself smiling up at him.

He gave her a little wave as he set off down the street. Jade put her head down and resolutely walked the other way. She would put all thoughts of what had happened today out of her mind. Anyway, he'd never shown any sign that he was attracted to her. He was a nice guy. Just nice, she told herself firmly. Some kindness after all she had gone through was making her a bit soppy. And that was all it was. She had to keep her focus on what she was really supposed to be doing here, which was making sure that Nick was OK. Building him a support network in Glasgow.

The walk back put her in a better mood. The dull grey streets all sparkled in the wet, and the freshness of the rain made a change from the stink of the cars. By the time she got back home she was smiling. She loved Glasgow. Weather and warts and all. This was her city. And she was proud of it. Roll on life. She was ready for it.

Nick had hoped his muscles would have held up after last week's class, but half-way through a yoga pose he felt his thighs beginning to tremble. Mind you, he hadn't had anything for breakfast, so it was probably all his fault. The black cloud in his brain had come on so fast last night that all he could do was lie in bed and wait for it to pass. He was still waiting. The beautiful spring sun shining in through the windows made even more of a mockery of his mood.

At least he had made it through the week. That was his main goal in life, to pass as normal. Only he knew just how much effort it had taken to drag himself out of bed this morning and walk across town. But he hadn't wanted to let Jade down. Or Archie.

Meeting Jade had given him some hope, and it felt as though she was the only thing that was getting him through his life right now. When he was with her the world seemed a little less grey and depressing. But he would never tell her how he felt about her though. Didn't want her to feel like he was somehow fixated on her in a creepy way. She seemed happy to just be friends. And he could see why. Who would want to take someone on who was miserable most of the time?

To his horror he felt his eyes fill with tears. Not here, not now, he begged himself. He beat his feelings back into submission until they slowly simmered inside him, although he knew they were ready to boil over again at a moment's notice. He shouldn't have come, he knew that now. The sound of Peter's voice as he ended the class felt like the biggest relief he had ever known.

He gathered up his mat, purposely not looking for Jade. He would go home. Sink into his bed. Never come out. And they would find his emaciated corpse when they finally broke down the door.

'Depression lies.' A voice spoke right next to his ear as he bent to put his mat back in the box. It was so quiet that he thought he must have imagined it. Was he starting to hear voices now?

He straightened and turned, only to find Jade not two feet away from him. 'What did you say?' He wanted to confirm what she had said. It felt so random.

'I said, depression lies.' She took his elbow and steered him towards the door. 'Whatever you're feeling right now, it's not you. Depression lies to you. It tells you things that aren't true.'

He looked suspiciously at her as they strolled down the corridor. 'How do you know what I'm thinking?'

She laughed. 'Not what. I'm not a bloody mind-reader. But it's pretty obvious that something's going on. You haven't said a word since you got here, and your eyes look kind of weird. In fact, I'm impressed you actually got here this morning.'

Nick's brain got caught between pride in the fact that she was impressed with him, and panic at the thought that what he was feeling was visible. Did everyone know? Is that why no one had talked to him today?

Jade must have caught some of his more negative thoughts, because she nudged him gently. 'Don't worry. I'm just good at noticing that kind of thing. I've had lots of practice. Now come on, let's get you something to eat. I could hear your stomach grumbling from halfway across the room.'

She disappeared into the changing rooms through the brown wooden door, leaving him staring after her. And one thought wound its way slowly through his tired brain, like a mole slowly carving its way through the dark soil. Who else did she know who felt like him?

Chapter 5

Jade put her arm around Nick's elbow as they walked up the road to the café, as if she knew he needed some mental help to drag himself up the hill. 'You will try the avocado today, won't you?' Her voice sounded almost accusing, as if she expected him to chicken out.

'Yes, although I still think it looks pretty much like someone has thrown up on your plate.'

Jade snorted. 'No more than that disgusting mess you made with your mix of egg, beans and mushrooms last time.'

'It's not the look, it's the taste.' Nick was defensive.

'Yeah. Wouldn't that be a good name for a café?' Jade waved her free arm expansively. '*Looks Shit. Tastes Amazing*.'

Nick had to laugh at that. 'I would go for *Shit Looks. Amazing Taste*. A bit more punchy. Bring in the customers.'

As they stopped outside the café, Nick turned to Jade. 'How is it possible to be happy and sad at the same time? Because that's what I'm feeling today. Like there's a black cloud over everything. But then you just made me laugh. Which just feels weird.'

She looked up at him, startled by the sudden change of topic, and for one unguarded moment he could see his own emotions mirrored in her eyes. 'I don't know. All I know is that it is.' She turned away, as if worried that he might see something on her face, but then suddenly turned back, an intensity in her eyes that surprised him.

'They say that everything passes. But I don't think it does. I think emotions are like the sea. It's sometimes smooth and sunny, and sometimes the wind is blowing so hard you think you're going to sink.' She opened the door, and motioned for him to go in. And as he passed her, she added, 'But it's when you think you're just about to drown that someone else tends to pass by with a life raft.'

She was his life raft, he realised. And he hoped she wasn't going to disappear any time soon, because the thought of swimming through the waves on his own was enough to make him panic.

Nick had to admit that Jade had been right about the breakfast. The bread was amazing, and the freshness of the taste went much better with his unsettled stomach that a cooked breakfast would have done.

'So, where are we going today?' He pushed his empty plate back, surprised that he had managed to eat at all. Still, Jade had distracted him with random stories about funny things that had happened at work, and he had hardly noticed himself eating until he had gone to take another bite and found it all gone.

'We were supposed to be going to the Kelvingrove Museum, but I got a text last night that with the weather as it is then we're just going to have a picnic in the park.'

'Sounds great.' Nick stretched his long legs out under the table, taking care to angle them so they wouldn't brush against Jade's. Last thing he wanted was for that to happen. Actually, he realised he was lying to himself. He was craving physical contact today just like a thirsty person desperate for water. But the last thing he wanted was for Jade to feel uncomfortable with him. He didn't think he would survive if he lost their easy friendship.

'Yeah.' Jade checked her watch. 'In fact, we'd better get ourselves off to the station or we'll be late.'

'It seems a long way to go all the way up there, just to come back here. Can't we just meet them there?'

Jade stood up and pulled him to his feet. 'Come on, lazy bones. A promise is a promise. Besides, Archie has been looking forward to seeing you since last time.'

'Really?' Nick couldn't quite believe what he had just heard. 'Looking forward to seeing me?'

'Oh God, did I not tell you?' Jade stopped in front of the till and rolled her eyes. 'Lily's been texting me. She says he hasn't stopped talking about you. What did you say to him?'

Nick started to say something, and then realised she was teasing him, and folded his arms. 'Any more of that, and you'll have to pay for breakfast.'

Jade shook a finger at him. 'No way. I'll skip off and leave you washing dishes. But seriously, he is really keen to see you. So you can't let him down.'

As they set off down the road Nick could feel the sunshine slowly warming the numbness in his body. Summer was coming. In fact, today almost felt like summer. He should take some time off. Get up north. Do some walking. Hang out by the rivers. Go kayaking. He hadn't had a break since Christmas. It was about time.

Jade had been right. Archie welcomed Nick warmly, shaking his hand firmly, and patting him heartily on the shoulders when he sat down. Lily enveloped him in a rose-scented hug.

'Is that a new perfume you're wearing?' He was good at smells, he realised. Enough to tell that it was different from what she had on last time.

Lily smiled, clearly impressed that he had noticed. 'Yes. Archie got it for my birthday. Came all the way from London.'

'They've been teaching us how to use the internet.' Archie looked smug. 'So I thought I would put my new skills to good use.'

'How old are you now, Lily?' A little smile lifted the corners of Jade's mouth.

Lily looked sternly at Jade, but Nick could see the twinkle in her eyes. This was clearly some sort of game that they had played before. 'Goodness! You know a lady never tells.' She clasped her hands in front of her dramatically, and all four of them laughed.

The bustle started to get everyone into the minibus, and soon they were speeding their way towards their destination. There was no singing this time. Everyone just seemed content to relax and enjoy the sunshine.

Keith dropped them off at the entrance to the park, and they made their way slowly along the winding path. The park was busy with the sounds of people playing football and kids shouting and screaming. It seemed like half of Glasgow was out to enjoy the sun. A group of park runners wove their way past the wheelchairs at one point, flowing around them like rocks in a stream.

'We need a flat bit to play croquet,' Jade said, just when Nick was starting to wonder if they were going to walk the whole length of the park.

'Ah, that's what that weirdly-shaped bag is for.' He pointed at the red bag that one of the other volunteers was carrying. 'I'd wondered that.'

'Yeah. Although we've only got four balls and mallets, so I think we're going to have to do some teams or something.'

'Some people won't be able to play,' Nick pointed out.

'Yeah.' Jade agreed. 'Although that guy over there,' she pointed at one of the wheelchairs up ahead of them, 'pretty much all he remembers how to do is play croquet. Can't even remember if he's had breakfast, but if you put a mallet in his hand, he's a bit of a pro.'

'Weird.' Nick couldn't help marvelling at the brain and how complex it was. People would probably never understand it all.

They finally found the perfect spot and settled themselves down. Someone offered Nick a camping chair, but he politely declined, preferring to lie himself down on a rug. He closed his eyes, feeling the warmth of people's affection wrapping around him like a warm winter jacket, staving off the cold feeling of loneliness. He really should keep on looking for other jobs again, he thought. It was awful to be stuck in that office five days a week. The dark feeling that came over him every time he thought about work started to pull him in, but he pushed it away. Don't think about that right now, he thought. Leave it until Monday morning.

He focused on the little things. The feel of grass under his right hand where it had slipped off the edge of the rug. The gentle breeze on this face. The sound of a blackbird singing in a tree somewhere. It was a beautiful day.

Jade watched Nick as he lay on the ground. His face looked different, she realised. The line in the middle of his forehead had smoothed out to almost nothing, and his breath rose and fell evenly. He even had a faint smile on his lips. She suddenly wished she could freeze him just like that. Life was so cruel to people with mental health problems. Break a leg, and everyone gave you sympathy. Go through a crisis that seemed to be entirely in your brain, and people didn't really have a clue about how to react.

There was a vigorous discussion going on around her about how to set up the croquet teams. Jade leaned back in her chair and closed her eyes, only half listening. The sun warmed her face, making her think that she should have brought sun cream. Lily would have some. But it could wait just a bit longer before she put some on.

Someone tapped her on the shoulder. 'It's three teams of four, and then the winners will all play each other.'

Jade opened her eyes, shading the sun with her hand as she looked up at Connie. 'OK. What are the teams?'

'Well, Archie and Nick, with—'

'Oh no.' Archie interrupted. 'I'm too old for all these shenanigans.'

Nick sat up. 'Oh, come on, Archie. I can't believe you're wimping out of this one.' His hair was all tousled from lying on the grass, and Jade longed to smooth it down for him.

Archie looked down at Nick, slightly affronted. 'Well, young man, unless you're going to invent a new sport called wheelchair croquet ...'

Nick's face broke out in a massive grin. 'I don't have to. It's already been invented. More than a hundred years ago in fact.' He jumped up and grabbed the back of Archie's wheelchair. 'And we are going to play it.'

Jade couldn't help laughing at the eager expression on Archie's face as Nick wheeled him over to the centre of the small patch of grass that had been chosen as their croquet lawn. There was much discussion about the best way to set out the hoops, and then the game began.

The croquet game was a lot of fun. Archie quickly adapted to his new skill, and Nick made fake racing noises as he steered the wheelchair around the grass. There were a lot of insults traded to try and put people off their game, and one of the helpers kept up an Olympic-style sports commentary which had them all in stitches.

It was in the middle of the first round, when he was waiting for Archie to take a shot, that Nick looked straight over at Jade. Focused on Archie, she caught the movement, and looked up just in time to see Nick's infectious grin and a wink. The action was so natural that she couldn't help winking back. Nick turned his attention back to the game, but Jade was caught, stunned by the realisation that despite her best efforts to not get sucked in, she had. She now cared about his happiness. Very deeply, in fact.

You're going to have to tell him about me, Ruby whispered in her mind, *if you care about him that much*.

Jade took a deep breath. She would, she thought. And actually, knowing about what had happened to someone else might even help Nick. And explain a lot of things to him about her own behaviour. But it wasn't like she could just casually drop into the conversation something she had never told anyone else: *you know what, my little sister committed suicide last year and it was all my fault ...*

Dinner, she thought, struggling to focus. She was planning to invite him to dinner at home next week. Mum had promised to cook because she was dying to meet Nick anyway. She could take Nick up to her room and show him the photos and tell him then. That was a good plan. And her anger at herself was just something she would have to deal with, if there was a chance to help someone else.

Lily, sitting next to her, touched her arm. 'Are you OK?'

That was Lily, just always quietly attuned to other people's feelings. No wonder she had been so successful as a social worker. But Jade's feelings of guilt connected with her sister's death were something that she had never been able to reveal to anyone, not even Lily.

'Yes actually.' Jade pulled herself up in her chair and squeezed the older woman's hand briefly. 'I am.' She twisted her neck from side to side, feeling the release of tension from her shoulders that had come from making the decision. She could do this. She would be strong.

Cheering and clapping brought her focus back onto the game in front of her. Archie had won the game, although she didn't know how much of that was due to his skill, or if the others had let him win. It didn't matter anyway, she reminded herself. The whole point of this was to have fun.

'Come on.' She took Lily's arm and helped her up. 'We're up next.'

Jade flopped onto the picnic blanket, badly in need of a drink and glad for the tree that had thrown its shade over their sitting area as the sun grew higher. She would have loved to say that the final had been close, but as usual Jim had trounced everyone again, although second place had been a tightly-fought battle between Archie and Connie, with Archie losing out narrowly to the woman who often took care of Jim on these outings.

'He's been giving her lessons,' Archie grumbled as Nick wheeled him back into position beside Lily's chair.

'Don't feel too bad,' Jade told him. 'Jim was the national croquet champion three years running back in the day. I looked him up.'

'I'm amazed that that's really a thing,' Nick said, throwing himself down beside her.

Jade could feel his presence only inches away from hers, and it felt sort of comforting. If they had been alone then she probably would have reached out and touched him, but instead she just lay with her face propped up on her hands, enjoying the feeling of being near to him.

Someone passed her a can. The cold metal felt amazing in her fingers, and when she cracked it open and felt the fizzy chill slide down her throat then she thanked whoever had invented ice boxes.

They sat enjoying their sandwiches, watching the world go by and saying very little.

'I bet the staff at your place are glad to get rid of everyone for a few hours,' Nick said.

Lily shook her head. 'Maybe. They always use the time to give everywhere a proper clean, so it's not like they're getting a rest.'

'Hmm.' Nick was surprised. 'They do work hard, don't they?' It made his nine to five, Monday to Friday seem pretty relaxed. But still, even eight hours in an office was too much if you hated it.

It was all too soon for Jade when they had to pack up. She could have stayed in the park all afternoon. But she could feel her face getting slightly warm, in spite of the sun cream. She pushed herself up off the grass with regret.

After everyone was settled back home, Jade walked Nick back to the station, despite his protests that he could find the way. It was starting to cloud over now and a strong breeze helped the fluffy masses through the sky.

'Thanks for coming,' she said, as they stopped by the station entrance.

'My pleasure,' Nick said. He put his palm on his face, which was already starting to look slightly pink. 'But I really should remember to wear sun cream next time.'

'Oh! I never thought!' Jade put a hand to her mouth. 'Lily had some in her handbag.'

'I'll just put some after sun on it when I get home.'

'Well, that's probably the summer over, so you should be OK.' Jade suddenly remembered something. 'Oh, next Saturday you're invited for dinner at my place. My mum's going to cook and she's amazing.'

Nick grinned. 'Is that the next thing on the list? Eat some amazing food?'

'Close. It's eat some good food that you haven't had to cook yourself.'

'Interesting that you picked that one. Regular chores seem to be the thing that get me down the most.'

Nick kissed her on the cheek and she could feel the warmth coming off his face. She badly wanted to reach for him, to pull him in for a hug, but by the time her thoughts crystal-lised into actions he was gone.

Chapter 6

Jade paced around in her bedroom, feeling a knot in the bottom of her stomach. Over the past week she had gone through a hundred different ways to tell Nick about her sister, and none of them seemed right. In fact, she had skipped going to yoga this morning because she was sure that he would see her mental turmoil written large on her face.

Pick up the photo, say this is her, act casual. *As if Ruby didn't matter to you?* Her brain frowned at her accusingly. What if he thought she didn't care? What if he rejected her once he knew the whole story? And what if she started crying? Made a fool of herself? Embarrassed him into leaving?

The doorbell rang, and she heard her mum go and answer it. It was too late. She would just have to wing it when the time came.

Nick checked the house number once again on his phone. Yep, this was definitely the right one. But when the door opened there stood a small Chinese woman with short black hair, which was definitely what he wasn't expecting.

'Hi,' she said with a big smile. 'You must be Nick. I'm Shirley.' Then, perhaps sensing his confusion, she added, 'Jade's mum. So pleased to meet you.' She held out her hand.

Nick was sure that she had been through this particular ritual many times. Feeling himself growing slightly red, he took her hand and grasped it tentatively. She had an unexpectedly firm grip, and he found his own hand tightening up in response, his shyness slowly retreating.

'I brought you this.' He held out a bottle of wine in the other hand.

Shirley took it from him. 'So kind of you. Please come in.'

She took him through the hall, but instead of turning into the sitting room, where he could hear the TV was on, she led him to the back of the house, where what was once presumably the dining room had been combined with the kitchen. She sat him down at the small wooden dining table and turned to stir something on the stove. The back door stood open, with the evening sun streaming in through the gap.

If the smell in the air was any indication, she was as good a cook as Jade had claimed. Nick inhaled deeply, savouring the scents that he couldn't define. His stomach rumbled.

'I am sure Jade will be down in just a minute.' Shirley pulled a glass out of a cupboard. 'We'll have your wine with the meal. Would you like some juice while we wait?'

Nick nodded. 'That would be great.'

Sure enough, a few moments later Jade opened the kitchen door.

'Hey.' Her smile was kind of tentative, and he wondered if it had anything to do with her missing yoga this morning. He had enjoyed the class, but it hadn't felt the same without her.

'Hey.' He started to get up, but the table sort of trapped him, and by the time he had got halfway then Jade had already pulled out the chair opposite. Her mother set another glass of orange juice on the table for her.

'Thanks, Mum.'

That was the thing about Jade that always surprised him. She had this kind of tough girl exterior. Swore a lot. But underneath she was so incredibly kind. And polite. She was such a contradiction.

'So,' he said, leaning towards her, 'what happened to yoga today? I was expecting to see you.'

A slightly guilty look came over Jade's face. 'Oh.' She blushed slightly. 'I had some things to do.'

Nick wondered if she was having second thoughts about their friendship. But still she would have hardly invited him here, to her house, scratch that, to her parents' house, if she didn't want to see him again. Jade, being Jade, would be the first one to tell him to get lost if she couldn't be bothered. And probably not even as politely as that.

Looking at them in the same room together, he could see the similarities between the two of them. Random gestures. The way they moved. They were pretty much the same height, although he had to look really closely to see any similarity in their faces. And then it suddenly dawned on him; Jade's hair wasn't dyed black at all. It was the exact same colour as her mother's. Obviously, the sparkly green highlights that shot through it were entirely her own creation, but the rest was completely natural.

'Jade, go and get your dad from the next room, darling.' Shirley leaned back against the kitchen counter.

'Is it dinner time already?' Jade sounded hopeful. Maybe she was as hungry as he was.

'No.' Shirley's reply was unexpected. 'But I'm just about to grill this young man about every aspect of his life, and I don't want him to have to repeat himself when your dad asks the same questions.'

As Jade disappeared, Nick considered Shirley's words. She was joking, right? He hoped she was joking, anyway. He didn't much like the idea of being grilled. He looked up and found her looking at him. She winked. 'Don't worry. No challenging questions.'

Jade's mum was definitely like no other mother he had ever met. But then, Jade was like no other woman he had ever met either. She was pretty unique. And kind of special.

He heard the sudden silence as the TV was switched off, and then the kitchen door opened again. Nick wasn't sure what he had been expecting from Jade's dad. But when he saw him he knew that it couldn't be anyone else. Jade had her father's face in miniature, but without that thick mass of grey hair. It started him wondering what bits of his own parents he had inherited, which wasn't something he had ever thought about before.

But the big hand that took his own in a welcoming grip was nothing like Jade's at all. Rough and slightly calloused, it felt very warm and reassuring. Nick found himself liking this man before they had even said a word to each other.

'I'm Martin. Welcome to our house, young man.' The big man sat himself down in one of the other chairs, while Jade resumed her seat opposite Nick. The size of the table was such that if he had just stretched out his legs a little their knees would have touched. The thought made him flush slightly, which surprised him. He wasn't attracted to Jade, was he?

Shirley set a bowl of crisps on the table, along with a bowl of roasted peanuts. 'Just so you won't die from hunger.' She gave him another wink. 'So, tell us where you're from.'

'I grew up in Fort William.' That was an easy one. 'My parents run a B&B just at the far end of the town.'

'Brothers? Sisters?' The older woman snagged a couple of crisps from the table and returned to her cooking.

Nick shook his head. 'Nope.' He paused, wondering how much to reveal. 'I think maybe they wanted to, but couldn't.'

'Ah.' Shirley nodded knowingly, and Nick wondered if she had experienced the same. After all, they just had Jade, and no one else.

'So what brought you down to Glasgow?' It was Martin this time. The man leaned forward, his elbows resting on the table, the rolled-up sleeves of his bright checked orange shirt stretching over his upped arms. Nick could see where Jade had got her liking for flashy colours. By contrast, her mother was dressed in muted black trousers and a dark maroon jumper. Nick found himself intrigued by these two people, they seemed so different. How had they even met? How had they got together?

He realised that Martin's question was still hanging. 'Work, really. It's been pretty hard since the recession. I studied up in Fort William, and then had to come down here for work.'

'What did you study?' It was Jade's question. And Nick realised that they had spent so much time talking about weird stuff that they had never really done the standard getting to know you questions.

'Oh, just an HND in computing.' He had enjoyed the course, he realised. 'I was hoping to do something locally, maybe with the Navy, but because of the cutbacks then I couldn't find anything. So I'm working for a small company that does consultancy work in cybersecurity.'

There, he thought. He had managed to talk about his job without feeling any sense of despair, or panic. He took some crisps from the bowl.

'So what do you both do?' The question slipped out before he really thought about it.

'Dad's a taxi driver,' Jade said proudly.

Martin nodded. 'Twenty-three years now. Took it up when Jade was born. Easier to look after a kid when you're working flexible hours.'

Nick nodded, impressed. He had casually assumed that just because Shirley was the one cooking that they had taken up traditional roles in the home, but it just showed that you could never tell.

'Shirley works in the CAB.' Martin, seeing Nick's puzzled face, added, 'Citizen's Advice Bureau.'

'Yeah, there's still loads of Chinese people in Glasgow who don't speak very good English,' Jade added. 'They were really happy for your skills, right Mum?'

'Not loads of people,' her mother corrected gently, grinding some pepper into a metal bowl an adding some salt. 'There are a few. But we help everyone, no matter where they come from.'

'So how did you two meet?'

At that question Martin laughed, while Shirley just smiled. She motioned at her husband. 'Go on, you tell it.'

Martin shook his head. Was the man actually blushing? 'No, you do it. You're so much better at stories than me.'

Jade leaned forward in her chair. 'Come on, Mum. It's a great story.'

'OK.' Shirley resumed her mixing. 'My parents came over from Hong Kong in the seventies. I don't really remember much before we moved here. I was pretty young. They set up a Chinese restaurant in town, on Sauchiehall Street. I used to work there after school, and when I left school, I joined them full time. I think my parents were always hoping I would take over the business. Anyway, Martin used to come in on a Saturday night with his mates, before they went out drinking. He became a bit of a regular, but I never worked out if that was because of me or just because of the food.' She winked at her husband, a big smile on her face.

'So do your parents come down to see you often?' Martin looked back at Nick.

'Not often. They're very busy with the B&B.' Nick frowned. He didn't want to say that they hadn't visited him at all, in case they thought that was strange.

'Right.' Nick jumped as Shirley placed two bowls in front of him on the table. One held something which looked like uncooked pastry, the other was full of mince mixed with grated vegetables.

He looked at her, puzzled, but Jade had already uttered a crow of delight and was reaching for the pastry. 'Oh Mum! We haven't had these for ages. But you didn't warn Nick that he'd be making his own dinner.' She looked straight at Nick, and he knew she was thinking of the list. He smiled at her, to let her know it was OK.

Shirley produced a rolling pin and a large round cookie cutter, and placed them on the table.

'You're going to have to show me what to do.' Nick looked back at Jade.

In the end, Martin rolled out the pastry, as Jade said he had the biggest muscles, and Nick wasn't about to argue with that. Jade cut rounds out of the resulting thin translucent layer, and Nick dolloped a small scoop of meat mixture carefully into the middle of each one. Shirley showed them how to crimp the edges together with just a touch of water, to make sure they didn't come apart when cooking. Then she dumped the first batch into the water, while Jade cleaned up the table and washed up the bowls.

Nick had eaten dim sum before, but these were like nothing he had ever tasted. Light and fluffy, they almost melted on his tongue. There was a complex combination of flavours that just blended into a subtle but perfect whole. He ate until he was full, and then managed to squeeze in three more.

'I told you it would be good.' Jade laughed at him as he leaned back in his chair, totally overcome. 'You won't believe it, but Mum hardly ever cooks Chinese food. We usually just have macaroni cheese or pasta or something.'

'It takes a lot of effort to get it right,' Shirley said. 'Too much effort for every day.'

'Couldn't you just freeze these and cook them later?' Nick wanted to know.

She nodded, then shook her head. 'You could. But once you taste them fresh, the frozen ones just miss something.' She rose, bringing the fruit bowl from the sideboard to put on the table. 'Dessert is just fruit. Good to have something fresh after all that meat.'

They ate the fruit, Nick enjoying the sharp contrast of fresh orange slices to the rest of what he had eaten. Shirley showed them how to carve an apple into beautifully artistic shapes. Nick wanted to take it home, but by the time everyone had finished admiring it then it was already starting to go brown, so Jade and he divided it in half and ate the delicate curls slowly, savouring the paper-thin strips.

Nick could feel the usual knot of tension in his shoulders slowly unwinding. It was almost as if the three other people in the room were bleeding away the darkness that usually eclipsed his happiness, and he thanked them all silently for it. This all seemed so normal. So cosy. Almost like home.

The thought made him still for a moment. He missed home terribly. He longed for the mountains. But tonight had shifted things somehow. Until this evening, he had thought there was nothing to tie him in Glasgow. But these people, these three people who had taken him into their home so naturally, were starting to make him feel like there might be something worth staying for.

When they had finished, Nick offered to help with the washing up, but Shirley waved him away. Martin left for work, but not before he had said goodbye to his wife with a kiss that left Nick not knowing where to look.

'Do you have to still do that when we have visitors?' Jade complained when her father had left.

Shirley stopped, her hands still in the washing up water, and looked straight at her. 'Do you know why we do that?'

Jade shrugged, looking at her mother.

A faint smile appeared on the other woman's face. 'I thought I told you this story before.'

Jade shook her head, obviously puzzled. 'No, never.' She leaned forward, elbows resting on the table, chin in her hands. 'Is it very romantic?'

Her mother laughed, drying her hands and sitting down at the table again. 'Yes and no. You see, just after you were born, I found it very hard. It was the middle of winter, things were very cold, the sky was always grey. Being a new mother is always hard. Your father and I used to argue all the time. He had just started his job with the taxi, and was working all the hours he could to pay for the three of us. We were both so tired.'

Jade reached across to find her mother's hand and squeezed it. Nick saw the other woman give a quick squeeze back.

'So one night we argued as usual. He left. About one in the morning I got a call from the hospital. He had been stabbed by someone who he picked up. Of course, I rushed to the hospital with you, terrified that I was going to lose him.

'You won't remember, you were too young.' She patted Jade's hand. 'But I swore after that whenever he left, I was going to show him how much I loved him. Every time.'

Jade swallowed, her eyes suspiciously shiny. 'That's a scary story, Mum.' She rose from the table, obviously uncomfortable. 'I was just going to show Nick my room, then I thought we could watch some TV. Is that OK?'

Shirley laughed. 'You're a grown up now, darling. You can do whatever you want.'

Then, as Nick also got up, she added, 'I forgot to tell you. Carina called. She said she really needs to speak to you.'

Nick caught a glimpse of Jade's face as she turned back towards her mother, and the look he saw there suddenly scared him. Her eyes flashed like granite in a winter sun. Whoever this Carina was, she definitely wasn't popular.

'I told you I wanted nothing to do with her.' Jade's voice was taught and barely controlled. 'You shouldn't even be taking calls from her.'

Shirley's shoulders slumped and Nick wondered what was going on. The tension between the two women drew out like a thin rope that was close to snapping. 'I just thought–'

'Well, don't just think.'

Nick couldn't believe the change that had come over Jade. Her face was white like he'd never seen it before. Her tone was harsh and unforgiving. And rude.

'Darling, she said it was important. Said she had something she needed to show you. She was your best friend. Won't you just talk to her?'

'I don't give a shit about anything she needs.' Jade's voice rose. 'And how can you even speak to her? After what she said at Ruby's funeral.'

Nick just stood in the corner, not knowing what to do. He felt like he was intruding in a very private conversation. Ruby? Who the hell was Ruby?

Then something clicked in his brain. Jade had said her grandmother had died not that long ago. That must be it. And whatever Carina had said, it couldn't have been good, to get Jade into such a state. He shifted uncomfortably, the tension in the room suddenly too much for him. The knot in his shoulders had reappeared and was twisting painfully.

Jade must have remembered that there was a third person with them. 'I'm really sorry, Nick. I didn't mean to drag you into this.' She suddenly deflated. She looked so lost that Nick wanted to just pull her into his arms and hug her.

She went across to her mum and put an arm around her shoulders. 'Sorry, Mum. I didn't mean to shout. I just don't want to talk to her, OK?'

Her mother reached up, smoothing a stray strand of hair back behind her daughter's ear. 'It's OK, darling. I know this is hard on you.'

Jade dropped a kiss on the top of her mother's head, then turned to Nick. 'Are you coming?'

The intensity of the longing that had sheared through Nick as he watched their exchange had surprised him. He missed his mum. And his dad. As a grown man he had a hard time admitting that, but it was true. He missed their cosy evenings in front of the big range in the kitchen, putting the world to rights while his mother did the ironing and his father folded towels. And to his horror he found he was close to tears.

'Actually, I think I'd better go home,' he mumbled, stuffing his hands in the pocket of his jeans. 'It's getting late. And I have to get up early tomorrow.' It was a lie, but he just had to get out of there.

Jade's face fell, as if she had been hoping for him to stay. The disappointment on her face speared his heart, just adding to the sadness he felt inside him. But now all he could think of was getting out of the house. He managed to hang on to his control long enough to thank her mother for the dinner, and then he turned away, desperate to get out before he made a fool of himself.

'Wait,' Jade called as he opened the front door. 'I'll walk you to the station.'

Nick wanted to tell her no, but found that speech was too much for him. Jade had already grabbed a jumper and followed him. It would be easier to just let her walk beside him, he thought. He could stop himself splintering for five more minutes, as long as he didn't say anything. After all, how different was it from what he had to do every day? He focused his mind on the steps he was taking. Of the feel of the pavement beneath his feet. He walked in silence, counting in his head. One hundred. Two hundred. Three hundred. They were almost at the station now.

'I know what you were doing on that bridge.'

Jade's statement almost made him stumble as he took the next step, her words so unexpected that they literally caught him off-balance. His brain whirled as he absorbed the weight of what she had just said. If she had figured that out, what else did she know?

He turned towards her. 'You what?'

Jade shrugged. 'I know. And I don't judge you for it. Life is hard sometimes.' Her tone of voice sounded as if she had some experience of what she was talking about. 'And I'm sorry about what happened back there. This thing with Carina is a bit of a sore point and I just flamed up. I'm sorry if it made you uncomfortable.'

How could he tell her that it wasn't the anger that had almost destroyed him, but the tenderness instead? Desperate to distract both Jade and his own mind from his own problems, he blurted out the first thing that came into his head. 'What did Carina say to you, that made you so angry?'

Jade looked at him, as if that was the last thing she'd expected him to ask. She hesitated a few moments. 'She said she wasn't surprised.' The shape of her mouth, and her arms that went to wrap around herself, told him how hard it was for her to relive the words.

'That she died? What an awful thing to say.' Nick felt a flash of anger at this person, who was supposed to be her best friend, but had caused her so much grief. But he could be a friend to Jade; he could be there for her. If he managed to hold himself together. He had to leave. Now. Before he totally broke apart.

'Look, Nick, I need to talk to you about Ruby.' Jade's words were rushed, as if it was something she had been waiting to say for a long time.

He forestalled her by touching her shoulder, feeling the bones barely covered by a thin layer of flesh. 'You don't have to. I worked it all out.'

Her face, still visible in the deepening twilight, showed its confusion. 'You did?'

'Yes. Losing anyone from your family is hard, but to lose someone so close to you must have been awful. My friend Jamie lost his dad a few years ago. He found it really hard too.'

Jade looked at him as if he'd just taken a weight off her shoulders. 'It was. I can't tell you how much she meant to me.'

Nick touched her gently on the shoulder again. Part of him longed to reach out and pull her towards him, but he knew if he did then he would splinter into a thousand pieces. 'You can tell me all about it when you're ready, but until then, it's fine.'

He heard a rumble from the tracks and looked at his watch. 'Look, I really need to catch this train, I'm going to have to run. Thank your mum again for the dinner, won't you? And thanks for inviting me.'

He sped off before she had the chance to reply. He barely made the train, jumping in just as the doors were closing, and sagged into a corner seat. He buried his head in his hands, squeezing his face as if it would somehow put back together all the chaotic pieces of his brain. Depression lies, he told himself. Depression lies. He repeated the words all the way back into town, holding onto the thought like a climber clinging to a rockface when the only alternative is to fall.

Jade looked at the place where Nick had been just moments before. She had been building herself up so much to telling him that his sudden departure and his revelations made her feel like a yawning hole had opened up at her feet. Relief settled in her heart, while confusion filled her head. He had figured it out, he told her. But how the hell had he done that? No one had mentioned anything. Just a name. And the funeral part. How had he done it?

The photo. It hit her with blinding clarity. The photo in the hall. The one of the four of them. Someone had taken it for them, during that idyllic summer holiday they'd spent on Arran. That had been a beautiful trip. The weather had been amazing. That had been the last summer before Ruby ...

She tried desperately to push the memories away. Leaving her phone at home by accident when she went on a night out with friends. The missed voicemail messages from her sister. Coming home to find Ruby not in her bed, and her mum not there either. The hospital. Her little sister. The bed. The tubes. The days of waiting. And the agonising decision to switch off her life support when it was clear there was nothing more that anyone could do.

Jade couldn't help it; the tears broke open and flowed down her cheeks. She found a wall not far away and leaned against it, hands over her face. The brick at her back felt like a rough caress, grounding her, connecting her back to the real world while she struggled with her thoughts.

You have to deal with this, especially the guilt, she thought. It's not going to go away. But somehow, meeting Nick had brought everything back to the surface. You should have never spoken to him, that day on the bridge. Should have stayed out of other people's business.

But really, maybe it would be good to talk about it with someone, she thought. Someone who might be able to give her some insight into why Ruby had done what she did. It seemed so incomprehensible. So out of character for her. So

... she didn't really want to say the word even to herself, but so selfish.

There. It was said now. Yes. Selfish. It had been selfish of her sister to take the easy way out, to disappear while she, Jade, had to carry on without her. To see the impact her death had on their parents. She was angry with her sister, she realised. And guilty about how angry she felt. And angry about how guilty she felt.

What a fuck up, she thought. What a total pile of shit this is.

'Y'allright, hen?' A voice nearby startled her into opening her eyes.

A round middle-aged woman stood a couple of metres away, a concerned look on her kind face.

Jade sniffed very unattractively, wiping the tears away from her face. God knows what she must look like. 'Yes ... yes. Just having a moment.'

The woman looked at her for another few seconds. 'PMT – a killer, eh?' Obviously satisfied, she started to carry on down the street. 'Just you wait for the menopause, hen, that's when the shit really hits the fan.'

Jade couldn't help but smile. This city, and its people, were probably the only thing that would save her. She turned, wrapping her arms around herself, and headed for home through the gathering darkness.

Once back in the warmth of her home, Jade paused in the hallway, to look at the photo which she had barely registered for months. She studied it carefully. They all had their arms around each other, but Ruby had her sunglasses on, hiding her eyes from the camera. Had she been having problems even then? She had been quiet in those last few months, but Jade had just put it down to the stresses of her final year at school and the big decision about what to do afterwards.

She took a deep breath. It was too late to ask her now. Her sister was gone, and that wouldn't change. She would talk to Nick, but only when she was ready. And until that time, she was just going to get on with things and savour the feeling of being alive. Of having a good friend. She used to have a lot of friends. Where had they all gone?

She had pushed them away one by one, she realised, tired of their efforts to drag her out of herself and cheer her up. But Nick didn't do that. He was just – well – funny. He had a great sense of humour. He was good for her, she thought, as she slowly climbed the stairs to her room. Long may it continue.

Chapter 7

Jade waited at the bottom of the station steps, sheltering under the railway bridge. There couldn't be more difference between the glorious sunshine of two weeks ago and today's weather. The steady drizzle seemed to find its way into everything. She had gone back to wearing Ruby's old red coat again, glad of its big comfy hood. The colour didn't really suit her, but she didn't care. She pushed her hands deeper into the soft wool pockets. When she was being fanciful, she pretended it was a hug from her sister. Sometimes it helped.

Jade was telling herself off at this very moment, too. Nick knew how to find his way to Sunnyside by now. She could be inside enjoying a brew with Lily. So why was she freezing her arse off in the rain just to meet him?

Because you've fallen for him. Jade shifted from one foot to the other, and back again. If she was completely honest with herself, she had. But not in a romantic way, just in an admiring way. That was it. She was full of admiration for him and how he was dealing with his issues. Anyway, Nick had missed the yoga class this morning, even though he had said he would be there. She didn't mind helping him out, but dating someone unreliable was a big no-no.

'Hi.' It was as if she had conjured him out of her thoughts; there he stood, in the bright blue jacket she had seen him in the first time they had met. She had been so busy with her thoughts that she hadn't noticed the rumble of the train above her.

'Hey.' She couldn't have cared what the weather was doing now. 'How's your week been?'

Nick shrugged. 'Not bad. The usual.' He fell into step beside her. 'I'm so sorry for not turning up this morning. Work's been pretty bad, and I didn't sleep well last night. I totally overslept.'

What could she say to that? She pushed her irritation away. Telling him off for something he clearly already felt bad about wouldn't help either of them.

'Anyway.' He touched her on the arm. 'I'm dying to know what the next thing on the list is. And actually, I'm dying to know about the whole list. I mean, I don't even know how long it is. The suspense is killing me!'

Jade couldn't help laughing at his melodramatic tone, which she was sure was put on for effect. 'Isn't it nice to get a surprise each week? Just think of it like a game.'

'Oh – come on.' Nick put a hand to his heart and looked towards the heavens. 'So cruel.'

'If I give you the list, then you might not be bothered to see me again. Or Lily. Or Archie. And we all know that he would pine away if he didn't see you regularly.' Jade tried to keep her voice light, but her words did hold a very real fear for her; if Nick had the list, then he had absolutely no reason to keep seeing her. And she knew that, in spite of all the issues he was having, he made her world just that little bit brighter. She didn't want to do without him.

'Ridiculous,' Nick scoffed. 'I couldn't do without my little Weegies.'

'You'd better not let Archie hear you lumping him in with all the Glasgow people,' Jade warned him. 'He always insists he comes from Milngavie.'

'Meh.' Nick seemed unimpressed with this statement. 'At least tell me what the next thing is on the list. What is our quest for today, fair lady?'

Jade couldn't help her irritation melting away. Nick in a good mood was just ... well, great.

'It's very simple. You have to hug someone.'

Nick stopped walking and turned towards her. 'Is that it?' His face showed his surprise. 'That's on your happy list?'

'Not just any hug.' Jade defended herself. 'Not just a passing thing. A proper hug. Really wrap your arms around someone. You'd be surprised at how good it feels. Besides, hugging is supposed to release that happy drug in your brain. I've forgotten its name.'

Nick was silent for a bit, as they tramped round puddles on the pavement.

'Am I allowed to hug you, or does it have to be someone else?'

She should have expected the question, really, but it still took her by surprise. A hug? With him? Did she even want to do that? Wouldn't it be overstepping the bounds of their friendship?

Friends hug all the time, she reminded herself. Yes, but not when one of them had a secret crush on the other one. There, she had admitted it. She had a crush on him, which was a total disaster. Which is why hugging him would be a very bad idea.

'Earth to Jade. Earth to Jade.' Nick made crackly radio noises.

Jade blinked, realising she was just about to walk right past the entrance to Sunnyside. She turned to him. 'I think you should hug someone else. Lily maybe. Or Archie. I bet he doesn't get many hugs.'

Nick looked at her, his face clearly sceptical. 'Okay.'

'Oh! Am I glad to see you!' Sandra greeted Nick with a fist pumped in the air as they entered the building. 'We've got two people off sick today, and I've barely got enough helpers. Jade, I think you're going to have to let Lily walk by herself today. I need you to push Jim.'

They had just got everyone on the minibus when the sky opened. The rain lashed the windows, and Keith drove carefully, windscreen wipers frantic. Nick couldn't believe that anyone would want to go out in this weather. 'Are we going to change our plans?' he asked. Jade was sitting right beside him in the front of the minibus this time, sandwiched between him and Keith. He tried to ignore the fact that both her shoulder and thigh was touching his, and the unexpected effect that it was having on him. Thank goodness he had his rucksack on his knees.

'I don't think so.' It was Jade who replied. Keith was too busy peering into the road ahead.

He could smell the faint scent of her perfume, something delicate that he couldn't define. It suited her though. Nick focused determinedly on the road in front of him. 'A picnic? On a day like this? Are you crazy?'

'It's just a passing shower. The weather is supposed to clear up soon.' A stray piece of damp hair was clinging to Jade's cheek, and Nick had to clench his hands together to stop himself from smoothing it away. If she had refused a hug from him earlier, she was bound to go apeshit about him doing something like that. This was turning out to be so more complicated than he had imagined. If it weren't for Archie, and the fact that he knew the old man was lonely, he would just walk away from the whole situation. But Jade was right. A promise was a promise. And he wasn't the type to let people down.

'I brought my camping tarpaulin, we can sit on that if the grass is damp.' Nick had seen the forecast and had been determined to be prepared.

'That was thoughtful of you.' Jade shifted slightly next to him, and Nick tried desperately to think of anything else.

The rain was still coming down by the time they drove through the entrance to the park. Nick was relieved when they stopped outside what was obviously a cafe. He pulled his hood up. 'You stay here. I'll give you a shout when it's time to run for it.' But Jade stubbornly got out right behind him.

They managed fairly well with a few umbrellas and waterproof jackets thrown over the wheelchairs, but by the time they were all through the door they were all partially soaked to some degree. The smell of fresh coffee was heavenly.

'What a day.' Lily pushed back her hood. 'I think I need a cuppa first after all that.'

While the group was all seated, conversation turned to the next trip they were doing. Everyone was very excited about the matinee visit, although there was some quite intense discussion about the quality of what they were seeing and whether a musical counted as real theatre.

'Who pays for these trips?' Nick turned to Jade, who was sitting on his left.

'Well, mostly people pay for the costs themselves.' Jade fiddled with one of her braids. 'But this time we put a bit of money in to help with the theatre tickets. And the minibus gets paid out of the grant too.'

'A grant?' Nick frowned, not quite understanding.

Jade nodded. 'Yeah. A charity grant. We got one to cover just the basic costs. Sandra's pretty good at sorting these things out.'

Nick stored this piece of information away for future reference. He had thought that charities only gave their money to life-threatening things, but seemingly not. Interesting.

By the time they had finished their tea the rain had stopped and everything was sparkling in the bright sunshine. Nick wheeled Archie out into the fresh damp air. It smelled amazing.

'Some of the people who don't want to walk so far are going to just go round the gardens here,' Jade said, wrapping her handbag around the handle of Jim's wheelchair. 'But some of us are going to go for a walk around the park if you want to come.' They said goodbye to Lily, who was going to the gardens, and set off.

The park was great. It felt like they were out in the countryside. Vast old trees spanned their branches high above their heads, and they had to steer around occasional puddles on the path. The rain-soaked grass in the sunshine sparkled like a million diamonds. The group stopped frequently to look at a particular tree, or a flower, or to watch a squirrel bouncing past. To his delight, they even came across a group of highland cows in an open field. When Nick checked his watch and saw that two hours had passed, he couldn't believe it.

He mentioned this to Jade, who suddenly looked panicked. 'Shit, I was supposed to be keeping track of time! They'll all be wondering where we've got to. We have to go.'

She turned Jim's wheelchair and set off determinedly. The sunshine had disappeared by now, and Nick zipped his jacket up before he set off after her. The other three helpers turned their wheelchairs and set off behind him.

When Nick caught up with Jade he could see that she was tiring, but she determinedly set her mouth and carried on. At the top of a small slope she stopped for a minute to rest her arms, and waved the others past them. 'You go on ahead. We won't be long.'

Nick refused to leave her and stopped just beside her. Archie was uncharacteristically quiet.

Suddenly a few fat drops of rain fell on them. Everyone looked upwards. A massive grey cloud lay directly above them.

Jade swore again and grabbed the handles of Jim's wheelchair. 'Sandra is going to kill me.'

They hurried on, Jade almost running now, and Nick stretched his long legs to match her pace. He was so busy trying to keep up with her that he forgot to look at the path in front of them. A big bump shook the wheelchair, and Archie went flying, crying out in pain as he hit the floor and then lay still.

Jade came running back towards them, shock and worry written on her face. 'What happened?'

Nick felt his own face flush with shame. He pointed to the ridge in the path where a tree root had pushed up the tarmac.

'What are we going to do?' Jade put a hand on Archie's shoulder, who groaned at her touch. He had fallen face down on the grass, and lay with one arm twisted under him.

Nick realised he had to think quickly; the rain was now coming down more steadily, and time was critical. 'You take Jim back to the rest of the group. No point in keeping him out here to get cold and wet. I'll stay with Archie and call an ambulance. They'll be here sooner than you think.'

Jade looked at him, as if not sure whether this was really a good idea, but then she nodded. The look of trust in her eyes only enhanced his feeling of guilt. 'Text me when you have any news.' She hurried off.

Nick knelt down beside Archie. He would call for an ambulance, but first he had to find out how badly Archie was hurt. He touched him gently on the shoulder, calling his name, and was relieved when the old man opened his eyes.

Nick opened his first aid kit and took out a foil blanket. Not only would this keep off the rain, but it might also keep in some heat. He placed it gently over Archie, then touched him on the shoulder again. 'Can you tell me what hurts?'

Archie seemed more with it now and smiled weakly up at him. 'Everything, lad. But then, when you get to my age, that's normal.'

Nick took a breath of relief. If Archie was cracking jokes, then things couldn't be that bad.

A few more minutes of exploration determined that Archie's left arm was the only thing that was really in trouble. Nick called the ambulance, who said they would do their best, but since it wasn't life-threatening then it wouldn't be immediately. Nick managed to get Archie to a sitting position on one foil blanket, with another wrapped around his shoulders, but it wasn't an ideal situation, not with the rain coming down all around them.

Then, inspiration struck him as he noticed a close-growing group of trees less than twenty metres away. He touched Archie briefly on the shoulder. 'I'll be back in a couple of minutes. Don't go anywhere.'

The old man let out a cackle of laughter, cradling his arm to his chest.

Nick pulled his tarp out of his rucksack as he walked towards the trees. He had brought it to sit on, but it would be just as easy to rig up a shelter for them both to sit under. In less than two minutes he had everything sorted and came running back to Archie.

'Do you think we could get you in the wheelchair?'

Archie nodded, obviously willing to try. It took them a couple of minutes of manoeuvring to get him up and in. Nick winced every time they jolted Archie's arm. But finally they were in, and Nick wheeled Archie ever so carefully over to the makeshift shelter he had made. The tarp formed a shape just like the top of a house, and they could be safe and dry underneath, while the rain ran off down the sides.

'Nice work, lad.' Archie nodded approvingly. Nick tied up the injured arm in a sling, and then wrapped the foil blankets carefully around him. It wasn't a particularly cold day, but he knew how fast someone could lose body heat when they weren't moving around. He silently thanked his first aid training.

Rooting around in his rucksack, he found his emergency plastic bag that he always kept in there because he always forgot to take one with him shopping. Spreading it out, he settled himself on the ground beside Archie's wheelchair. And he had found something else in his bag that he had forgotten about.

He held up the two muffins that he had bought from the cafe in case he got hungry. 'Chocolate or blueberry?'

They munched in silence for a while, listening to the steady beat of the rain drumming on the green fabric surface above them. 'I'm really sorry about what happened.' Nick felt he had to apologise.

Archie waved his good arm. 'Don't worry, lad. These things happen. I've been in worse situations.' He finished his last bit of muffin, carefully brushing a few dropped crumbs from his lap. 'There was the time I fell off a cliff face and broke both arms. Had to get someone to feed me for six weeks.'

Nick smiled, thinking of the old man, in his younger days, tramping up and down lofty peaks. 'I miss the mountains.'

He felt a hand descend onto his head, and a gentle movement tousled his hair. 'You just need to decide what's most important in your life, lad. Don't get stuck in this money trap.'

Nick's shoulders slumped. 'That's so easy to say, but so hard to do.'

This time a finger reached under his chin and gently lifted it until he was staring right into Archie's eyes. 'You'll know when the call hits you, lad.' Bright blue eyes peered intensely at him out of the wrinkled face. 'But also don't forget things can change. What you need at one point in your life might not be the same some other time. Look at me. Twenty years ago I couldn't have thought of leaving the mountains. Now I'm really happy to be close to our Maisie and the family. You just have to listen to your heart, lad.'

Nick considered this for a couple of minutes. He had been so tied up in everything that he hadn't stopped to think about what he really wanted. Hadn't thought that there might be another way to stay at home. But then come to think of it, did he really want to stay at home? Or did he want to strike off on his own and make his own mark?

And what did his heart truly want? He tried to ask himself that question, reached into the depths of the dark pool that lay there. And the first thing that came out was Jade. He hadn't realised until that very moment how much she meant to him as a friend. It was something to do with her smile, and her badass but caring attitude to her life. And how she made him feel as if he could find a way to solve his problems. She was pretty special.

Nick let out a sigh of relief as he saw the two paramedics coming towards them across the grass. They wore sturdy waterproofs and seemed well-prepared for the weather.

'Great day for a camping holiday, eh, lads?' one of them joked.

Jade made her way through the entrance doors to the hospital, Lily on her arm. The other woman had insisted on coming after they had dropped everyone off at the home, and she hadn't had the heart to put her off. They had left the others having the missed picnic in the communal sitting room. Jade's dad had dropped them off at the hospital, promising to come and pick them up later. The two of them had eaten their sandwiches in the car on the way over. Nick had messaged her to say that Archie was OK, but that he thought his arm might be broken.

Jade had pretty much forgotten what the building looked like inside. The last time she had been in the place she had been so focused on Ruby and what was happening to her that she hadn't really registered anything else. But it all came back to her as they came through the doors. A huge atrium rose five or six floors high in the middle of the building, with glass set in the roof to let in natural light. There were a couple of cafes, and even a small supermarket. Tables and chairs were dotted around for people to sit on. The walls were painted in warm colours instead of unrelenting white. Despite the massive size of the place, it almost felt cosy.

Scanning the area, she saw Nick sitting at one of the tables. He waved a hand when he saw them.

'They think it's a broken arm.' He greeted them as they sat down not with a hello but with the news they both really wanted to know. 'But they're checking his head out too in case he hit it in the fall. They were talking about maybe keeping him in overnight just in case.' He leaned back in his chair, wrapping his arms around him. 'They chucked me out while they were doing all the tests and stuff. It'll be another hour or so.'

Jade leaned over and twisted his wrist so she could see his watch. His skin felt slightly chilly, and she remembered that he must have missed his lunch.

'I'll get everyone a brew.' She rose from the table and walked towards one of the cafés. The prices made her wince slightly, but she took three cups of tea, and picked up a sandwich for Nick. He looked at her gratefully when she slid it across the table and it disappeared in a couple of bites.

'Thanks. I kind of forgot about food what with everything else. Did you guys get back OK?'

Jade nodded. 'Everyone got a bit damp, but there was no harm done.' She rubbed her upper arms. 'That's the last time I push a wheelchair that far though. It's better than a workout at the gym.'

'Better than a yoga class?' His teasing gaze had also more than a hint of tenderness in it, as if he knew she was purposely trying to lighten the mood, and happy to go along with it. Jade could tell that Nick felt guilty about what had happened, although he didn't say anything.

Finally Nick looked at his watch. 'I think we should head on up and see what's happening.'

They made their way towards the lifts and stepped inside the sleek shiny metal box. Jade was glad for the pressure of

Lily's hand on her elbow. It anchored her into the present, for which she was very grateful. She knew what guilt felt like. Guilt about leaving her sister on her own that night. Guilt about forgetting her phone at home. Guilt about–

Lily's gentle squeeze on her arm interrupted her thoughts and Jade took a couple of deep breaths. This was all about Archie. She should leave the past in the past right now.

Archie was in good spirits when they finally got to see him, although slightly disgruntled about being kept in overnight. Nick looked slightly happier when he saw him. But Jade was still unsettled. The room he was in looked almost exactly the same as the one her sister had been in. She hadn't thought about the fact that they would probably all be the same.

'Look, why don't you two young ones get yourself off, and I'll stay with Archie?' Lily had probably picked up on her unease, Jade thought ruefully.

'Sounds like a good idea.' Jade found herself agreeing. 'We can take the bus back into town. Dad can give you a pick up later.'

She looked at Nick. 'What do you think?'

The rain had finally stopped by the time Nick and Jade got into the centre of the city.

'Archie said he wouldn't go to a musical even if we paid him, so we don't really need you next time.' Jade laughed.

Nick smiled down at her, happy to just have her walking beside him. 'That's OK. Musicals aren't really my thing either. But I will miss seeing you. And Lily and the man himself.'

'You know you can visit any time. I think Archie would love to have you come to see him. And you've got an excuse now that he's an invalid.' Jade looped an arm round his in a friendly fashion.

Her gesture suddenly reminded Nick of something. 'Wait.' He stopped. 'The hug. We didn't do it.'

Jade released his arm as if it suddenly burned her. 'You did. Lily gave you a hug when we left.'

Nick shook his head. 'That was half an arm and a peck on the cheek. You said a proper hug.'

Jade rolled her eyes and gave a rueful half-smile, as if she knew she had been beaten. She held out her arms. 'Go on then. If you really have to.'

Nick opened his own and wrapped them around her, pulling her close. Her head fit perfectly under his chin. He could smell that faint scent again in her hair. He took a deep breath and let it out, feeling his shoulders relax. She felt so good. He never wanted to let her go. He felt her give a similar sigh, and she leaned against him, her head on his chest. He so desperately wanted to freeze that moment forever in time. But he couldn't. So he was the first one to start to pull away. But somehow, his hands refused to let go of her.

She looked up at him, a small smile on her face. 'You give pretty good hugs.' Her hands were still resting on his hips, as if they didn't quite want to let go either.

He looked at her, standing there so close to him. *Do it*, his body said. He bent his head towards her. She tilted her face up to meet his. Their lips touched, ever so gently.

Suddenly Jade pulled away, arms clamped by her sides. 'I'm really sorry, Nick. I just can't do this.' Her face had bloomed a brilliant red. 'I'm so sorry. I just–' She backed away a few paces, then turned and ran.

Nick was still lost in the feel of her soft lips on his, and the sudden change felt like a foothold disappearing on a cliff face he had thought would hold him. It took him precious seconds to regain his stability, and by the time he recovered she had disappeared.

Nick ruffled his hair with one hand. *You really screwed it up there, mate.* But he wasn't sure what had happened. He hadn't imagined her movement towards him. In that moment she had wanted the kiss just as much as he had. So how had everything changed?

He would phone her. Speak with her directly and talk things through. He couldn't give up. Not when he had only just found her. He trudged wearily towards home, deflated but determined. They would sort this out. He would call her this evening.

Jade walked through the streets, not really caring where she went. In the films when this sort of thing happened then it was always raining, but the sky stubbornly refused to reflect her mood. The day had finally cleared up, and fluffy white clouds raced through the sky. She glared at them. They were ruining everything.

She sighed. She was the one who had ruined everything. Clinging onto Nick like an idiot. And then, going in for that kiss. What had she been thinking? No better way to ruin a friendship than that.

She stomped onwards, barely noticing that she had turned onto the canal and the path was now gravel under her feet.

Why had she run away like that? He must think she was a total nutcase. But the truth was she had been afraid. Scared of her response to him. When he had put his arms around her it had felt like all her troubles had been smoothed away. And the kiss ... even the brief touch of his lips had woken things in her she had never felt before. Sure, she was no virgin, but she was in no sense of the word experienced in this sort of stuff.

Flinging herself down on a black metal bench, she stared at the water. Feelings hurt.

The path was busy now the sun was out. Lots of cyclists, and people pushing prams. Having a good time together. She suddenly wished she could speak to Lily. But she knew what the other woman would say. She would tell her to go for it. To not be afraid. To fall in love. But it wasn't the love she was worried about, it was the loss on the other side of it.

A pair of graceful swans swam by, followed by two smaller brown cygnets. She felt like that most days. Serene on the surface, but desperately pedalling underneath to keep up.

She sat for a while longer, letting the sunshine warm her face. Her hand brushed against her phone in her pocket, and she pulled it out. Given where the blue dot said she was, it was time to make tracks for home. It was much further than she had intended to come. She didn't want her mother to worry.

Jade could hear the TV on when she opened the front door but didn't bother going in to the sitting room. She climbed slowly up the stairs and lay down on her bed, staring over at the other single bed on the far side of the room. Her parents had offered to take out Ruby's bed, but Jade had said no, wanting to keep at least something that reminded her of the times that she and Ruby had shared. They had always been close. When her baby sister had been put carefully into her arms when she was only four years old, Jade had known that they would always be friends. Even when Jade had met Carina and the two girls became inseparable, Ruby had always come along with them on their adventures, like a sort of mini shadow.

She heard a creak on the stairs, and seconds later her mother opened the door. Jade smiled up at her as she came to sit on the bed beside her.

Her mother smoothed a hand over Jade's hair. 'Everything OK?'

Jade grimaced. 'Depends.' She told her about what had happened with Nick.

Her mother said nothing, just put her arms around her, and held her tightly while Jade cried hot tears.

Pulling away, Jade reached for a tissue. 'I was just thinking about Ruby's bed.' She blew her nose loudly.

Her mother looked at her, expression unreadable. 'You want your dad to take us shopping next week?'

As ever, Jade was grateful that she didn't have to put things in words. She hugged the other woman tightly, resting her head on the soft wool shoulder. 'That would be great, Mum. Let's do it.'

She slept early, exhausted by the day's events, and her dreams were jumbled and confused. She was woken by the sun poking through the window, and a smile crossed her face before she remembered what had happened the day before. She should send Nick a message, she thought. It wasn't his fault things had turned out the way they had. Well, not his alone. They would have to sort things out between them. Or, just agree to call it a day and go their separate ways.

She finally found her bag under the desk where she had flung it the night before. And when she pulled it out there was a missed call from Nick. And a voicemail message. Her heart beat faster as she sat down on the bed and pressed the button to play it.

'*Hey Jade.*' He paused, and it was if she could sense his hesitation. '*I – um – Sorry for what happened today. It was out of order and I'm sorry. I would never do anything to hurt you.*' There was another pause. '*Just, er, give me a call when you get this. I just want to know that you're OK. As a friend.*'

Shame swept through Jade's body in a hot flush that left her face burning. He cared about her. As a friend. And she had just run off and left him last night without a word of explanation. Of course, he would be worried.

But, she thought, drawing her legs up and hugging them to her, she didn't know if she wanted to be friends any more. She had to admit that she wanted more. She wanted to feel his arms around him again. It was just ...

She had to be brave and say what was on her mind. 'You're worried about losing him just like you did with Ruby.' She said it out loud to the empty room, wishing desperately that Ruby was there. The two girls had often snuggled up in bed together, talking about their plans for the future, or commiserating about a tough day at school. But what was the quote? Better to live one day as a lion than a thousand years as a sheep? That was Mussolini though, and look what happened to him. The sudden humour made her grin and hug herself again, and she quickly typed out a message to Nick before she could change her mind.

I'm OK. Thanks for caring about me.

Her stomach rumbled. Time for breakfast. And then time for work. Things would sort themselves out. All she had to do was deal with one thing at a time.

Her phone beeped when she was half way through breakfast.

Glad you're OK. Have a good day at work. Drive some cars for me.

She caught herself smiling, and when she looked up and found her mother's eyes on her then she blushed. You are so screwed, she told herself.

I'll be lucky, she sent back.

She had just finished dressing for work – black jeans, company sweatshirt – when another message came through.

I feel like I got lucky last night. But if you want then we can just be friends.

Jade blew out a breath. Here he was, offering her a get out. She should take it. Take them both back to a safer place. At least, until they had a chance to get to know each other. But then, wouldn't being friends be just as bad? If she lost him? Was it not just better just not to get close at all?

She was still considering this as she slung her bag over her shoulder. It was like having two boxes to choose from. One box, she knew what was inside. Her current life. Predictable but safe. The other box, she hadn't opened yet. It could hold wonderful treasures, or it could be full of shit. But the trouble was, she wouldn't know until she opened it.

By the time she got through to her break at work she still hadn't made up her mind but knew that not replying would seem as if she didn't care.

It was a bit unexpected. I just need a bit of space. Just a lot going on in my life right now. Her fingers trembled as she typed. What happened if he got pissed off at her?

She stared at the screen for a couple of minutes, waiting for the signal that would mean he was typing a reply. But nothing happened. Swearing under her breath, she put the phone away and firmly went to concentrate on giving other people a good time.

But by the time she finished work there was another message waiting and it was so not what she had been expecting that it actually made her laugh out loud.

Sorry not to reply sooner, I went out for a walk. Beautiful day. At least tell me what the next thing is on the list. You can't leave me hanging on that …

She smiled as she read it again.

Read a good book, she typed back.

The reply came back with lightning speed. *Is that it?*

What do you mean, is that it?

It doesn't sound very inspiring.

Maybe you've been reading the wrong books.

There was a pause before the next message came back. *TBH I haven't read many books at all.*

Another person who didn't read. How did they live? How could they not see how much it enriched their lives? She rolled her eyes.

It's never too late to start.

So what would you recommend?

Jade had reached home by this point. She kicked off her shoes and gently placed them in the rack by the door. Her dad was in the sitting room, watching the roundup of the day's football in his favourite chair.

'Where's Mum?' She gave him a quick kiss on the top of his head and threw herself on the couch.

'Out having a drink with some friends.'

'Really? On a Sunday night?' Jade was surprised. Her mum hadn't been out for ages. And definitely not on a Sunday.

Her dad shrugged. 'Well, it was supposed to just be a shopping trip into town, but she texted me about four to say they were just going for drink. I haven't heard from her since.' His tone sounded morose, but Jade knew he was actually really happy about it.

Swinging her legs up onto the couch, she considered Nick's question. She could just recommend him some of her favourites, but he might not actually like them. Knowing how keen he was on the outdoors, he'd be more likely to enjoy some desperate tale of Arctic adventures. Although he might also like the sci-fi she loved so much. She mused for a few minutes, wondering what to write. Then a better idea struck her.

Go and check out your local library and get them to give you some recommendations.

A few minutes later another message came through. *Going in my lunch break tomorrow. Wish me luck.*

'What are you smirking at?' She looked up to find her dad looking at her quizzically.

She shook her head, knowing she was smirking as she did so. 'Nothing.'

Chapter 8

Nick rubbed a hand across his forehead. How an office could feel both cold and stifling he didn't know. The air conditioning units above him wafted out stale air, but that was nothing new. Maybe it was the new deodorant from the guy across the desk, which seemed to have an invasive personality all of its own.

His hand went unconsciously to the window right next to him, before he remembered that they wouldn't open. Well, technically they did open, but it wasn't allowed. Small red stickers on each window announced the health and safety concerns. Nick knew that the double set of windows helped to retain heat in the old building during the winter months, and for that he was very grateful, but they made the outside seem even further away.

'Yeah, pity about the windows.' An extra waft of deodorant rolled over as the other man leaned forward to speak. Nick jumped guiltily. He shouldn't just sit here dreaming. He should be working.

'I don't know, maybe it's a good thing.' Someone else from further down the office took up the banter. This often happened; a chance remark sparked off a whole round of discussion and joking. Nick smiled. They were often quite funny, providing he wasn't the target. No matter what other feelings he had about his colleagues, he had to admit they were quick on the uptake.

'What d'you mean?' Nick couldn't see who had said that.

'Well, you wouldn't want anyone jumping out, would you?'

'I don't know. Let 'em, I say. If that's what they want to do. I'm not going to stop someone committing suicide if that's how they want to go.'

'Yeah. Selfish gits. Taking the easy way out. Jacking it all in while the rest of us have to sit here and work for a living.' There was a wave of laughter.

Nick realised he was shaking. He gripped the edge of his keyboard to still the movement. He had a sudden memory of the day on the bridge. How hard it had been to make that decision, knowing full well the implications of what he was doing. Not an easy way out at all.

His stomach twisted, and for a few seconds he thought he

was going to throw up. Desperate, he looked at his watch. Eleven thirty. He could take an early lunch. Get some fresh air. Go for a walk along the river like he normally did.

Then he remembered that he was supposed to be going to the library.

For one moment he considered skipping it. The thought of spending his lunch break in a musty old library, shut away from the fresh air again, was almost too much for him. But then, the library was only a five-minute walk from the office, so it wouldn't take him long. And how hard could it be? Go in, pick up a book, walk out. He'd brought all the things he needed to join.

But when he finally got to the place, it was much bigger than he had expected. Rows upon rows of books. And then he got his second surprise. Instead of a kindly white-haired lady with glasses, there was a young girl at the front desk. With a nose ring. And loads of tattoos. She didn't even look grown up, but Nick wasn't going to jump to conclusions about someone's age a second time around.

'Is it possible to join the library?' Nick almost didn't know if she should ask her.

The girl looked at him. 'Sure. Sean!' She yelled into the back. 'Customer!'

The rule of silence in libraries obviously didn't apply any more either, Nick thought. Although it did seem very peaceful in here. It would be a nice place to come and sit. Large comfy chairs were dotted around, and there was a kids' corner with tiny chairs and toys.

'Sorry, I can't do registrations yet.' The girl seemed to feel like she had to explain herself. 'I'm just here for a week on work experience. As part of my course.'

'Don't worry about it.' Nick replied as another man joined them on the front desk.

'Can I help you?' Sean wasn't old or grey-haired either, maybe only a few years older than Nick. In actual fact, he looked pretty hench and like he spent quite a bit of time outdoors.

It only took two minutes for them to take Nick's details and produce a library card, even though the girl did it under Sean's instruction.

'Ten books at a time, for three weeks each.' Sean waved his hands. 'DVDs are a bit different, so if you think you might want to borrow any of those then I can take you through the rules.'

'I think books'll be fine for now, thanks.' Nick was sure that DVDs wouldn't count with Jade. 'Could you recommend anything?'

'Hm.' Sean stroked his carefully trimmed beard. 'Hm.'

'Sean won't admit it, but at least ninety percent of the books in here are not his thing.' The girl spoke up. 'He doesn't read crime, romance, or any kind of genre fiction really.'

'Shush, Charlotte, you'll get me fired for comments like that.' Sean winked at her. Then he looked back at Nick. 'What sort of books do you generally like to read?'

Nick felt himself growing warm. 'Well, I can't say I've read much at all really.'

'Brilliant, we've got ourselves another book virgin.' Although Charlotte's tone didn't sound like she thought it was a bad thing. More like a win, to get him even as far as joining the library.

'Shush, you, you'll get yourself fired for comments like that.' Sean wagged a finger at her. The two of them laughed, and Nick couldn't help joining in.

'So, what would you recommend for a book virgin like me?'

Sean stroked his beard again, considering, but it was Charlotte who spoke. 'What do you like to do in your free time?'

'Mountains.' The word tumbled out before Nick even had time to think.

Charlotte shrugged, as if mountains were for crazy people. 'That's your area, Sean. You're always going on about them. I'll stay here. You show him around.'

Sean led him off up one of the aisles. 'We've got a whole shelf on Arctic adventures if you think you might like to try one of those.' He stopped, looking along an upper shelf, then pulled out a book and handed it across. 'You'll have seen the film about Shackleton, but the book is pretty compelling.' He looked at Nick. 'What about some fiction?'

Nick shrugged. 'Whatever you think.'

Sean considered for a moment. 'Well, there's a lot of books which are sort of action or crime, or both. I'm not that keen on them, but they're usually an easy read, and pretty exciting.'

He took Nick down another aisle and pulled out a book. 'Here you go. That's probably one of the better ones. Local author actually. First one in a series, so if you like it there's plenty more where that came from.' He pulled out another one from further along. 'This one's not bad either.'

He handed the books across. 'That'll get you started. Feel free to have bit more of a browse and pick up anything which looks interesting.'

'Thanks.' Nick balanced the books under one arm. 'Really appreciate your help.'

'No problem.' Sean disappeared round the end of the shelf.

Conscious of time, Nick just spent a couple more minutes browsing the fiction shelves. The shelves headed 'Scottish authors' looked a bit more eclectic. And in the next aisle was the start of the non-fiction section, which was quite impressive. He picked out a couple more Scottish writers, and a book on Norway. It was somewhere he had always wanted to go.

By now his arms were beginning to protest about carrying the weight, and he took them back to the desk, thankful that he had brought his rucksack. Charlotte scanned them through for him and wished him all the best. 'I won't be here when you come back,' she said. 'But Sean will. So don't be afraid to ask for any help. All the people in here are really lovely.'

'Good luck with your course.' Nick waved to her as he left.

All that afternoon the books felt like they were burning a hole through his bag. He hardly noticed what he was doing, or the people around him. He would get a takeaway, he decided and sit and read as he ate. Carefully though. If he damaged a library book then Jade would probably disown him.

Jade. He missed her so much. But really, it was probably only because of how lonely he was in Glasgow. He missed the tightly-knit circle of friends that he had built up back home. Especially Jamie. Working together for those twelve months had been a blast.

And he was worried. Maybe he was only attracted to Jade because she was nice to him. Maybe he was just so desperate for human contact that he was throwing himself at any little crumb of kindness that came his way.

He sent Jade a picture of the book before he opened it. He didn't expect an immediate reply, because he knew she'd be working. But he wanted to share with her the momentous occasion.

Nick ate, book propped up at first against a tin of tomatoes, but as he got deeper into the story he abandoned the tin and grasped the book in his left hand while he ate with his right. It was only when the fork that he lifted to his mouth came up empty that he realised that his curry was gone and he was already a hundred pages in. He dumped the plate in the sink and retired to the sofa, book now more comfortable in both hands. And it was only when his eyes started complaining that he lifted his head and looked at the time. He had been reading for more than two hours.

And suddenly he realised why Jade had put reading books on the list. For the last two hours, he had not been in Glasgow, but in America. It was totally different from watching a film on a screen. Instead of watching the characters, he had been the characters – well, the lead character anyway – living his struggles and fighting his enemies.

It was still light, but that didn't mean anything. This time of year, it didn't get dark until late. He checked his watch. There was still time to go for a run. And he would definitely go and visit Archie after work tomorrow.

When he got back from his run there was a text from Jade. *Interesting choice.*

Want to meet up to discuss it? He barely dared to breathe as he waited for the reply.

You got me. Never can resist talking about books. Yoga and brunch again on Saturday? It was followed by a combination of emojis that included prayer hands, food and a muscly arm.

Nick pumped his own fist in the air and went for a shower.

Chapter 9

'I have this theory about books,' Jade said, her mouth still half-full of toast. She was enjoying her usual favourite, while Nick went all out on a cooked breakfast. 'There are people who are good at writing, and there are people who are good at crafting storylines, and they don't necessarily go together.'

'Hm.' Nick considered this idea while he munched on a piece of black pudding. 'So what would you classify my book under?'

Jade thought for a moment. She didn't really like the book that much herself, but didn't want to be too scathing, as Nick had obviously enjoyed it. 'Your guy, I think he's really good at writing words. I mean, I do get the sense of really being there. All the sounds and smells and stuff.'

Nick nodded. 'Yeah. I felt that. And I've never even been to America.'

Jade took another bit of toast, and chewed it slowly, considering. 'But I thought that his storylines were a bit far-fetched sometimes. That bit where he walks into the bar and those two guys he knows from years ago just happen to be in there? That seemed a bit incredible.'

'Yeah.' Nick nodded. 'I thought that at first. But then, if that didn't happen, there wouldn't have been a story.'

Sound logic, Jade thought. 'It still seems pretty improbable.'

Nick pointed his fork at her. 'Well, it is his twelfth book. Maybe he ran out of good ideas.'

The topic devolved into a discussion about writers of series, and which ones had managed to keep up the quality. Nick's claim of not being much of a reader wasn't entirely true, Jade found. He had read a lot of crime when he was younger, books stolen from his mother's collection.

'I only read them because they were full of gruesome details and sex,' Nick admitted. 'You know what teenage boys are like. My parents never let me play computer games when I was growing up so I had to at least do something with my time. There's lots of variation in the quality of those books though.' He had finished his food by this time and was slowly sipping from a cappuccino.

'You know, I had you pegged as more of an espresso man,' Jade said.

Nick raised one eyebrow with a smile. 'What, smooth, dark, and sexy?'

Jade laughed, but she felt herself growing slightly warm as she thought about it. He was sexy, especially engrossed in conversation about a topic he was interested in. 'Didn't you have a double one last time?'

Nick nodded. 'I've been trying to stay off the coffee recently. Caffeine really isn't good for me. This is just a bit of a treat today.'

He tipped his drink to her. 'Going back to that book ... the way we met was quite a coincidence.'

'What made you go there that day?' Jade found the words slipping out before she even thought about it.

Nick toyed with his cup. 'I can't say I'm proud of it. I just didn't think there was anything left to live for.' He picked up his teaspoon, running his fingers over it as if he was trying to polish it up. 'That day was particularly bad. I'd had an interview for another job the previous week where a mate works with a company that does outdoor adventures for kids. They'd offered me a job, and I was so excited at the thought of finally going back to something that I really love. But then that Friday they called me to say that they didn't need me anymore. And then, my mate texted me Friday evening saying he was sorry, but that they'd picked a friend of the boss's son to help them out instead and that was why everything had changed.'

He shifted in his seat, looking straight at her. 'I didn't sleep much that night. It just seemed to be as if the whole universe was against me. You know, just dangling that in front of me, getting my hopes up, and then taking it away. After everything else that had happened, what with the tossers at work and the walking group, I just seemed to hit a wall.'

'The walking group? What walking group?' Jade frowned.

'Oh, didn't I tell you about that?' Nick told her the whole story, and Jade found herself angry for him about the way he had been treated.

'Bastards.' She didn't mince her words.

Nick sighed. 'Maybe. I'd like to give them the benefit of the doubt though.'

'I wouldn't.' Jade clasped her hands together angrily on the table.

Nick put down his cup and gently separated her fingers. 'And that's why I like you so much.' He squeezed her hands tenderly.

'Look,' he said, still not letting go, 'I do like you. A lot. And if you really want to deny what's happening between us, then we can just stay friends. But I would hate to miss out on something so special.' His voice was low, as if he didn't want anyone else to hear him. Not that it would have mattered; the people on either side of them were engrossed in their own conversations and definitely weren't listening.

His thumbs were stroking her palms now, almost unconsciously, and Jade couldn't deny the current of attraction that was flowing through her. She squeezed his hands back before withdrawing. She had originally not wanted to get involved with Nick because she hadn't wanted to take on his problems, but that was pointless now. She cared about him very deeply, and she couldn't change that. But dealing with his problems as a friend was completely different from having a relationship with him. To get so close ... to be the primary person in his life who would be worried how he was thinking and feeling ... that was something that she didn't know if she wanted to do. No, scrap that. It wasn't about wanting. She honestly didn't know if she could do it. She honestly didn't know if she could put herself in a position again where her happiness depended on someone else's unstable moods.

'I like you a lot too, Nick.' She found herself leaning forward across the table, as if anxious to convince him. 'It's just ... well ... we've only known each other a few weeks. Could we just spend a bit of time together before we jump into anything? Get to know each other a bit better?'

Nick put his head to one side for a few moments, as if considering her words. Jade found that she cared very much indeed about his answer.

'Will hugs be allowed?' It was so totally not the response she had been expecting that Jade had to smile. Relief flooded through her.

'Yes, hugs are allowed.' Jade had to hand it to him. 'After all we're friends, aren't we? Wouldn't want your oxytocin levels dropping too low.'

'Friends.' Nick took one of her hands and squeezed them again, and Jade felt anything but. Still, she would try to guard her heart just a bit longer. Although she had to admit that it might be a losing battle already.

'Hey.' Nick suddenly thumped his fist in his palm, startling Jade. 'You looked it up.' He must have seen her puzzled face. 'Oxytocin. The happy drug.'

Jade laughed. She loved how his brain could jump around from one random topic to the other. 'Yeah. I looked it up. Seemed like both of us could do with a bit more of it in our lives.'

Nick nodded. 'Yep. Never going to complain about a bit of that.' He winked at her, and Jade felt her heart melt just a little bit more.

'So, what's the next thing on the list?' He drained the dregs of his cup and set it down, wincing at the bitterness.

'Well.' Jade had to smile again. 'The next thing is, do some exercise. But,' she held up her hand as he looked like he was going to speak, 'not something like yoga. A proper cardio workout. Like a spinning class or something.'

Nick considered a minute. 'Well, I could take you for a run, but you'd never make it.'

She had already opened her mouth to blast off a retort when she realised he was teasing her and shut it again. Besides, he was probably right. She was pretty fit from the yoga and all the walking she did – Glasgow was pretty hilly – but running? That was a different ball game. Or a different sport actually. She smiled at her own humour.

'Are you going to let me in on the joke?' Nick looked at her questioningly.

She shook her head. 'Not important. What is important is this running thing. And there's only one way to find out.'

Chapter 10

Much to Nick's surprise, Saturday did actually dawn bright and fair. It was only the beginning of May, but then that was no guide at all in this part of the country. They had planned to go to the yoga class and then for a run afterwards, but Jade had texted him on Friday evening to say that given the beautiful weather forecast it would be better to take the bus up to Loch Lomond and have a picnic, and then go for a run. Nick was always suspicious when the weather predictions were so good, but for once it looked like the forecasters had got it bang on.

He met Jade at the bus station, and they swung into their seats, giggling like teenagers and causing the driver to look at them suspiciously. Jade was wearing a close-fitting khaki t-shirt that curved delightfully around her breasts. It was another reason to be happy for the warm weather.

The bus took its time, winding through the low hills, which were patched with grass and heather. After almost an hour they got off in Balmaha at the edge of the loch. It was a tiny place really, not much more than a collection of a few white-painted houses with a pub and a tiny shop.

Nick motioned to Jade. 'The beach is about another mile up the road.'

'Hang on.' Jade was already wandering across to a small park. 'I just want to have a look at this.'

It was a bronze statue of a cheery walker, with a bobble hat on his head.

'Tom Weir.' Jade read from the plaque which was standing beside it. 'Looks like he was a pretty keen walker.'

'Yeah, my dad knew him. He used to stay in our B&B when he came up our way.' Having seen the man in real life, Nick thought it was a pretty good likeness.

Jade turned to him, surprise obvious on her face. 'Really? That's pretty cool. You can use it as your claim to fame.'

'Claim to fame?' Nick hadn't thought about it before. To him Tom had just been the guy who had shown him how to tie knots and lace up his boots properly. But he realised she wasn't really being serious.

'So what's your claim to fame then?' He started off down the path that would take them to his favourite bit of beach.

Jade almost stumbled over his feet as he turned to check that she was following him. He put out a hand to steady her, and his fingers brushed against the edge of one of the breasts that he had been admiring when they were on the bus. He pulled his hand back as if he had been burned. Looking was one thing, but touching was a completely different matter. Touching was dangerous. Touching made him want to pull her into his arms and kiss her. He started off down the path again, his face burning, not waiting to see if she was right behind him.

Jade had felt the touch on her right boob as Nick had grasped her arms to steady her. If she hadn't already been wobbling after almost tripping over him, she probably would have anyway. She could tell it had been by accident, but it had felt like a lover's caress. It made her wonder what it would be like to have him touch her there again. But then again, her experience with those sorts of things was not exactly extensive. In her first relationship neither of them had had enough experience to really know what they were doing. And the other one ... well, let's just say it had been OK. Sex, really, she could take it or leave it.

She suddenly realised that Nick was waiting for her at a bend in the path and hurried to catch up. She had read in books about great sex, but really, wasn't that just fantasy? It was important to keep a good line between fantasy and reality. She smiled as she caught up with Nick. It was a good thing he couldn't read her thoughts. If he knew how far they had fallen into the gutter then he would probably be shocked.

They continued in silence up a small slope and down another, just enjoying the sunshine and the sounds of the birds. The path curved towards the loch, and Nick stopped for a minute, just to take in the amazing view. Two tiny clouds above the hills on the opposite shore were all that broke up the amazing colour of the sky. The loch twinkled blue to match the sky above. A sigh that was obviously delight escaped his lips.

'My vote,' he looked at his watch, 'is have some lunch, sunbathe for a bit to let things settle, go for a run, and then jump in the loch to cool off.'

Jade had been nodding along until he came to the last bit. 'Jump in the loch? Are you crazy? It'll be freezing.'

Nick raised one eyebrow at her. 'Are you saying you didn't bring your swimmers then like I told you to?'

Jade had, but she still wasn't keen on the idea. 'Yessss, but I was still hoping to talk you out of that bit.' She set off again towards the beach. 'Let's discuss that bit later, OK?'

By the time they got down onto the beach it was pretty hot and Jade was starting to feel a bit more amenable to the idea of a dip. There were already a few other people on the beach. Two small children were fishing in the shallows with tiny nets. They found a patch of shade further along the beach where a gnarled grey tree spread its green leaves over the pebbles on the shore and sat themselves down. The picnic soon disappeared, and they lay on their backs on the gravel, staring up at a single tiny cloud that was travelling slowly but surely towards the sun.

'I went to see Archie this week.' Nick's voice sounded quiet, as if he was reluctant to break the silence that had stolen over them.

'I know. Lily told me.' Jade matched his tone, then yawned. She was feeling pretty sleepy after all the food.

Nick laughed. 'I forgot you have a hotline to the heart of the action.'

'How is he doing anyway?'

'The usual. Everything seems to be healing up fine. Lily said any bump to his head could only make him less crazy, but I don't think he did actually have any head injuries at all. It's just the arm. He says it itches like crazy though. He's borrowed a knitting needle from Sandra so he can have a good scratch.'

He scratched his chin, and Jade could hear the sound of his fingers against the stubble that he hadn't shaved that morning. 'I do still feel a bit guilty though. If I had been looking where I was going ...' His voice trailed off.

Jade rolled over onto one elbow, looking down at him. He had one hand tucked behind his head, stretching his t-shirt up so she could see just a glimpse of his toned stomach. For someone who worked in an office he was pretty fit.

'You can't change the past.' Her heart twisted as she thought of how many times she told herself that every day. How easy it was to give advice. But how hard it was to follow it. 'I was the one who was rushing you. I was just worried about the weather. So stupid.'

'A good friend told me that you can't change the past.' Nick smiled up at her, turning his head towards her a fraction. It felt really good to have him next to her like this. And in that moment, she felt a longing that was so intense that she almost bent her head and kissed him. Wasn't it better to just seize the day instead of worrying about the future? Wouldn't the good part of being with him outweigh the bad?

You are so overthinking this. You just need to jump in with both feet or back off totally, otherwise this is going to drive you crazy. She lay back down, folding her hands underneath her head as she gazed at the view across the loch towards the green and purple slopes opposite. It was so peaceful here.

There were a few other people on the beach, but they also seemed caught by the calm of the day and were speaking in low voices as they chatted. A gentle breeze kept the midges away.

'I would have thought there'd be more people here.' Jade stretched again. The warmth of the sun felt so good on her skin.

'Most people get stuck in Balmaha and never find out this place exists. I only found out because someone else told me about it.' Nick closed his eyes. He knew he shouldn't have been watching Jade out of the corner of his eye, but he couldn't help it. If she knew just how amazing she looked every time she stretched ...

It was time to go for a run. It had been at least an hour since lunch, and they should probably wait longer, but if they spent any more time like this then he was going to do something that he would regret. Well, he wouldn't regret it, but Jade probably would. Which was even worse.

He pushed himself to his feet. 'Come on. Time for you to put your money where your mouth is. Let's do this thing.'

Jade looked up at him, shading her eyes against the sun. 'Really? Are you sure?'

He nodded, reaching out a hand to pull her up. 'Come on, lazy bones. We can leave our bags here. We can do short circuits so we can keep an eye on them. And,' he gave her a wicked grin, 'it means that if you bomb out then we won't be far away.'

Jade's mouth set in a stubborn line. 'Never. I'd rather die first.'

Nick reached out and roughed up her hair. 'You just might do that on the way.'

Jade made a mock horrified face at him, smoothing down her hair as if she was really offended, and they both had to laugh.

They stuffed their bags under the root of a tree and made their way back onto the gravel path. 'Right, it's a bad idea to try to run a long way if you've not done it before, so what we're going to do is do two-minute bursts.' Nick pressed a few buttons on his watch to call up the pre-set timings he had worked out the night before. So we run for two minutes, then walk for ninety seconds, then run again, then walk. So we'll do it like five times, and warm up and cool down with a walk.'

'I'm pretty warm already.' Jade pretended to fan herself dramatically.

Nick couldn't help laughing again. 'You could do a one-woman comedy show. Seriously.'

'Not by myself. I'd need my fall guy with me.' She winked at him.

'Much more of that and you'll find yourself running away from me instead of with me, while I try to strangle you.' He tried to keep his tone serious, but he knew that she could hear the laughter in his voice. He pressed the start on his watch. 'Three minutes warm up walk. Let's go.'

Jade was uncharacteristically quiet as they walked down the path, and Nick wondered what she was thinking about. It was a perfect place for a run. The gravel under their feet would absorb some of the impact, and the trees arching above their heads turned it into a cool tunnel where the warmth of the sun was lessened. Not a problem that was common in Scotland, Nick reflected ruefully, but today was an exception. His watch beeped. 'Right, that's time to go. Just keep it to a slow jog. You don't want to overdo it.'

They set off slowly. Nick kept an eye on Jade to see how she was doing. Her form was pretty good actually. She ran in an efficient manner, arms close to her sides. When two minutes were up he slowed them down to a walk. Jade was pink and breathing heavily, but otherwise seemed OK.

'Everything OK?' He turned them back the way they had come so that they didn't get too far away.

Jade nodded. 'I'm fine. Raring to go for the next one.'

He could tell that she was tiring by the time they finished the third run, although she steadfastly refused to admit it.

'We don't have to do the last one if you don't want to,' he said as they slowed down after they finished the fourth burst.

The stubborn line had crept into her mouth again, but her eyes were still smiling, which was a good sign. 'Bring it on.'

He could hear her breath labouring beside him all through the next two minutes, but at no time did she slow her pace or complain and he admired her all the more for that. He kept her going with a countdown all the way through, and when they came to the end she leaned against a tree with a groan, fighting to get her breath back.

'None of that.' He pulled her arm to keep her moving. 'You've got to keep walking or you'll stiffen up too much.'

She walked beside him as her breaths slowly returned to normal. Nick looked at her anxiously. She was still very quiet. Had he killed her off? Then she turned to him, and the look on her face was like nothing he had ever seen before. Her eyes sparkled. Her cheeks had a healthy tinge of pink. Her hair was tumbling out of her messy bun in such a sexy way that it took his breath away.

'Oh. My. God. I did it!' Her excited shriek sent two magpies chattering off in fright. She threw her arms around his neck and jumped into his arms with a massive hug.

The unexpected movement sent him stumbling a little, but he managed to keep standing and swung her round and round until she begged him to stop and put her down. But when he did, she looked up at him with such a happy look on her face that he just had to bend his head and kiss her. He started with a gentle touch of his lips to hers, and when he felt her mouth curve under his then he took the courage to deepen the kiss. His hand slid down to the base of her spine. Oh, that bum! He had been dying to get his hands on it since that first yoga class.

He could feel Jade's hands curving round his own body tentatively, and he pulled her closer to him so she could feel exactly what she was doing to him. And then – with difficulty because the kiss was so good – he broke it off gently and looked down at her.

He needn't have worried. Jade grinned up at him. 'That was pretty good. Can we do it again?'

He laughed as he bent his head.

They kept their hands entwined as they walked back to the beach, as if anxious not to lose the contact that they had created between them. Nick looked over at Jade. 'Not that I'm complaining, but a week ago you said that you just wanted to be friends. What's changed?'

She looked up at him, her eyes serious, a slight blush on her face. 'I think it was what we were talking about earlier. Not being able to change the past made me wonder if I was just worrying too much about the future too.'

He slung an arm around her shoulders and pulled her towards him with a squeeze. Her shoulder fit under his arm as if it was made to be there. 'We can only live one day at a time.'

'That's true.' She wrapped an arm around his waist.

'Yeah. My mum always used to say that whenever my dad would get too hung up on something. He's the worrier in our family. My mum's the one who's a bit more chilled out.'

'It's the other way round in ours. My dad's the chilled out one, while my mum always worries. I guess it's not surprising after what she said about him ending up in the hospital.'

The heat of the sun hit them as they stepped out onto the beach. Their bags were still there, and they both gratefully swigged from their water bottles. A couple of people were already out swimming.

'I'm really looking forward to that dip.' He pulled off his t-shirt and kicked off his shoes. 'I would say I'd race you, but I'd probably just faceplant and knock myself out on a rock.'

Jade was looking at him, a wry smile on her face. 'I know this sounds like a cliché, but you look pretty hench without your top on.'

He wrapped his arms around himself, unused to all this attention. 'Thanks. I think.' He did a few weightlifting poses, just to cover his embarrassment, while Jade giggled.

'Anyway, what about you?' He motioned towards her. 'Time to take your top off.'

Her t-shirt and shorts came off to reveal a dark green bikini which was brief enough to take his breath away. He gave her a wolf whistle, and she flipped him a finger as she walked towards the water's edge.

The water was cold, but very inviting after the heat of the afternoon and the exercise they had done. They splashed around for a bit, then lay in the shallows, shoulders just touching.

'So what did you think of the run?' Nick wanted to know.

Jade sighed. 'Knackering. But I could imagine doing it again.'

'There's lots of apps you can get for your phone if you do want to start.'

'Yeah. It sort of felt like – I mean, when I walk I tend to think about stuff, but not really think about it. A bit like the meditation class really. I could see running doing the same thing.'

Nick considered this for a minute. 'I guess you could say that. I know I usually come out of a run feeling much less stressed than when I started.'

Silence fell for a few minutes, then Jade looked up at Nick. 'You do know that this relationship is doomed from the start, right? What with me working evenings, and Sundays and stuff, we're only going to be able to meet up once a week, at best.'

She should tell him exactly what had happened with Ruby now. Before they got in too deep. If he was going to reject her for not caring enough about her sister then better sooner than later. But just then Nick smiled down at her, and the tender look in his eyes made the words die in her throat.

Coward. She felt as if the word was branded across her forehead.

But Nick didn't seem to notice anything. 'They say it's quality, not quantity. Let's just see how it goes.' He pulled her towards him and kissed her again. Jade had never quite been kissed in the way that he did it. His mouth was neither to hard nor too soft, and his tongue, when it touched hers was ... well ... anyway, it felt amazing. She gave up thinking for a while.

They were very wrinkly by the time they finally dried themselves off and flung themselves down on their towels. Jade pulled some sun cream out of her bag and tossed it over. 'You should probably put some of this on. Your top half looks like it hasn't seen much sun this year. If ever.' She dodged as Nick threw the bottle back at her in mock disgust.

'Will you rub some into my back?' His eyes sparkled at her, as if he knew he was using another cliché.

She affected casual nonchalance, lifting her chin. 'Only if you'll do mine.'

'With more pleasure than you will ever know.' He reached over her to retrieve the bottle and squeezed out a massive dollop. 'Go on. Roll over.'

She was luxuriating in the touch of his hand on her skin when her phone beeped in her bag.

'Do you want to get that?' Nick stopped, his hand just resting on her shoulder.

'Only if you don't stop what you're doing.' She reached for the backpack.

'Don't forget you still have to do mine.' Nick squirted out some more cream.

She looked over her shoulder at him, a wicked grin on her face. 'With more pleasure than you will ever know.'

She dug out her phone. 'Oh. It's Dad. He said they were thinking of coming up to pick us up and go for an early dinner at the pub in Balmaha.'

'Oh.' Nick sounded surprised.

'Is that OK?' Jade couldn't work out if there was disappointment in his tone.

'No, no.' Nick looked slightly pink, but whether it was from the sun or something else then she couldn't tell. 'It's just I was enjoying having you all to myself. Selfish, I know. It's a great idea. Especially because it means we get to stay here a bit longer. But what about his work?'

'He's going to start a bit later tonight. Said he didn't want to waste a day like this. He and Mum have been sitting out in the garden all day apparently.'

'What time are they going to come down?'

'About half five.'

Nick looked at his watch. 'That still gives us another couple of hours down here.'

'Well, I'd better get some of that cream into your white patches before they turn red then.' She typed a quick reply into the phone and grabbed the bottle from him, giving him a quick kiss as she did so. 'Can't wait to get my hands on those hench muscles of yours.'

Later, they walked hand in hand up the path back towards the village. The sun was slightly lower now, but still pretty warm. It really had been a perfect day. Being around Nick made her forget her worries and just focus on the present. Something she really hadn't been doing enough of lately. And touching him. It just felt so good, she thought, squeezing his fingers with hers.

He looked down at her. 'You OK?'

She smiled up happily at him. 'Yeah. Thanks for everything. It's been great.'

He draped an arm over her shoulders and pulled her towards him as they walked. 'I'm so glad you changed your mind. Being just friends with you was starting to be a bit challenging.'

She snorted. 'Why, because of my stunning looks?'

He stopped and turned to face her, placing one hand on each of her shoulders. 'You are stunning, you know.'

His tone was so earnest that she looked up at him in surprise. 'Come on, you're kidding me on.'

He shook his head. 'I wish I could hold up a mirror that reflects you as I see you. I think you'd be surprised.'

Jade took his hand again, and planted a quick kiss on his cheek. 'You'll have to behave when we see my parents. Otherwise they'll realise just how crazy you are.'

He looped his arm over her shoulders again. 'Don't worry. I'll behave.'

As they came in sight of the pub Jade could see her parents sitting outside with their drinks. Just orange juice – Dad wouldn't drink when he was going to drive, and Mum never drank much anyway – but they looked happy and relaxed.

'Had a good day?' her mum asked, as they rounded the end of the low stone wall.

'Yeah.' Jade smiled up at Nick. 'It's been a great day.'

As Nick excused himself to go to the toilet, Jade sank down gratefully into one of the metal chairs.

Her mother was looking at the wooden door through which Nick had disappeared. 'I'm glad you worked things out with him. He's a good lad.'

Jade knew she was blushing, but she didn't care. 'Yeah, we worked things out. We'll just see how it goes.' She didn't want to reveal anything more than that.

She fell asleep on the way back, nestled up against Nick in the back of the car, and she only awoke when the car stopped outside his front door. He just gave her hand a quick squeeze as he got out, and she knew he didn't want to make a big show of affection in front of her parents. She mimed texting him as she waved goodbye, and he gave her a big thumbs up.

She got her first text from him within seconds. He must have barely opened the front door.

Great day. Really wanted to kiss you, especially with your face all sleepy like that.

She typed back quickly. *There'll be another chance. Next Saturday?*

Aren't you taking out the oldies again? To the matinee?

Only in the afternoon. The rest of the day is yours.

Let's make a plan nearer the time. Depends on the weather. But you could come over Friday night after work and we could wake up together … This was accompanied by both a rain and a sun emoji and a winking face.

Sure. She sent back her trademark smiling face and strong arm emojis.

'Seems like he likes you.' Her mother spoke from the passenger seat in front.

'Yeah.' Jade settled back into the seat with a satisfied sigh. 'Seems that way.'

But then her phone beeped again. *So what is the next thing on the list anyway?*

Jade grinned to herself. *Turn off your smartphone for 24 hours.*

Sounds like a great plan. I'll totally go for that.

She was surprised at how enthusiastically he had agreed; he had seemed pretty wedded to his fancy watch. Still, she hadn't said that he had to turn that off too. Maybe she should include it into the deal.

Talk later in the week? She texted back, smiling at the thought.

Sure thing. His reply came back almost immediately.

Chapter 11

They texted back and forth so much over the next couple of days that Jade began to wonder what life had been like without Nick. He was pretty romantic; and funny pictures and messages were obviously carefully chosen to make her laugh. So it was a bit disappointing when the message she found waiting for her when she woke up on Monday morning was not in the least bit romantic.

Really sorry, but I don't think I'll make our plans for Friday night, I've just been asked to work that evening. Client in the States needs some help and support and we probably won't finish before midnight. Tried to get out of it but there's no escape, no one else wanted to do it. Five crying emojis gave her some clue about how he felt.

He had obviously felt bad about it, because half an hour later he had sent another message. *Can I cook you dinner at mine on Saturday night?*

Jade pushed down her irritation. It wasn't his fault that he had a crappy job with a crappy boss. Although, she did wish he would do something about it. Still, there wasn't any guarantee that if he got another job then it would be any better as far as hours were concerned. Maybe she was the one who should try and get another job. Something that gave her more evenings off. But then, it wasn't a bad job. Bill was a pretty good boss. She gave up thinking about it and went for a shower.

It was only when she got out of the shower that she realised she hadn't texted him back and reached for the phone, holding the towel round herself with her other hand as she closed the bedroom door with a foot. She remembered just in time that her dad would still be sleeping and managed not to slam it closed.

Would be great. You want me to bring anything?

He had obviously been watching the phone, anxious for her reply, because his answer came back almost immediately. *Just your stunning self.*

She sent him a blushing emoji. Now that she thought about it, she kind of fancied another run. Although, she'd only got out of the shower, so that was a bit stupid. Maybe it could wait until tomorrow? Or, she could always have another quick shower when she got back.

She opened the cupboard and dragged out a pair of shorts and a t-shirt. No time like the present. All she had to do was find that app.

Sunday had been predictably rainy, as if to make up for the beautiful weather the day before, so Nick had spent most of his time reading his library books, only stopping to sort out food to keep himself going. Food that you could eat with one hand was the way to go, he decided. Anything that needed both a knife and fork just slowed you down. By the time the fading summer light made him realise it was past eleven in the evening, he was half way through the last of his books and hungry for some more. It was time for another visit to the library.

He nipped out at lunchtime on Monday again, taking the books he had finished. As predicted, Charlotte wasn't there, but Sean was, and greeted him enthusiastically.

'Hey. You finished your books already?'

'Most of them.' Nick placed his books on the counter.

'Any you particularly liked?'

Nick nodded enthusiastically. 'You were right about the Shackleton. It's amazing. That bit where they get to the island and then realise they have to climb over the mountains to the other side ...'

Sean smiled. 'Yeah. That's my favourite bit too.'

'But some of the others were pretty good. I know you're not that keen on crime, but this one's pretty exciting.' He pointed to the one he had read first.

'Hey.' Sean held up his hands. 'I'm not going to rubbish anyone else's taste in books. Just because it's not for me, doesn't mean it's a bad book.'

Nick hesitated, an idea suddenly occurring to him. There was something he was afraid to ask, but then again, who was Sean going to tell? 'Do you think ... I mean, do you have any books on career changes?'

A big grin split Sean's face. 'Oh yeah, loads. Let me show you where they are.'

He led Nick over to a row of shelves. 'This one was a great help to me, when I was trying to work out what to do.'

He pulled out a slim book. 'It was written quite a while ago, but it's got lots of useful exercises to do to find out what sort of job might suit you.'

Another book was pulled off and placed in Nick's hands. 'This one has great advice about interviews, CVs etc. It's also very useful.'

He gestured towards the shelf. 'Anyway, have a look at the other ones. Most of them have at least something useful in them.' He strode off.

Sean always tended to stride everywhere, Nick had noticed. Forget about his mental image of a soft-voiced librarian who always tiptoed around. Anyway, he took the two books Sean had recommended. They would do for now. He could always go back for some more. He selected some more fiction books. Escapism was especially valuable on his bad days. Although really, since he had met Jade, his good days definitely outnumbered his bad.

Nick took the books to the desk, where Sean was looking up something on the computer. As Sean scanned the books through, he hesitated for a moment. 'Look, me and a couple of guys are going out for a walk at the weekend. I was wondering if you'd like to come?'

'Me? Really?' Nick knew his surprise was showing on his face.

'Yeah.' The other guy seemed slightly embarrassed. 'Only if you want to though.'

'Yeah.' Nick suddenly realised that his surprise might have been taken for reluctance. 'Yeah. Yeah. Sure. I mean, that would be great.'

Then, he suddenly remembered what his other plans were. 'Oh. I'm busy on Saturday though.'

Sean flashed him a grin. 'That's fine, because we're going on Sunday.'

Nick felt his own face break out into a happy smile. 'Great. Great. That would be great. Only–' he hesitated, 'only if you're sure?'

Sean nodded. 'Yeah. It would be great. There used to be a group of four of us that always went out together, but one guy had to move down to London a couple of months ago and since then things just haven't been the same. It would be good to have some fresh blood.'

He looked down at the crime novel in his hand. 'Actually, that sounds really creepy with me standing here holding this.' A laugh escaped him. 'Just come. Only a short walk this time as the weather's not supposed to be great. Pick you up about eleven?'

'Yeah. Yeah. Great.' Nick just didn't know what to say. They swapped numbers and he wandered back to work in a happy haze.

He couldn't wait to get home and start on his new cache of books. When the time came to go home he zoomed along as if he had wings on his feet, and was soon settled on his sofa. He left his half-finished book for later and opened up the fatter of the career books. But even more than that, he couldn't wait for the weekend. The idea that he had not just one but two things to look forward to was amazing. Sean seemed like a really solid guy. And Jade ... well. Dinner with her was going to be great.

Dinner. He suddenly sat up straight, pushing a hand through his hair. What the hell was he going to cook? It had to be something special. But then again, if he tried something too complicated then he would be sure to screw it up. He flicked the pages of the book absentmindedly while he tried to think. And then he knew what he had to do. He pulled out his phone and dialled home.

'Hey, son.' The voice that greeted him was his father's. 'Everything OK? You don't normally call during the week.'

'Yeah. Yeah. Fine. Is Mum around? I just wanted to ask her something.'

'Not at the moment. We had an unexpected group booking so she's gone out to get more breakfast stuff.'

'Oh.' Nick rubbed his cheek. It would just have to wait.

'I'll tell her you called, shall I?'

'Yeah, thanks. I was just after her for some of her recipes, that's all. I'm cooking on Saturday and wanted to do something special.'

'Oh. Sure. Will do.' There was a long pause. 'I could give you my shepherd's pie recipe if you want. It's a bit basic, but pretty good. And pretty easy too.'

Nick had a sudden vision of a shepherd's pie coming out of the oven, crispy and golden on top with the rich juices bubbling underneath. His mouth started watering. 'Yeah, Dad. That would be great. In fact, that would be perfect. Let me just get a pen.'

He scribbled frantically as his dad recited ingredients and quantities.

'And then, you just bake it for about half an hour and that's it. So who's coming to this dinner anyway?'

Nick should have seen the question coming but had been too busy trying to keep up with writing things down. He flailed. 'Oh ... just a ... just a friend.'

His dad laughed. 'Is it a girl?'

Nick could feel a flush creeping up the back of his neck. 'Yeah. But don't tell Mum, otherwise she'll never stop with the questions.'

'Scout's honour.' His dad laughed. 'I'm doing the gesture too, just so you know I'm serious.'

'Thanks, Dad.'

They chatted for another couple of minutes and then hung up.

All that talk of food had made Nick hungry. It was time for dinner. He texted Jade. *Got some more great books at the library. Just settling down for a quiet night in.*

He knew she'd be at work, so didn't expect an answer back straight away. He was in his bed by the time his phone beeped.

Hope you had a good time. Had some right tossers today. Three poo emojis completed the message.

Want to talk about it?

Nah. Just the usual corporate aholes. I'm used to it. All I want is my bed.

Sleep well. Nick sent back three kisses and a hug.

You too. Have a good day at work tomorrow.

Nick had made it through most of the first career book during the evening, although he had skipped a few bits. There were some pretty interesting exercises and some great suggestions on CVs that he would have to incorporate next time he sent one out. But the book was more orientated towards trying to work out what you wanted to do. He knew what he wanted to do, but just didn't know how to do it. Still, there was no point worrying about it for now. He got himself comfy on the pillows and yawned. He could worry about things later.

It always felt a bit weird when he shifted his working day to match a different time zone. East coast wasn't too bad at only five hours, but this was west coast, a full eight hours behind. He wouldn't be finished until gone midnight. At least they would pay for some dinner.

It felt quite weird to get into the office just as everyone else was leaving. This was the first time he'd done this by himself. He should be proud of himself, actually. It meant they trusted him to do a good job. Which was definitely something.

He got some snarky comments from some people, and some commiserations. But when everyone had finally left, the office seemed strangely peaceful. He opened a couple of the forbidden windows, and let the fresh air flood in, breathing deeply and feeling his shoulders relax. He put his own music on, and let it waft around the office. And then he sat down at his computer.

About three hours later he yawned and stretched; it was time for dinner. It was great to think that he had the pick of the places nearby, and he didn't even have to pay for it. It was getting a bit chilly now though; he would have to shut the windows.

He and his contact in the States had been messaging back and forth, occasionally calling each other when things got tricky.

He typed on the screen. *Just going to get some food. Back in 15.*

Sure thing. The reply came back almost immediately. *Should be OK here while you stuff your face.*

Nick couldn't help but smile. He really liked this client actually. Waiting for processes to run had given them quite a bit of a chance to chat, and he seemed like a pretty nice guy.

It was almost one when they finally finished, and the message he had been waiting for flashed up on the screen. *I think we're done here. You get yourself to bed.*

OK.

Thanks for all your help. Really appreciate it.

No worries.

It felt good to be appreciated. He stretched again. He had been sitting at his computer for far too long. But the work had been interesting. And working with someone he liked had made it fun.

He looked around the office, drinking in the unusual feeling of satisfaction. Really, his actual job, the actual things he was doing, wasn't that bad. If he could just get rid of his colleagues somehow, and this awful airless office, he would probably be able to live with it. He laughed out loud at that thought. Unless, somehow, they would let him work remotely? A picture of himself, living up in Fort William, working from there, flashed into his mind. Then he shook his head. His boss didn't even trust anyone enough to work from home. That was never going to happen.

Saturday morning Jade woke up feeling happy. It took her a couple seconds to work out what the reason was for it. Nick. She was going to see Nick today. Go to his place. He was cooking her dinner. A little thrill of excitement went through her.

She checked the time. She had been thinking about the early morning yoga class, but it was already half over.

'Yeah, as if.' She rolled over onto her stomach again. It had been a tiring week. Big groups that needed lots of taking care of and organising. She could still make the late morning class though. It would be a good idea. Get rid of all the stresses of the week.

She reached for her phone again and texted Nick.

Thinking about the yoga class. You going, or are you still asleep?

Slept really well last night. Just lying in bed thinking the same thing. See you there?

Sure. She added a couple of prayer hands, and then jumped out of bed and wandered down to the kitchen in search of some breakfast.

The class was just what she needed. A good stretch, a few laughs, and she was feeling good. Oh, and the sight of Nick's delicious bum in front of her was an added bonus. And the thought that she might be touching it later on was just the icing on the cake.

She hummed softly to herself as she rolled up her mat.

Nick came over to her and pulled her to her feet, giving her a quick kiss in greeting. 'It's good to see you. What time do you want to come over?'

The touch of his lips made her want more, but she resisted the temptation, aware that there were others still in the room. 'I'll come straight over once the matinee's finished. Should be some time between five and six?'

He slung his arm round her shoulders as they walked towards the door and kissed the top of her head. 'Sounds great. Looking forward to it.'

As they paused in front of the entrance to the changing rooms, he pulled her in for a long lingering kiss, his hands cupping the curves of her backside. 'Actually, I lied.' He murmured in her ear. 'I can't wait.'

She pulled away, somehow feeling self-conscious with all the people passing in the corridor. 'I'll see you later. I can't wait either.' She flashed him a blinding grin and then slipped through the door to the women's changing room.

The musical was surprisingly good. Many of the audience sang along with the songs and Lily was no exception. Even Jim piped up in a thin reedy voice. Archie should have come. But then, there was no accounting for taste. They had left him listening to one of his favourite adventure biographies and he had seemed pretty happy.

As soon as they had got everyone back on the minibus, she waved goodbye to them and sped off towards Nick's place. She was really curious to see what it would look like. The Merchant City area was pretty posh these days. She found the address pretty easily. It was a great location. Tucked away in a quieter side street but only just around the corner from some great bars and restaurants.

The buzzer was one of those fancy ones where you had to type in the number.

'Hello?' The crackly voice came through the intercom.

'It's me.' She almost said her name, but then changed her mind. He was expecting her after all.

'Come on up.' The lock buzzed, and she pushed the door open.

It was very posh. There was polished grey marble on the floor, and it looked like the white walls had been freshly painted. She walked slowly up the stairs. There was no point taking the lift for just two floors.

The door was already open by the time she rounded the corner, and Nick was standing there. He was wearing a long-sleeved grey t-shirt that fit him neatly, and scruffy blue jeans that looked like they had seen a lot of wear.

'Hey.' His voice was soft, almost hesitant, but his smile was clearly just for her. 'Come on in.'

Jade expected him to kiss her in greeting, but instead he held the door open for her and motioned her in. She found herself in a tiny entrance hall with just enough room for a row of coat hooks and a shoe rack that doubled as a small bench. She toed off her trainers and hung her jacket and handbag on a hook.

Nick was already opening a second door. 'Well, this is it. Welcome to my humble abode.'

It was pretty tiny. It was all one room. A bedsit. To her left a small kitchen sideboard contained a cooker, sink and washing machine, while a tiny table and two chairs for eating stood in front of a large bay window. In front of her a small sofa was arranged with a TV. To her right, in a corner, was a double bed. Her skin grew warm at the thought of the small packet of condoms she had bought on the way over. It never hurt to be prepared.

'Sorry it's a bit small.' Nick must have mistaken the look on her face for disappointment.

'No. No. It's great.' Jade looked at him with a smile. 'I think it's what estate agents would call bijou, but really, it's great. It has everything you need.'

He looked at her for a few seconds, as if weighing up the truth of her words, then smiled. 'Come here. I've been wanting to kiss you properly all day.'

Jade closed the distance between them, reaching her hands up to wind around the back of his neck and into his hair. He lifted her up and sat her on the table, and she wrapped her legs around him to draw him closer while she closed her eyes and luxuriated in the feel of lips against hers. He used one hand to hold her firmly to him while the other played through her hair. Then his mouth left hers and he kissed his way slowly down towards her neck.

The way things were going Jade fully expected him to start taking off her clothes. But instead he levered one hand under her legs and lifted her off the table. Jade yelped in surprise as he swung her towards the sofa and sat down with her on top of his lap.

'Sorry, I didn't mean to jump on you like that.' His hand reached for her head where it lay on the arm of the sofa and started massaging her scalp. 'I don't want you to think that I invited you here just to have sex. When I said dinner, I really did mean dinner.'

Jade closed her eyes and let out a sigh. The movement of his hand felt like heaven. 'We can do what you like, as long as you don't stop doing that.' She opened one eye and looked across at him. 'But I won't say no to dinner. What is that amazing smell anyway?'

'Shepherd's pie.' Nick smiled at her smugly.

'What, a real one? Not bought from the supermarket?' She curled herself up in his lap, resting her head on his shoulder. 'I think you must be my favourite person.'

'I thought I already was your favourite person.' The rumble of his voice came through his chest.

'Well. I don't know.' She thought she had to tease him. 'There's Mum, and Dad, and Lily, and Archie, and Bill and Mandy from work ...'

He squeezed her in a tight hug that took away the breath for whatever else she was going to say. 'Yeah, yeah. I'm the bottom of the list. Obviously.'

She didn't have anything to say to that, so instead she just kissed him again.

They lay on the sofa for a while, just listening to the whirr of the oven and the faint noise of traffic. Jade turned her nose into his chest and breathed in the smell of him, just enjoying being curled up in his arms.

'I picked out a film for us to watch.' Nick broke the silence. 'Since you said you liked Deadpool. It's got Ryan Reynolds in it too.'

'Oh. I do like him. What's it called?' She squirmed around, changing position until she could see his face properly.

'The Hitman's Bodyguard. You haven't seen it, have you?' His right arm was resting on top of her, and his hand was gently moving up and down the outside of her leg. It felt so good to be touched like that. Jade could feel her whole body relaxing.

'I haven't actually. Must have missed that one.' Jade stretched, yawning. The size of the sofa was perfect actually. Her head was resting against one fabric-covered arm, and her legs were draped over the other side.

'Yeah. I haven't seen it either, but it looks funny. It's got Samuel L. Jackson in it too.'

'Let's get it started. Why not.' Jade stretched again.

'Let me just check on the dinner.' Nick lifted her gently off him. He opened the door to the oven. 'Looks pretty good. Probably about another half an hour? I'll just set a timer.' He patted his pocket, then smiled sheepishly. 'Of course. I already turned off my phone.'

'So did I.' Jade patted the grey fabric beside her. 'Come and sit down. We'll smell it if it starts to burn. Besides, we'll know how far we are in by how long the film has left.'

'How did you turn out so clever?' Nick sat back down next to her, wrapping his arm around her shoulders and reaching for the remote.

'I just can't help it. My natural brilliance just shines through.' Jade pretended to preen.

The first twenty minutes of the film were pretty funny, but they paused it when the dinner was ready, and sat at the small table while they ate, looking out through the large double window. Nick poured two glasses of wine, and they clinked them together in salutation.

'This is what I love about being grown up.' Jade sipped her wine.

'What, drinking alcohol?' Nick grinned at her.

'No. Not really. Just the freedom. Sure, I have to work, but I can do whatever I want in my spare time. No adults to tell me what to do.'

'Maybe.' Nick didn't sound so convinced. 'My mum still thinks she knows what's best for me.' He slowly chewed a mouthful of salad. 'But don't you think that being grown up means more choices? And aren't choices hard?'

Jade took another sip from her glass, considering. 'I guess ... I guess it depends on what kind of weight you attach to those choices. If you think that they're really important, I can see how that might be stressful. But if you have a belief that whatever choices you make then things are going to be fundamentally OK, then the choices become less important and the principles behind them are what really matters?'

'Hm. That's an interesting viewpoint.' Nick did sound like

he meant it. 'But what happens if you make a choice just because there's no other alternative?'

Jade reached out and touched the back of his hand gently. 'You're talking about your job, aren't you?'

Nick blew out a long breath. 'Spot on the money, as always.' He smiled wryly at her. 'And not just the job. I miss all my friends from back home. Especially Jamie. He was like a brother to me.'

'He still is, surely?'

'I don't know.' Nick extracted his hand and took another drink from his glass. 'I've asked him down to visit loads of times, and he just seems to make excuses. Says things are too busy. But I know he's not. I just wonder if he's annoyed with me for leaving.'

'No.' Jade couldn't help the word that slipped out. She tried again. 'Look, friendships are just tricky.' She winced as she thought of Carina, and how they still weren't talking.

'Yeah.' Nick nodded in agreement. 'I was kind of hoping that I would be able to make some new friends here, but people just don't seem interested. It's like they already have enough friends. I know that sounds a bit weird, but it's the best way I can think of putting it.' He made a face. 'I was thinking that walking group would be somewhere to get to know people, but you know all about what happened with that.'

'I'd still like to punch them both.' Jade curled her fist and made an angry face. But he knew she was joking this time. Kind of.

'Anyway, how come all your friends are about three times as old as you?' Nick obviously wanted to divert the topic away from what had happened. 'I would've thought that you'd have loads of friends your own age. From school. Or from uni. I mean, I know what happened with Carina, but what about all the others? You don't seem like that kind of person.'

He must have seen something of what was on her mind pass through her face, because he touched her hand gently, causing her to look straight up at him. 'I'm sorry. I shouldn't have asked. Just forget it.'

She saw the concern in his eyes, and her heart went out to him.

'No, you're right, it's a valid question.' Jade just wished she knew the answer to it herself. 'I did have a lot of friends. But ... I don't know really. I guess I changed somehow. Or they changed. Or we both did. This last year has been pretty tough for me. And I think I just let people go who didn't know how to handle it. Lily seemed to be the only one who was willing to accept me just as I am.'

Nick put his head in his hands. 'I wish my colleagues would accept me just as I am.'

Jade shrugged. Somehow she had to get him away from these destructive thoughts which kept cropping up. 'I think there's some good in everything. Just think, if you hadn't come down to Glasgow you wouldn't have met me. Or Archie.'

'True.' Nick straightened his shoulders. 'Or Sean.'

'Who's Sean?' Jade couldn't remember him having mentioned a Sean before.

'Oh. I forgot to tell you. He's the librarian.'

As Nick told her about his experiences at the library, and the planned walking trip, Jade felt a strange sense of relief. Finally, he had met someone who sounded like a friend. And the worry that he might be totally dependent on her and her actions eased up just a little.

'I vote for ice cream while we watch the rest of the film.' Nick rose to put the empty plates in the sink. 'And for doing the washing up later.'

'I vote for that too.' Jade plonked herself on the sofa, stretching out. 'But I don't know where you're going to sit, because this seems just the right size for me.'

'If I can't sit beside you then I'll just have to sit on top of you.' Nick squished himself on top of her, his long legs sticking off the end of the sofa.

'Can't ... breathe ...' Jade pretended to gasp.

Nick looked horrified for a minute, hurriedly pulling himself off her. When he realised she was joking he just stuck out his tongue at her and lay back down again.

'I can breathe, but if you put too much weight on me then all that nice shepherd's pie is going to come right back up again, which would be a pity.'

'That would be a travesty.' Nick rolled off her and went to fetch the pudding.

The rest of the film went down as smoothly as the ice cream. Jade loved action films for their predictable endings.

When the credits rolled Jade looked at Nick. He reached around her for the remote, switching off the TV.

'I'd normally put some music on now, but it's all on my phone.' He shrugged apologetically.

'I quite like the silence, actually.' Jade wasn't bothered by it at all.

She moved to straddle his hips, running her fingers through the tangles of his hair.

'I need a haircut.' Nick lifted one of his own hands to tug at a brown strand.

'I quite like it.' Jade buried her fingers in it. 'Anyway, I can't believe that you're thinking about haircuts when you clearly should be thinking about something else. What kind of man are you?'

Nick just laughed, and kissed her.

Jade never worked out how they got from the sofa to the bed; she was too focused on making the most of the moment. Her jumper had disappeared somewhere too. But it was when she went to pull off Nick's t-shirt that he drew back a little, looking down at her.

'Stay the night. Will you? I want to do this properly. Give you a good time ...' His voice trailed off, as if he was unsure of what to say.

Her heart suddenly melted for him, at the same time as her body responded to the suggestion in his words. 'Sure. I'd love that. But,' she placed one hand on his shoulder as he went to kiss her again, 'if I'm going to do that then I'd better text my mum so she doesn't worry. Smartphone ban or not.'

He nodded, then pushed her back down gently as she went to sit up. 'I'll get it for you.'

She lay back on the pillows, smiling at him. 'Just grab it from my bag.'

Nick opened the door to the hallway. For a minute he couldn't remember where she had put it, but when he closed the door there it was, hanging on a peg. He opened the zip on the tiny black thing, reaching his hand in, but he couldn't feel a phone anywhere.

He tipped everything gently out onto the floor, kneeling beside the pile. It would be quicker. Seeing the packet of condoms made him smile. If he had held onto any worries about her intentions in that respect then he could put them aside. Still, they wouldn't need them; he had his own small box stashed in a drawer beside the bed. He sifted through the items. Just the usual. Lip gloss, tissues, sanitary towel. Book. But no phone. So where was it?

Feeling back inside the bag, he came across a zipped compartment. That would be it. He opened it up and there was the phone. But as he pulled it out, a worn piece of paper fluttered to the ground. He picked it up, glancing at it without thinking.

Hug someone. The words jumped out at him, and his eyes were drawn to the page. *Read a good book. Do some exercise.*

This must be the original copy of the happy list. Intrigued, he opened out the paper.

Dear Ruby, it started,

I have written you this list of happy things, for you to do when you get sad. I know that things haven't been easy for you over the last couple of weeks, but I love you very much and I wish that I could take everything bad away.

He started, suddenly painfully aware that he was reading something intensely personal that he probably shouldn't be. A hot flush of shame went up the back of his neck. He folded up the paper carefully and gently placed it back where it had come from, and then did the same with the rest of Jade's things.

He was going to have to tell her that he had seen the letter. Not doing that would be almost like lying.

Stepping back into the living room, he closed the door firmly behind him. Jade smiled at him and reached for her phone. 'Thanks.' Then she saw his face. 'What's up?'

He lay down beside her, propping himself up on one elbow. 'I saw the letter. I didn't mean to. It just fell out when I got your phone out.'

'Ah. Jade's face suddenly became blank. 'I'd forgotten that was in there.'

'I'm sorry. I didn't read all of it. Only the first few words.' Nick felt terrible.

Jade lay back, arms behind her head, phone forgotten. 'I don't even know why I carry it around, really.' Then she looked at him. 'You can read it if you want.' She propped herself up on her elbow, unconsciously mirroring his position. 'In fact, you probably should read it. After all, you already know the main details of the story.' She tugged her t-shirt down nervously.

'Are you sure?' Nick didn't want to push into her personal life unless it was something she wanted to share.

'Yeah.' He knew her off-hand manner was hiding a lot of emotion. But this was a chance to get to know her better. Which he should be happy for.

Before he could say anything else, she rolled off the bed and went to fetch her bag. Then she pulled out the paper and handed it to him. 'Read.' She perched on the end of the bed.

He unfolded it carefully, aware that the creases were already very worn. The beginning of the letter was just as he had read it earlier. This was followed by the list of things that Jade had already told him about. Then there followed another four things. He read through them, marvelling at their simplicity. At the bottom of the list it was just signed 'with much love, Jade xx'

Jade's face was a picture of sadness. 'I just feel guilty about it really, because I never got to give it to her. I guess that's why I've been carrying around. But maybe it was just waiting for you instead.' She shrugged.

'Thanks for letting me read it.' He folded the paper carefully and laid it gently on the bedside table, then pulled her to him in a hug. She hugged him back, and they lay side by side for a few minutes, legs intertwined.

Nick couldn't help thinking about the list. 'It seems a strange sort of list, really.'

Jade propped herself up on one elbow. 'What do you mean?'

'Well, for an old person.' Nick couldn't really explain what he meant. If her grandmother had been sick, how would she have been able to do all that kind of stuff?

Jade looked at him as if he was crazy. 'She wasn't old. She was just seventeen.'

'Wait. Wait.' Nick rubbed his forehead. 'Aren't we talking about your grandmother?'

Jade made a silent O with her mouth, and her eyes went wide. 'Oh. Oh. You didn't know. Oh. Shit. You thought it was ... Oh.'

She paused, pinching the sides of her nose as if her head hurt. 'How did you get that idea?'

Nick shook his head, confused now. 'You mentioned that you'd started going to see Lily after your grandmother had died. And then, when your mum mentioned Ruby's funeral, I just thought ...'

'Oh. Shit. Yes. Of course.' Jade flipped over onto her stomach, resting her head on her arms. 'No. No. Ruby was my sister.'

'Oh. God.' It was Nick's turn to have his mouth drop open, and he could feel the heat flush his skin in embarrassment at his mistake. 'What happened to her?'

'She committed suicide. Off the bridge. A year ago last February.' Jade turned her head away.

'Off the ...' Nick's brain was struggling to process what she had just said, and then it all fell into place. 'The bridge.' He looked at her with new understanding. 'God.'

'I thought you knew, otherwise I would have told you sooner. I'm so sorry. I should go.' Her face bright red, Jade gathered up her bag and phone, and scrambled off the bed, searching for her jumper.

'No. No. Please stay. I'm sorry. We don't have to – I mean – just stay.' He rubbed the back of his neck, cursing his inability with words at the crucial moment.

She looked at him for a long moment, and the silence stretched out between them. Then she nodded slowly. 'OK.'

She lay back down, and he gathered her into his arms. He rested his chin on her head while his mind raced, thinking back through every single conversation. What a cock up. Serve him right for thinking he was so clever. Assumptions. Always a bad idea. They were what got you killed in the mountains. His face burned hot again as he thought about it. He wanted to apologise again, but he knew it wouldn't help. He felt so inadequate at that point that he couldn't have even begun to think about what to say.

But silence seemed to be what she wanted, although she lay so still that the movement of her breathing was the only sign of life.

After a long while she stirred.

'You OK?' he murmured quietly.

'I thought you'd seen the picture.' Jade rubbed her face against his chest. Her voice was flat and emotionless.

'What picture?'

'The one in the hallway. The four of us on holiday.'

Nick frowned. 'Never noticed it.'

There was another long silence. The light outside slowly faded as they lay there, and the gathering dusk enfolded them.

'You're hopeless, you know. Massive picture in the hallway, and you never noticed it.'

It didn't sound as if she was angry at him. In fact, the tone in her voice was that of fond exasperation.

'I was too busy looking at you.' He said it with the same light teasing tone, but in actual fact it was the honest truth.

There was a snort. 'Charmer.'

Nick let out the breath he didn't know he'd been holding. That was his real Jade back. Things were going to be OK. He just kissed the top of her head and squeezed her gently again.

'I'd better text my mum before she starts to worry that I've fallen under a bus.' Jade reached for her phone.

'You do that.' Nick stripped off his trousers and pulled back the covers. He tossed her a t-shirt. 'Have this if you want. Bathroom's through that door there.'

'Thanks.' She gathered it up and disappeared, returning in a few minutes with her hair plaited back. The t-shirt reached her mid-thigh in a very attractive way, but he pushed those thoughts away for now. He was still in shock that he had got things so wrong. And now so many of her comments made much more sense. The comments about Ruby's funeral. Her knowledge about depression. The way she had felt like her friends didn't understand. And as they lay down together, Jade curling her body into his, the thoughts were still whirling through his head, piecing everything together. Now her reluctance to get involved with him was completely logical. If you had lost one person you loved in your life, why would you want to risk losing another?

His heart went out to her. She was so brave. To jump into something like this with him after what had happened to her already. He took a deep breath and let it out slowly. He would just have to try to be the best version of himself that he could be. For her. And for himself too.

He lay there, a quiet resolve growing on him as he listened to her gentle breathing as she slept.

He didn't realise he had fallen asleep until he felt Jade stir beside him. The light was streaming into the room. He had forgotten to draw the curtains last night.

Jade yawned, and stretched. 'What time is it?'

He checked his watch. 'It's only seven.'

Jade stretched again, and sat up. 'I'd better get going. We start at ten on Sundays, and I still have to get home and change.'

He pulled her in for a lingering kiss, which she willingly indulged in. But finally she pushed him away. 'Come on, Romeo. Some of us have jobs to get to.'

'I'll see you next Saturday?' He desperately wanted to make sure that things were alright between them, but didn't know how to ask.

'Yeah. Sure. And since you've seen the list now, why don't you pick what we do? You know what's coming next.'

She disappeared into the bathroom.

Chapter 12

Jade hurried towards the station. The grey clouds threatened rain, and she didn't want to get caught out in her light summer jacket. Her parents wouldn't mind about her staying out all night. All they seemed to want from her was for her to be happy. But then, in some ways, that was the hardest request of all. To be happy. What did that even mean? And how the hell did she go about doing it?

Sometimes she caught a glimpse of happiness. Sometimes, for a fleeting moment, she managed to think of herself as not one of two sisters, but an individual in her own right. And that was what she liked most about Nick. He made her feel like a real person. Took her exactly as she was, without the shadow of her sister following her.

Maybe that would change now. Maybe he would see her differently. The look on his face last night when she had told him, that that had been painful to watch. The look in his eyes as he realised. And, to make things worse, she still hadn't shared the whole story with him. She had been so close to doing it, but somehow the words had passed her by.

She shook off the thought. They could only go forward now. One day at a time. As she had been doing ever since her sister had died. She had never intended to fall for someone like Nick. And it was kind of ironic that he seemed to be the one person who was actually good for her. They were either going to manage to help each other through this, or just crash and burn in flames together. But she had to tell him the whole story. The next time she saw him.

The house was quiet when she pushed open the door. She tiptoed upstairs, anxious not to wake anyone. Still, she would need a shower. And clean underwear. The noise of the shower would probably wake her mum up. Not her dad, though, who slept like a log. Although she'd never come across a log that snored quite as much as he did.

Sure enough, when she came downstairs, hair scraped up into her usual messy bun, her mum had already brewed a pot of tea. Jade poured herself a cup and sipped it slowly, savouring the delicate taste. No tea bags were allowed in the house; it was always brewed directly from fresh leaves. Silence settled in the kitchen as they both sipped their drinks and munched through their breakfast. Jade had shared many weekend mornings like this with her mum. Ruby hadn't been a morning person either. So often, while the other two had slumbered above, the two women had shared a pot of tea and a chat about what was going on in their lives.

Was that a factor in what had happened, Jade suddenly thought. She had talked it all out while Ruby had kept it all in?

She found herself telling her mum about what had happened with Nick. His assumptions, her assumptions, the big misunderstanding, the lot. And then she flinched as she realised what she had done. This was the first time that she had really spoken openly to either of her parents about Ruby and how she felt about it all.

She looked into the older woman's face, to try to gauge her reaction. There was pain there, sure, but also a smile on her face, as if she was happy about something. Before she could ask what it was, her mum rose, gently placing the empty teapot on the sideboard.

'You're right. You should tell him the whole story about Ruby and what happened. I think it would be good for you. And for him. But first,' she looked towards the clock on the wall, 'you need to get yourself off to work.'

Jade dumped her teacup in the sink, grabbed her bag from the corner and gave her mum a squeeze and a quick kiss on the cheek. Her mum's eyes were suspiciously bright, but she gave her a gentle shove. 'You get yourself off. I'll see you tonight.'

'Bye Mum. Love you.' She ran out the door.

Nick packed his daysack carefully. Picnic, snacks, water, waterproofs. Emergency shelter, because you never knew. The days were so long at the moment that he didn't bother with a torch. If he was desperate then he could always use his phone. He was torn between excitement at actually having someone to spend the day with, and desperate dread that it would end as badly as the other walking trip.

He was waiting outside on the pavement bang on time. A couple of minutes later a tiny red car pulled up beside him. Sean hopped out of the driver's seat and pulled it forward so Nick could squeeze in the back. Then he slammed the door and they started off. Nick settled himself into the corner of his seat, placing his bag beside him.

'This is Stevie,' Sean indicated the guy sitting next to him, 'and sitting next to you is Pete.' He jerked a thumb over his shoulder. 'But we sometimes call him Stumpy Stevie, when he's being a pain, and Pete is often Prof, because of all the long words he uses.'

'Says the librarian.' Stevie grinned backwards over his shoulder towards Nick. He was a bit of a stumpy sort of person; quite stocky and not that tall. Unremarkable brown hair was cut in an unremarkable style. In contrast, Pete was thin and wiry, with a thick brown shock of wavy hair not too dissimilar to Nick's own. Pete looked like he'd spent quite a bit of time outdoors, whereas Stevie's complexion was fairly pale. A bit like Nick's own really, there was still a long way to go before he was back to the brown he used to be when he spent most of his time outdoors.

'Great to meet you.' Nick smiled at Pete. 'So where are we going?'

'Well, Stevie's not been out walking for a while, so we're going to take it easy today. We're just going to do a low-level peak near Loch Lomond and then we'll probably stop for a drink in a pub somewhere.'

'Sounds good.' Nick envied the way that the three of them seemed so comfortable with each other. Still, they had invited him along, which was nice of them.

Over the course of the journey, Nick found out that Pete was working as a post-doc, although the specifics of what he was working on completely went over his head. Stevie worked in an office doing admin. Pete and Sean were pretty much the same age, late twenties, while Stevie was only a year older than Nick. All three were single.

'Although,' Pete admitted, 'I did meet someone last night. And he gave me his number.'

Stevie let out a wolf whistle, while Sean thumped the steering wheel in excitement, inadvertently sounding the horn.

'Go on! Give us all the details.' Sean sounded like he couldn't contain his excitement. 'Were you out for the night?'

'Actually, it was in the university library.' Pete sounded both slightly embarrassed and slightly pleased with himself.

Stevie let out a theatrical groan. 'Oh my god. Another academic. You're going to end up happily married with lots of disgustingly intelligent children.'

'Actually not.' Pete winked at Nick. 'He's a mature student. Not in my department, luckily. Said he was finding his course pretty challenging, that's why he was in the library late on a Saturday night. He used to be in the army.' Stevie let out another wolf whistle, and Pete pretended to hit him over the head in retaliation. 'Anyway, we're going to meet up some time this week.'

And of course the next question was about Nick's love life. He found himself telling them all about Jade. He left out the happy list, and the bit about her sister, and how they had met. Those things were private.

'She does sound pretty amazing.' Stevie sounded a bit wistful.

'Stevie here used to be married,' Sean looked in the rear-view mirror directly at Nick. 'But she ditched him when things got tough.'

'I don't know.' Stevie hastened to correct him. 'We kind of ditched each other. I think we both just realised that we'd become different people.'

There was a bit of a silence, as if no one quite knew how to follow that. But Sean taking a turn off the main road turned the conversation back to where they were going, and what the plan for the day was.

They soon pulled up in a small car park by the side of the road, and Sean let the two in the back out.

Nick stretched, enjoying the feeling of being free to move after being curled up in the cramped car. Still, he wasn't complaining. There was a hill to be climbed, and a picnic to be had. Anticipation curled through him, making his face break out into a grin.

'What's so funny?' He hadn't realised until the other man spoke that Sean was standing looking at him.

Nick shrugged. 'Nothing. Well, everything. It's just – well, mountains.'

Sean laughed, and gave Nick a friendly thump on the shoulder. 'I knew it was a good idea to invite you along.'

They did a quick poll and decided to wait for lunch until they got to the top. Nick was glad they had chosen one of the lower hills. Dark grey clouds drifted around the mountain tops, which looked very forbidding in this weather. There was no way he'd want to be up there; it would be wet and cold. In fact, they'd be lucky if they didn't get rained on this afternoon. Still, they all looked well-prepared for the weather. And at least it wasn't that windy. Could be much worse.

They set off. Stevie walked with a slight limp, Nick noticed. Maybe that was why he hadn't been out for a while.

It took them about two hours to get to the top. They took plenty of rest stops, but Stevie was still visibly tired by the time they reached the summit. He sat down heavily on a clump of heather.

'Shit. I can't believe I made it.' He looked up happily at the three of them.

'Whoop!' Sean gave him a high five.

The rest of them sat down next to him and lunch was doled out. Nick ate his ravenously. The wind was slightly stronger now that they were exposed, but the weather was still pretty decent, and he was snug and warm in his waterproofs.

'Sorry gents, I'm just going to have to take this thing off.' Stevie put his sandwich aside. He pulled up his trouser leg and before Nick could really work out what he was doing then he had unclipped the lower part of his leg – knee, boot and all – and put it to one side. He heaved a sigh of relief. 'Ah, that's better.'

Nick stared. He knew it was rude, but he just couldn't help it. So that was where the limp came from. And, he now saw, his nickname.

'Cycling accident.' Sean saw where he was looking. 'Stevie – before he became Stumpy Stevie here – was knocked down by a car.'

'Isn't it a bit harsh, calling him that?' Was Nick's first reaction.

Stevie laughed. 'Actually, I started calling myself that. Right after the accident actually. It started out as a way to bash myself at first, but after a while it kind of stuck and I'm proud of it now.'

As they ate the rest of their lunch, the three of them filled Nick in on what had happened. Nick found himself telling them about how much he hated his job.

'Yeah, I hear you.' Stevie spoke again. 'I'm not that keen on my new job either. I mean, it's OK. But not what I really want to do.'

'What did you do before the accident?'

'Outdoor activity coach for kids. Mountain biking, canoeing, camping, whatever.'

'Hm.' Nick could see how that could be challenging. 'Surely you can do all those things with a prosthetic though?'

'Oh yeah. It's just I don't have the stamina these days. Everything is just so much more tiring. I might go back at some point, but as you can see I'm still trying to build up my fitness levels.'

'Talking about fitness levels, it's probably time we started back.' Sean heaved himself up. 'I'm glad we're going downhill after the size of that lunch we've had.'

He pulled Stevie to his feet, and Pete and Nick scrambled to pack everything away. On the walk back down they talked about lighter topics. The music they liked. Films they'd seen. Nick joined in, just happy to be part of the close-knit group.

'We're going out again in a couple of weeks,' Sean said, as they drew up in front of Nick's building and he let him out of the back. 'If you'd like to come with us then it would be great to have you.'

'Yeah.' Nick couldn't help a grin escaping him. 'Great. Just let me know where and when.'

'It'll depend on the weather as usual,' Sean got back in the car. 'But we were thinking about something a bit bigger next time. Give this guy a bit of a challenge.'

Stevie made a rude gesture. The four of them were all laughing as the car sped off.

As Nick dumped his bag in the hallway he was still smiling. Maybe life wasn't so bad after all. But he would relive the good memories later. First, he had to take a shower, and then, he had to do some research for the next thing on the list. He already had some good ideas floating around in his head.

When Jade got home from work she just felt restless. She would have thought after standing on her feet all day she would have been tired, but she just couldn't stay put. Her mum was in the kitchen cooking, didn't need her help, and didn't want the distraction of her presence while she tried a new recipe. She needed to do something with herself. Something outside, but not walking. She was tired of walking. She was tired of —

She cut off the negative thoughts and batted them away. Exercise. She had the sudden urge to go for a run. Well, a jog was all it would probably be, but still. She went out into the hallway to grab her phone.

She heard an audible sigh of relief from her father as soon as the living room door closed, which made her smile.

The run was just enough to keep her mind busy, but not so much of a challenge that she got disheartened. Just like last time, it took her through the same sort of routine that she had done with Nick; run a bit, walk a bit. And repeat. It made her wonder how he was getting on. How his walk had been. She would text him when she got back.

She returned home feeling much more settled, and she hummed as she took a quick shower. Maybe she should keep up with this running thing, if it put her in such a good mood. The house smelled amazing. She was just putting on her fluffy cotton pyjamas when she heard her mum calling dinnertime. She ran lightly downstairs and settled herself at the table, now totally ravenous.

It wasn't until after dinner was finished that she thought to check her phone. There was a message from Nick waiting.

Had a great day. Will tell you all about it when I see you next. Lots of stuff we could do for the next thing on the list. How about brunch on Saturday to talk about it? There was a sunglasses emoji and one with a kiss.

It made sense to plan it out, Jade reflected.

Sure. Yoga beforehand? She added a couple of prayer hands and a winking face.

A thumbs up emoji came straight back. *See you there.*

Chapter 13

It felt good, going through the motions of the yoga class, knowing that Nick was there with her too. Somehow just his presence made everything so much better. As they headed up to the café she held onto his hand tightly. Seeing him only once a week was starting to get slightly frustrating. Still, she would make the most of the time they had together.

'I found loads of scary things to do,' Nick said as they settled themselves at a table. 'But then, I realised that first of all, I don't know what you find scary, and secondly, there's so many things to do I thought that it'd be better to decide together.'

'Sometimes just getting up in the morning scares me.' Jade was surprised by her own honesty.

Nick nodded. 'I'm glad I'm not the only one who feels like that.'

'I think everyone probably feels like that some days, don't you think?'

Nick looked at her in surprise. 'You really think that?'

'Yeah. I just think we don't really talk about it. You know, stiff upper lip, mustn't grumble, keep calm and carry on, all that.' She put on a posh accent and was rewarded by seeing him laugh.

'I hadn't really thought about it. That's the danger of getting too involved in my own problems and not thinking about anyone else's. Oh!' he continued, 'I did start giving hugs to my colleagues. That was pretty scary. But it's become quite a thing. Man-hugs all round every morning.'

'What, even the Tosser himself?' Jade wanted to know.

Nick knew exactly who she meant. 'Well, not him. Not yet anyway. But you never know.' He winked at her.

Nick digressed from scary stuff to tell her about his Sunday outing, and Jade just listened, happy to see that he had met some people who would probably end up as firm friends. It took the pressure off her somewhat. If he had other people who were looking out for him – and people who had been through some crazy stuff in their lives too – then maybe she could relax a bit and stop worrying about him so much.

'Anyway. Enough about that. Let's talk about what we're going to do next Saturday.' Nick got out his phone. 'I had a look at loads of things. Jumping out of a plane sounds pretty cool, but it's pretty expensive really.'

'Yeah. Too expensive. Plus you'd never get me going near a plane. What else?'

Their food came, and Jade dug in. She had opted for the cooked breakfast this morning. She was starving. Maybe it was all the running she had been doing this week. Three times already. She was pretty proud of herself.

'Well, there's lots of stuff like white water rafting, but then I came across this.' Nick held out his phone across the table.

Jade took it, looking at the webpage he had open. 'Abseil off the Titan.' She read aloud. She looked up at Nick. 'You have got to be kidding me. No way. Abseil off a crane? Not gonna happen.' She found her palms sweating just at the thought of it.

Nick shook his head. 'Not kidding. And, if you're up for it, we can do it next Saturday. At the moment it's normally only open for corporate and charity events, but apparently a mate of Sean's is the one who runs it, and he's said he could squeeze us in over lunchtime as a favour.'

'Oh, well, we definitely can't do it then.' Jade was relieved. 'We're taking the oldies out next Saturday.'

Nick shook his head. 'I went to see Archie on Wednesday evening and they're not doing a trip next week. Something's happened to the minibus and it's had to go in for some serious repairs.'

'Damn.' Looked like that excuse was gone. 'It's alright for you, you're used to abseiling off tall things.'

Another shake of the head. 'Not that tall. It's pretty scary for me too.'

Jade ate for a bit while she considered the idea. 'OK. But you're not to tell anyone about it until we've done it, in case I wimp out in a panic. Deal?'

'Deal.'

'How is Archie doing, anyway?' Finding her plate empty, Jade pushed it away.

'Pretty good. They're going to swap him to a flexible support next week, I think. He says he'll be glad to get the thing off. There were a lot of swear words in what he said though that I've edited out.' Nick laughed.

'Yeah, that sounds like him.' Jade laughed too. 'I'll have to pop in to see Lily sometime this week then, if I'm not going to see her on the weekend.'

They went to the park after that, anxious to soak up as much as much of the sunshine as they could. Propped up on her elbows, looking down at Nick as he lay on the grass, Jade realised that there was no better time to tackle a difficult topic. She gathered her courage together and opened her mouth. 'I really need to tell you exactly what happened the night Ruby jumped off the bridge.'

Nick looked up at her, the pain in his eyes clearly evident, although whether it was pain for himself or what she'd gone through she couldn't tell. He took a deep breath. 'Look, I'm really sorry to put you off, but could we leave it for another time? I don't know if I have the mental strength to get into that kind of thing right now, and I really want to listen to you carefully when you tell me all about it, because it's obviously so important to you. Could we do it next weekend? You could come back to mine after we've done the abseil and we could talk about it all then.'

Jade wasn't sure quite how she felt – perhaps a mixture of relief and irritation? The adrenaline that had been pumping through her veins as she steeled herself to tell him everything suddenly had nowhere to go, and she jumped up restlessly. 'In that case, I'm going to go and get us some ice cream. Do you want a flake in yours?'

They spent the rest of the afternoon lying on the grass in the park, not saying very much. Jade was half-wondering if Nick would invite her back to his flat again, but he didn't, and she didn't ask. The idea of sex was a little bit scary too. She was sure it would be great with Nick when the time came, because he was such a great guy, but she was happy with the hugging and kissing for now. Ah ... the kissing ... now that was something special. Nick made her feel special, she realised, just by the way he touched her.

Eventually she sat up regretfully. 'I really need to go. I'm going to a wedding celebration tonight with my parents.' She turned to look at him where he lay on the grass, one arm behind his head. 'I would have invited you, but it's not my party.'

Nick squeezed her where his arm was still wrapped around her waist. 'It's fine. I'm meeting Sean and the others for a drink tonight. I was kind of hoping you'd come along, but if you've got other plans then I'll just have to see you next weekend.'

'Yeah. For the abseil.' Jade looked at him sternly. 'I'm still not sure this is a good idea.'

'Just think how you'll feel when you've done it, though.' Nick sat up and hugged her tightly, then kissed her again.

Jade just leaned her head on his chest, luxuriating in the feeling of the moment. Then she withdrew reluctantly. 'I have to go. I need to get my posh togs on and my mum has threatened to style my hair.'

'Ooh – that is scary.' Nick jumped up and pulled her to her feet. 'I'll walk you to the station.'

'I'm going to get the bus from the edge of the park. There's one that'll take me almost all the way home.'

'Well, I'll wait for you at the bus stop then until the bus comes.' He looped his fingers through hers. Strange how the warmth of a hand could reach as far as her heart.

In the end they didn't even get a kiss goodbye. She saw the bus coming up the street and ran for it, waving over her shoulder as she took long strides towards the bus stop. He waved back as she sped past him on the bus, and blew her some theatrical kisses. She hugged herself half the way home.

Chapter 14

Jade could feel the butterflies in her stomach when she woke up on Saturday morning. Although to be honest, they felt more like a box of frogs jumping around. She texted Nick.

Are we really doing this?

The reply came back almost immediately. *Yep. Terrifying, isn't it?*

She stuck her head out of the window to try and gauge the weather. Overcast, but not raining. And definitely not windy. She had almost been hoping for wind, so that it would be cancelled, but it seemed as if the weather was not going to help her today.

A cup of tea helped to calm her nerves. She hadn't told her parents what she was going to do. Firstly, she didn't want them to worry, and second, she knew they would want to come and watch. And she didn't want anyone watching. In fact, the only person she had told was Bill from work, who had just smiled and wished her luck. Jade hoped luck didn't come into any part of what she was going to do. She didn't want luck to be the deciding factor in whether she got down to the ground in one piece. She sincerely hoped that safety was the determining factor in the ultimate outcome.

Her mum was suspiciously absent from the kitchen this morning. Normally she was up and about by now. Still, she was an adult. If she wanted to have a lie in then that was up to her. She had heard laughter coming from her parents' room when her dad had got back in the early hours of the morning, and was glad that her parents had started to laugh again. Some of that weird grey tautness had disappeared from around their eyes these last few weeks.

Besides, if her mum wasn't up that meant that Jade didn't have to be evasive when the inevitable question would come about what she was going to do that day.

Hunger finally broke through her nerves, and she managed a whole bowl of cereal without feeling like she was going to throw up. At least it wouldn't take long to get down the rope. A few minutes, tops. She had watched people come off the crane a couple of times, completely unaware that she would one day be doing the same. She shuddered. At least it wasn't bungee jumping. The thought of being suspended high in the air by her feet was just too awful to contemplate.

There's always something worse than what you have, she thought. With that in mind, she went upstairs to get dressed. But what to wear? What was the appropriate clothing for a death-defying descent from a crane? Something comfy, she guessed, going for a pair of black jeans. No hoodie – in case it got caught in the rope – but she took her dark green fleece in case it was cold up top. When she heard her mum go into the bathroom she fled, leaving a note on the kitchen table.

With time to kill, and not wanting to be alone with her own thoughts, she went to the library, and disappeared into the book stacks for a couple of hours. She purposely picked a book with a kickass heroine who always got the job done. When she finally surfaced she was ready.

Nick waved to her as she made her way through the glass doors to the tiny office at the foot of the crane. He wrapped an arm around her in welcome, and gave her a very quick kiss.

'This is Ruaridh, Sean's mate.' He motioned to a heavily built man who was standing beside him. Ruaridh was someone who looked like he spent a lot of time outside. He had a stubble of grey hair on his balding head, and muscles which looked like he either spent a lot of time in the gym, or had some kind of job in construction. The latter, Jade suspected, given the sun-weathered face.

Ruaridh stuck out his hand. 'Great to meet you.'

Jade grasped the big rough hand firmly, proud of the fact that there wasn't any tremor in her own.

Ruaridh took them through a quick safety briefing and fitted their harnesses on. Unlike the standard climbing ones these were full body harnesses that went up and over the shoulders as well. It made sense. Much safer. They had a test rig in the office, and both she and Nick got clipped up to the rope and had a turn at feeding the rope through the ring that would bring them down to the ground. There seemingly wasn't any way things could go wrong really. There was also going to be a second safety rope attached to her, in case the first one broke. It all seemed very simple, and very safe.

Jade suddenly had a thought. 'What happens if something gets stuck?'

'Oh, then I'll abseil down to rescue you. Like an overweight version of Spiderman.' Ruaridh winked at her. 'And there'll be someone waiting for you at the bottom, just to make sure you touch the ground OK.'

Jade took a deep breath and let it out again. 'OK. Let's do this.'

She turned to Nick, who was looking remarkably cool about the whole thing. Her mouth was open to make a jibe about it when she noticed his hands were trembling. It was a relief to know that he was as scared about it as she was.

She was fine in the lift as they rode up to the top, but as soon as they stepped out onto the iron walkway then the frogs in her stomach were back. Down at the bottom it had seemed relatively calm, but up here the wind whipped through her hair and made her very glad for the warmth of her fleece. Still, the view was pretty amazing. Even better than the one from the Necropolis. The river stretched out below them. She followed the road up from the river until she found her parents' house.

'Look.' She nudged Nick, one hand tightly grasping the rough metal railing. 'You can see the red table in our back yard. And the grey roof.'

Nick followed the line of her finger and nodded. 'And Sunnyside.'

'Yeah. They'll all be having their lunch right about now.'

Ruaridh had been readying the equipment, but he saw where they were pointing and smiled at them. 'Beautiful, isn't it? I never get tired of looking.'

Jade had never really thought of calling Glasgow beautiful, really. Majestic, maybe. Impressive, definitely. But beautiful? She took another look at the view. The river wound away into the distance, like a carpet of grey specifically chosen to match the colour of the sky. Green parks mingled in a patchwork with red roofs and the black lines of the roads criss-crossed like braiding on the city tapestry. And further away the hills framed the whole scene in purple and brown. Up here the sound of the cars were muted, and all that reached them was a gentle rumble which could have been the city snoring in slumber. There was a faint tang of salt in the air blowing in from the coast. Yeah. She would give it beautiful.

She saw the other two looking at her expectantly, and suddenly remembered why they were here.

'Right. Who wants to go first?' Ruaridh held out a hand.

'Me,' Jade found herself saying. 'I want to go first.'

Ruaridh clipped her into all the ropes and then pointed towards the edge. 'Off you go.'

She inched towards the edge, not daring to look down.

'Me. Look at me.' Nick said.

'Can't I just close my eyes?' Her legs were shaking now.

'You could, but then you'd miss that amazing view you were just admiring a few moments ago.' She knew Ruaridh was just trying to put her at her ease, but it didn't make her feel any better. As she swung out over the opening, she suddenly panicked, gripping the rope with both hands and closing her eyes. 'I can't do this.'

'Jade. Look at me.' Nick's voice was right next to her ear, and surprise startled her into opening her eyes. He was crouched down behind the barrier so his face was right next to hers.

'You can do this. Find the free end of the rope with your hands.'

She reached down until she grasped the rope in her hand. It felt comforting somehow, as if by grasping it she had control over her own destiny.

'OK. You got this. I'll see you at the bottom.' Jade nodded, unable to speak. 'Push the rope slowly through the ring.'

She gasped as the movement made her go down a couple of inches, but she could feel the strength of the harness around her body and mustered the courage to touch the rope again. Once she got it working, she started to move more quickly. The two men waved as she dropped away from them.

It was definitely a bonus to have something to do with her hands. It kept her mind off the drop to the ground below. Although it was kind of cool how everything just got magnified as she got closer. Little toy cars became bigger toy cars. Tiny scurrying ants became stick people with proper arms and legs.

When she felt as if she wouldn't be scared by it, she dared to look straight below her. A crowd of people had gathered around the barriers. She groaned. The last thing she wanted was a group of strangers witnessing her ungainly descent. But as she got closer, she realised that it wasn't a group of strangers at all. There was Lily, leaning against the barrier, looking straight up at her, and beside her was Archie in his wheelchair. In fact, it looked as if the whole Sunnyside crew were there. Even Sandra, still clad in her pink scrubs. And as she touched down on the platform and everyone clapped and cheered, she noticed her parents leaning on the barrier too. Her dad gave her a big thumbs up.

'I'm going to kill him.' Jade turned her face upwards and shook a fist towards where Nick would be standing, knowing he probably wouldn't be able to see her, but not caring. Everyone laughed.

When she was finally unhooked from the harness she ran over to her parents and gave them a big hug, then did the same for Lily. 'I'm going to kill him,' she repeated.

'Don't be too harsh on him.' Lily had a wicked look in her eyes. 'I worked out something was up when he came to see Archie last week and squeezed it out of him.'

Jade clambered over the barrier. 'I'm still going to kill him.' But her eyes were sparkling now.

Nick saw Jade reach the bottom and disappear into the crowd and crossed his fingers for just a second. Hopefully she wouldn't be too mad at him. Ruaridh nodded at him. 'Ready?'

'Yeah.' He waited until he was clipped in, and then looked at the other man. 'Thanks for doing this for us. Really appreciated.'

The older man shrugged. 'Happy to. I'd do anything for Sean. He rescued me out of a bad patch. Ask him to tell you the story sometime.'

Nick took a deep breath as he steadied himself against the platform. Sure, he had abseiled before, but not from such a great height. And usually, there was rock to plant his feet on. None of this crazy swinging out into open space.

He gritted his teeth. If Jade had done it, then so could he.

Ruaridh gave him a salute as he started to descend. Nick waved back with his free hand.

Working the mechanism was surprisingly simple. Being out in open space he had expected he would start swinging round and round, but the safety rope kept him anchored. He was facing the centre of town, but by the time he had thought to look for his building, he had already dropped below the height of the roofs. As he touched down there was clapping and cheering from the crowd.

It took only a couple of moments to get rid of the harness, and then he was searching the crowd for Jade. She was standing next to her parents. He reached across the barrier to give her a big hug.

'I'm going to kill you,' she murmured in his ear.

He swung himself over the barrier and gave her a quick kiss on the top of the head. 'Can you kill me after lunch? Because that's the next thing on the plan. We're all having lunch back at Sunnyside. And I think Sandra's even made cake.'

He held his breath, waiting to see her reaction. And then she laughed, brown eyes sparkling, and slid an arm around his waist. 'I think we can defer the killing until after some cake. Or maybe it can wait until tomorrow. I'll probably be too lazy after a big lunch.'

It was only a short walk back to Sunnyside, where a massive spread of sandwiches waited for them, and indeed, the promised cake.

'We all made it, really. Sandra supervised, but three of us mixed up the mixture, and everyone iced a bit of the top.' Lily was back in her favourite chair in the bay window, looking out over the garden. Jade was sat in the window seat just by her left elbow.

Jade looked over to where the big cake lay in pride of place in the middle of the table. 'I'm guessing that's supposed to be a crane.'

Lily laughed. 'It was, but then Jim got his hands on the icing bag.'

Jade munched through her third sandwich. Nick was over in another corner of the room, having an animated conversation with Archie. From the gestures he was making she could tell he was explaining just how the abseil mechanism had worked.

Now that it was all over it seemed a bit of an anti-climax. It hadn't been that scary at all. She would do it again without a second thought. Still, that was the same with many things. Do them once, they were scary. After that they just became familiar.

'I thought Nick said that there wasn't going to be a trip today, because of the minibus? Or was that all a lie?'

Lily nodded. 'It's true, the minibus is out of action. They're waiting for a spare part apparently. But then Sandra worked out that we could all just walk down to the crane. And that was when we came up with the plan.'

By the time the cake was finished and the plates had been cleared away, the adrenaline rush had drained and Jade felt pretty tired.

'Fancy getting away from this crowd?' She slid an arm around Nick's waist and reached up on her tiptoes to give him a kiss.

'Yeah.' He looked down at her fondly, his hand reaching around her to pull her closer to him and squeeze her bum. 'You still coming back to mine?'

Something curled in her stomach at such a blatant invitation. 'Sure. Let me just say goodbye to everyone and then we can scarper. Let's say fifteen minutes?'

He nodded and kissed her one more time before letting her go.

It took her a while to go around everyone, to thank them all for coming to see her. She gave Lily a long hug.

'Not angry at us, are you?' The older woman smoothed a hand over Jade's hair as she kneeled by the side of her chair.

Jade shook her head. 'Not at all. Thanks for making it special.' She gave Lily a fond kiss on the cheek as she stood up.

The last ones she went to were her parents, who sat on one of the comfy sofas, listening to Archie talk about his childhood. 'I'll see you later. Don't wait up.'

Her mum squeezed her hand, then pulled her in for a quick hug. 'Have fun. Don't do anything I wouldn't do.'

Jade just laughed, disentangling herself from the sofa and going to rescue Nick from Jim, who was explaining the rules of croquet to him in minute detail.

As they walked away from the building Jade placed her hand in Nick's larger one, feeling the warmth of his fingers seeping through to her own. 'Train?' She looked up at him. 'It's quicker than the bus.'

All he did was rest his hand on her thigh while they sat on the train, but even that simple contact made her hairs feel like they were standing on end. The twenty minutes it took to get back into town felt both incredibly short and horrendously long.

Chapter 15

The apartment door made a soft click as it closed.

'I can't believe we just did that. I mean, abseil off a crane? We must be crazy.' Jade looked at Nick with a massive grin on her face.

'Yeah. Feels kind of surreal, doesn't it?' Nick's face sported a similar expression to her own.

They stood there looking at each other for a couple of seconds, and then Jade couldn't help it; she jumped into his arms. Her bag fell forgotten to the floor.

He carried her easily to the bed, and they both tumbled onto it. She reached for Nick's belt, but he stopped her. 'Wait. That comes later. I want to do some stuff first.'

He took his time, kissing her slowly, legs wrapped around hers. One hand moved through her hair, massaging her scalp, and the other held her tightly to him. It already felt amazing, and they had barely done anything.

Her fleece and t-shirt came off, and he kissed his way down her neck. Jade closed her eyes. If she was a cat she would be purring right now. She gasped as his mouth closed around one of her nipples, and opened her eyes.

Nick raised his head. 'OK?' His eyebrows had drawn together, as if he was worried.

She shook her head. 'Yes. It's very OK. Just a bit of a surprise.'

He laughed, and bent his head again, undoing her bra with his hands and casting it to one side.

Jade had never known that such pleasure was there for the taking in that part of her body. Just when she felt it might be getting too much, he moved to her other nipple and did exactly the same. It was pleasure, but it almost felt like a sort of torture, for it made her want so much more from him.

She tugged at his t-shirt, wanting to feel his skin under her hands, and they both pulled it off over his head. She ran her hands over the muscles of his back, and up his arms. 'You're pretty ripped.'

Nick laughed. 'Not compared with what I used to be. I've let myself go a bit since I've been working in an office.'

She ran a hand over his back again, feeling the soft skin where it met the line of his trousers. 'Feels just perfect to me.'

He propped himself up on one elbow, tracing a pattern around her breasts with one finger. 'You're very beautiful, you know.'

'Me?' Jade was surprised. 'I've always been too short, or too skinny, or too pale.' She cupped a breast with one hand. 'And my boobs aren't big enough.'

He cupped the other one gently, and lightly kissed the tip. 'Feels just perfect to me.'

'There's something else I've been wanting to touch as well.' He reached for the button on her jeans. It took some un-sexy wiggling before they came off, but soon she was free.

Nick trailed a hand down across her stomach and down between her legs. One of his legs was still flung over one of hers, and she tried to reach for his belt again, but he gently pulled her hand away and winked at her. 'Don't be so impatient. I want to make sure you have a good time first.' He kissed her again, and while he was kissing his fingers slipped gently under her underwear. And for the second time Jade found herself surprised. That the touch of his hand could do such things to her. And the fact that he took the time, experimenting to see what gave her pleasure.

When he finally took his hand away she felt almost bereft. But he was kissing his way down her body, and down to her stomach. She arched her back in pleasure at the touch of his lips on her skin. But he kept on going, moving her legs apart and bending his mouth down to reach for the place between her thighs. She gasped as he gently licked, then took her into his mouth just has he had with her nipples. When had her underwear disappeared? She didn't even know.

'Are you sure you want to do that?' Somehow even through the pleasure she couldn't quite relax. 'I mean, I haven't had a shower since this morning.'

He laughed, his mouth still touching her, and she felt the vibrations give her another wave of pleasure. 'Don't worry. You'll be squeaky clean by the time I've finished.'

She was about to ask when Nick started moving his tongue in a way that threw all thoughts out of her head, and she twisted a hand in his hair, abandoning herself to the waves of pleasure that flooded through her.

He seemed to know when she had had enough, and lifted his head and kissed his way slowly back up, finishing with a light kiss on her nose that made her laugh. He propped himself up on one elbow again while his hand trailed lightly across her body.

Jade felt like she had just walked a hundred miles, or ran a marathon, or danced all night. Her body refused to do anything she told it to, so she just lay there for a while, enjoying the feel of his touch.

'That was pretty amazing.' She finally looked up at him, studying his face. 'I never – I mean, I read about that sort of thing, but ...' She found herself lost for words.

Nick frowned slightly. 'Don't tell me – I mean, you're not ...' He trailed off.

'A virgin, no.' She supplied the word he was too embarrassed to say. 'But it wasn't like that. Anyway. I definitely think it's your turn now.' She reached for his belt and gave him a theatrical wiggle of her eyebrows as she pulled down his jeans.

Jade took her time as well, experimenting to find out what Nick found good. She had read a lot of magazines, but it was so different in real life. To really take the time, and to have someone who had the patience to bear with her inexperienced touch, was really a new experience for her. And she wanted to make the most of it.

She found things that were unexpected for both of them. Most unexpected for her was the realisation that it turned her on to watch what she was capable of doing to him. Maybe it was the same for him. She would have to remember to ask him afterwards. She was so engrossed in what she was doing that it surprised her when he came, sticky warmth flooding out over her hand. She scrambled across the room for the kitchen roll, anxious to mop up before it made a proper mess.

Afterwards they snuggled under the duvet together. Nick yawned, then apologised, then laughed as Jade's mouth split in a huge yawn of her own.

'Guess it might be time for a little nap.' He kissed her on the top of her head. 'That was pretty amazing.'

'But we didn't actually do anything.' It didn't really count as real sex, was what she really meant.

Nick shrugged. 'There's no rush. As long as it's good, that's what counts.' He yawned again and wrapped his arms tighter. 'Just don't go anywhere.'

Jade listened to the soft sound of his breathing, and after a while heard it deepen as he fell asleep. She didn't really feel sleepy. Maybe she would just close her eyes ...

She woke some time later when Nick stirred beside her. It felt good to have him lying next to her with nothing but skin to separate them.

'Mmm.' His breath tickled her ear. 'I'll have to remember that spooning puts my hands in all the right places.' He reached up to gently roll a nipple between his fingers, while the other one dipped down between her legs. 'Are you up for another round?'

Jade suddenly found that yes, she was definitely in the mood for wherever he wanted to take her. And, leaning back against him, she could feel that he was pretty ready for it too.

Still, he took his time again, making sure she was thoroughly wet before he took a condom out of the bedside table and rolled it on. Jade braced herself for it to hurt as he went in, but somehow it didn't, and she felt a rush of something she couldn't quite describe. It was like he filled her up not just physically, but mentally too. As if he filled a place in her mind that had somehow been empty. But then there was no time for thoughts, because they were moving together, and he took her away again to the place of pleasure that she hadn't known existed until such a short time ago.

'Wow.' She didn't have any other words to describe what had happened, as they lay in each other's arms afterwards. 'I mean, just, wow.'

Nick drew the bedcover up to make sure they didn't get cold. 'Now that's a word that every guy wants to hear.' He kissed her on the forehead.

Jade was still trying to process what had happened. 'If I'd known it could be like that ... well.'

Nick laughed softly. 'You mean, you might have jumped on me earlier?'

Jade opened her mouth to give a cutting retort, and then realised he was teasing her. 'Maybe.' She reached her mouth up for another kiss, which he gave her willingly.

Her stomach rumbled loudly, and they both laughed. 'I am starving. What time is it?'

Nick reached over her for his watch. 'Probably about dinner time. What do you want to do? Go out? Get takeaway? Cook something here?' He squinted at the dial. 'Yeah, it's already almost six.'

Jade considered for a minute. 'We could cook something, if you want. What have you got in?' The thought of creating a dinner with Nick kind of appealed to her.

She yelped as he got out of bed and cold air rushed in. He crossed to the fridge, still completely naked, and bent to open the door. Jade stayed where she was, admiring the view. She liked how he wasn't self-conscious at all.

He lifted a packet out. 'There's sausages here.' He bent again to open a drawer. 'And I think I've got some potatoes.' He turned. 'Bangers and mash? I think I might have some peas in the freezer.'

'Meat and two veg? I think I could be happy with that.' Jade flashed him a wicked smile.

He looked down to where her gaze was focused and then made a dive for the bed, wrapping her up in the duvet and tickling her until she squealed for mercy.

'You're a wicked, wicked woman.' His smile was broad. 'But I like you.'

It didn't take long to prepare the dinner, for which Jade was thankful. They ate at the small table, hands often touching, as if they were reluctant to let go of each other after the experiences they had shared.

'Will you stay the night?' Nick looked at her when they had finished eating.

'Sure.' Jade squeezed his hand. 'Let me just text my mum to say that I won't be back.'

She retrieved her bag from where she had flung it, and sat down on the sofa to write her message. But when she pressed the button to activate the screen nothing happened. Somehow the battery was dead. Then she remembered. She had been in such a worry about the abseiling last night, she had forgotten to plug it in. She'd been worried about telling Nick everything too, she suddenly remembered, the guilt flooding back. But everything that had happened today had just driven it completely from her mind. She had been so busy enjoying herself that she had forgotten all about Ruby.

'I've got no battery.' At the sound of her voice Nick turned around from the sink, his hands covered in soap suds.

'Don't worry, you can use mine. It's by the bed.' He pointed to where his bright blue phone lay on the bedside table.

'But I don't know her number. It's in my phone.' She could feel the anxiety hit her. 'If I don't text her she'll worry.'

Nick dried his hands on a towel. 'Now you're acting all weird. It's just a phone.'

'No. You don't understand. I have to have my phone. If I don't then how will people get hold of me if something happens?' She knew she was being short with him, but she couldn't stop herself. She felt a tightening in her chest. *Oh please no. Not a panic attack. Not here. Not now.*

'Hey. Hey.' Nick couldn't work out where all this had come from. He crossed to the sofa and kneeled down beside her. Gently prising the phone out of her grip, he took her hands in his own. 'Something tells me that this is about more than just a phone. What's going on?'

Jade just looked at him and burst into tears.

Oh, God. What had he done now? All this about a phone battery. What was going on?

He looked at the phone. It wasn't the same as his, but it looked as if it had the same charger as his watch. It only took two seconds to plug it in.

He turned back to Jade. She was still sobbing as if her heart was broken, head laid down on the arm of the sofa. He sat down next to her, putting an uncertain arm around her shoulders. It was only a couple of minutes until she lifted her head.

Kitchen roll. That was all he had. He lifted the roll from where it still lay beside the bed and tore off a piece for her. Angry Jade, prickly Jade, defensive Jade, all these things he could deal with. But seeing her this upset was almost too much for him.

Jade wiped her eyes with the paper towel. 'I'm sorry. I over-reacted. It's just—' she swallowed, sniffing loudly, 'I left my phone at home that night.'

His face must have betrayed some of his total confusion, because she collected herself, obviously realising that he didn't have a clue what she was talking about. 'The night Ruby jumped off the bridge.' She took a deep breath to steady her breathing and sniffed again. A loud sound came from her as she blew her nose.

Nick racked his brains for something that would sound sympathetic but not trite and came up with exactly nothing. So he squeezed her shoulder, rubbing his hand up and down the top of her arm.

Jade pulled away and squished herself into the corner of the sofa. Despite her retreat, he took some comfort from the fact that she hadn't pulled away from him completely; her feet were still resting against his leg.

She swivelled herself around until she was looking directly at him. Her eyes looked dark black in her pale face. 'I've been meaning to tell you for ages. That's what I wanted to tell you last weekend. When we were in the park. I never meant to leave it behind. I always took it everywhere, especially after the first time. But that night ...' She rubbed a hand over her eyes. 'I left it in my room. What an idiot.'

Her hands went around herself as if she was cold, and she rubbed her arms, although it wasn't that cold in the tiny flat.

'Everyone makes mistakes.' Nick spoke automatically. He still didn't really know what the significance of her comments were, but it was obviously something important to her. He found himself wanting to reach for her, but she seemed so remote from him somehow.

Jade made a face. 'Sure. But not everyone forgets their phone at home when their sister is suicidal.'

Nick felt a rush of anger at her words. 'You can't blame yourself for what she did.'

Jade let out a short, humourless laugh. 'You know, everyone said that. But funny really, somehow I still do.' The sarcasm in her tone was obvious.

She stretched out, draping her legs over his lap, clasping her hands behind her head. 'She tried to call me that night. A couple of times. Once, early on in the evening, and then once just before midnight. Dad was out working. Mum was supposed to be keeping an eye on her. But we worked out she'd climbed out the bedroom window and jumped down onto the front grass.'

'Still not your fault.' Nick touched one of Jade's feet; it was ice cold. He took it in his hands and started rubbing it gently.

Jade nibbled at a nail. 'I have wondered, many times, if my subconscious left my phone behind on purpose. It was my birthday, you see. I almost didn't go out. We were all on tenterhooks after the thing with the pills. And Carina had a bad cold that night, so she wasn't going to go either. I sometimes wonder if my brain just wanted to ditch everything for a few hours. To not have to worry about anything.'

Shit. Nick's brain was only capable of one thought. *Her sister killed herself on her birthday*. Then something else she had said permeated through. 'You said, pills? What happened with the pills?'

Jade looked at him again. 'Sorry. I keep jumping around. Ruby tried to commit suicide a couple of weeks before she jumped off the bridge. Luckily my mum found her not long after and worked out what had happened.' She grimaced. 'You can imagine what happened. Lots of shouting and crying. My parents took her straight to the hospital to get her stomach pumped.'

She made another face, leaning back until she was staring at the ceiling. 'The hospital suggested it was probably just a cry for help, that she wasn't serious. Guess they were wrong about that one.' The casual way she spoke masked a whole bucket of emotions that she wasn't sharing, Nick could tell.

'Still not your fault,' Nick repeated. His hands moved to her other foot, kneading and massaging, trying to show with his fingers how much he cared.

'I know. I blamed the staff for that for a long time too. But really, everyone was just doing their best in a tricky situation.' Jade took a deep breath and let out a sigh. 'But the worst part about the night my sister jumped wasn't coming home to two voicemail messages from her and then a text from my mum a few hours later to say they were at the hospital. It was sitting in that hospital for five fucking days, waiting to see if she would wake up. Waiting while the doctors ran all their stupid tests, just so they could prove to us that she was really dead.'

An image flashed in her mind, of her sister, attached to a hundred tubes, chest rising and falling in time with the machine that made her breathe. She spoke the words that she had never yet said aloud. 'And knowing, if, just maybe, that I'd not left my phone behind, then she might still be here today.'

This time when Nick held out his arms she crawled gratefully into them, wishing his warm strength could help her blot out the memories.

'I deleted her voicemails. I was getting kind of obsessed with them, playing them over and over again, and I knew it wasn't good for me. But now, just sometimes, I wish I'd kept them. To have just a little piece of her left in my life. To be able to hear her voice again ...' Words failed her, and she broke down again and wept.

Nick didn't speak for the longest time, and she just nestled against him, glad of his solid warmth. The silence stretched out in the room, but this time it felt somehow comforting.

'Will you stay tonight?' Nick gently stroked her hair.

Jade loved him in that moment. Loved him for the fact that he didn't try to make her feel better, or give her some corny piece of advice.

'If you want.' She rubbed a hand along the top of his thigh. 'I'll have to leave early for work though.'

'I'd love you to.' Nick squeezed her tightly until she protested for air.

They took a long shower together, savouring the feel of each other's bodies, and then crashed into bed. But somehow neither of them felt sleepy. Nick ended up telling Jade all about back home, and his parents. He had her laughing with some of the tales about guests who had stayed at the B&B.

'It sounds like a great life you had.' Jade lay on her back, arms clasped behind her head. 'I'm not surprised you feel lonely in the big city.' She looked over at him. 'I'm sorry I dumped all of that on you earlier. It's a lot to take in.'

Nick shook his head. 'To be honest, I'm glad I know the whole story.' He was silent for a few moments. 'I just don't know why you didn't tell me right at the start. It would have explained a lot of things.'

Jade put her hands over her face. 'I just don't know. At the beginning, it was because I'd never told anyone else about how guilty I felt. After that, I wanted to tell you, but I was worried what you might think of me.'

'It was your fucking birthday, for goodness sake.' Nick's use of a swearword that she had never heard him use before startled her into sitting up. 'And you made an honest mistake. Don't ruin the rest of your life stuck on that.'

She blinked at him, surprised by the anger in his voice. 'I guess you're right. I have been so wrapped up in that. What an idiot I've been.' She could see it all so clearly now.

'Anyway, at least you can say you've done the next thing on the list. Wasn't it talk to someone and have a good cry?'

Jade laughed, surprised by his turn of thought. 'I guess so.' Then her expression soon sobered. 'But you haven't. You really tend to stick to conversation about the positive things in life. All the bad things you've told me about I've had to wring out of you by asking questions. And sure, you've told me about your work, and all that kind of shit, but you've never once mentioned how things make you feel.'

Nick stiffened. He knew she was right, and yet ... 'It's my protection mode.' He surprised himself with his honesty. Still, after the confidences she had trusted him with tonight, she deserved nothing less. 'I don't talk about my feelings.'

'Yeah, I get that.' Jade sounded like she had heard it all before and wasn't buying it. 'I mean, have you even told your parents about how you're feeling?'

He knew that his expression betrayed his answer. She nodded. 'Really, I think you should talk to someone. Not to me, necessarily.' She held up a hand as he opened his mouth. 'But to someone. Maybe your parents. Someone professional would be even better.'

Nick felt the old anxiety start to rise inside him. 'I'm just scared.' He spoke the words even as they formed in his mind. 'I already feel some days as if I'm hanging onto my sanity by a thread. I'm scared that if I start talking about things then it will snap and something terrible will happen.' He realised that he had raised his voice, and took a deep breath to calm himself. 'I don't want to lose my job. Or lose you.'

He shifted uncomfortably beside her. 'Besides, I'm much better now. I've got you, and Archie, and Sean and the guys. I don't feel lonely any more. And if I could just find out a way to sort out the job situation, then my life would be perfect.'

Jade frowned. 'Yeah, I can see that. But what happens if you don't have me any more at some point? Or Archie or whoever? What will happen then?'

'That's not going to happen. You won't all suddenly disappear. What's the chance of that?'

Jade snuggled into him. 'Let's not argue. I just really think you should talk to someone. Get some help. Look at what happened to Ruby. She knew we all loved her and she still did what she did.'

He really got what she was trying to say. But that didn't mean that talking was the right solution for him. He didn't need to talk. He needed mountains. And wild rivers. And the comfort of home, where no one would ask him any questions. Where people understood him.

He was about to escape by faking a yawn when a real one hit him, almost splitting his face in two. 'I'm pretty tired. Shall we get some sleep?' He was glad to have been saved the guilty burden of pretending.

'Shattered,' Jade agreed. She turned over and they lay like spoons, his arm wrapped tightly around her.

Chapter 16

Nick awoke in the darkness. Jade was still snuggled against him. His arm was still around her waist. He had been dreaming of home again, only this time Jade had been there, laughing as she helped his dad to cook dinner on the big range. Nick had gone to give his mum a hug just as he had woken up. The noises of the city around him only served to deepen the chasm between his dreams and reality. He felt his eyes fill with tears, and cried silently, his heart painfully full, while Jade slept unaware beside him. When he eventually managed to regain his control, he lay there for a long time, listening to the soft sound of breathing coming from the woman lying next to him. He couldn't quite believe that she was really real, that this was really happening to him. She was so amazing. He would fix this moment in his memory forever. And he would use her strength to sort his life out.

Nick finally drifted off into confused dreams where he was grasping at something he couldn't quite reach.

When Jade felt the first tear drop she almost turned towards him. But she knew what would happen if she did. He would brush them away and pretend it had never happened. So instead she lay still in the darkness, feeling the tears fall one by one onto her hair. She listened as his breathing returned to normal, and finally returned again to the steady breathing that meant he was asleep. And it was then, and only then, that she had to admit to herself that she couldn't do this thing. Not if she was going to keep her own sanity. She knew how it would play out. He would refuse to talk about things, just like Ruby had done. She would watch him warily, waiting for any sign that he was going to crack. It was no basis for a good relationship. Her thoughts went round and round, looking for another solution, until she finally fell asleep. But by the time she woke in the morning she knew what she had to do.

A rustling noise woke Nick out of a deep sleep, and he turned over, wondering what it was. Jade was sat on the sofa, pulling on her jeans. When she saw him looking at her she smiled, 'Morning. You looked so peaceful sleeping there that I didn't have the heart to wake you.' Her weight dipped the edge of the bed as she sat down.

'I have to go.' She stroked his cheek gently.

'I know.' He smiled lazily up at her. 'So I'll see you next Saturday?'

Her smile faded as she gazed at him steadily. 'Look, Nick ...' Her voice trailed off.

His heart sank. That was never a good start to a sentence.

'Nick.' she tried again, her voice firmer this time. 'I've been thinking. I just don't think that I can do this. Us, I mean.' She rested one hand on his chest, and he felt the warmth of her hand through the thin summer duvet.

Nick had thought her words would be a surprise, but he realised that a vast part of him had always been expecting them to come. At some point, anyway. Just not now. Not after the beautiful day they had shared yesterday.

His heart twisted inside him. 'Is this ... because of who I am?' He couldn't say it straight out, say the word he had been avoiding as hard as he could. Lose a leg, he thought viciously, and everyone feels sorry for you. Lose yourself, and nobody cares. Then he caught his thoughts, mentally slapping himself. That wasn't a fair way to think. And it wasn't true. Even if it felt that way right now.

Jade shifted on the bed, withdrawing her hands and stuffing them under her arms. Her hair, that beautiful mass of silky black, fell over her face, hiding her expression from view.

'No.' Her voice sounded tired, as if all the weight of his problems had somehow shifted to her shoulders. 'But it is partly to do with what you're doing.'

She pushed back the mass of hair, reaching for the tiny hairband that lay on the bedside table. She bound it up into the same haphazard style that he had seen on her the first time they had met.

'You need help. Professional help. It's obvious.' She turned away from him to pick up her jumper from where it had fallen on the floor. 'And I can't be a substitute for that.' She started towards the door.

Nick sat up in bed, irritated now. 'But I don't want you to be a substitute. I just want you to be you.' He started to get out of bed and realised that he was still completely naked. A pair of shorts pulled from a drawer had him feeling slightly less vulnerable.

Jade had her hand on the door handle now. 'But can't you see? I can't be me if you're like this. I can't stand the watching. The waiting. The wondering. And if I ever lost you ...' Her voice choked, and she turned away.

Nick wanted to grab her and shake her, but he knew that it wouldn't help. He just folded his arms and glared at her. 'So you're throwing it all away, just for the outside chance that it all goes wrong? I'm not your sister, you know. Don't try to judge me by what she did.'

When she looked at him he could see the tears in her eyes, although she stubbornly refused to let them fall. 'No, Nick. I'm giving it away, to save my sanity right now.'

About to open the door, she paused and turned back to him. 'I'll always be there for you, if you need me, Nick. Any time you need a friend, or if you're in trouble, just call me. But I can't offer you more than that right now. I just can't.' And with that she was gone. A few seconds later he heard the front door slam.

Nick sat down suddenly on the bed, feeling as if someone had punched him in the stomach. What the hell had just happened? How had they gone from what they had shared the previous night to such a sudden departure? He threw a pillow across the room in frustration. Just when it had started to seem like life was finally giving him a break, she was gone. Just like that. He rubbed his hands over his face, feeling the stubble scratch on his chin. What was he going to do now?

Sean. He was supposed to be going out with the guys today. They had planned to climb Ben Lomond. He flopped backwards onto the bed, staring at the ceiling. Surely he couldn't do it. He couldn't pretend to be normal, today of all days.

On reflection though, he didn't see a way of getting out of it. He could pretend to be ill, but Sean would never buy it and he didn't want to lie to them. And anyway, those guys would be the type to come banging on his door if he just didn't show up.

He lay there for a long while, time ticking by, until he came to the realisation that he would just have to go. Anyway, it was a trip to the mountains. His happy place. What possible reason was there not to go?

As he pulled himself up he suddenly caught sight of a scrap of paper on the bedside table. The list. Jade had forgotten it. Or had she left it because she no longer needed it? And no longer needed him?

Chapter 17

With every step she took it felt like her heart was breaking.

Every time Jade had come across something similar to those lines in a book she had either winced or snorted. She had never been one for drama. But the trouble was, these words where a pretty accurate portrayal of how she was feeling right now. Or more like, that there was a thin thread connecting her and Nick that was getting ever thinner the further she got from him, until the point when it would eventually snap ...

She gave up. This was just shit. Really shit. Too fucking shit for analogies. It had been bad enough being broken up with. But to be the one to do the breaking up, well, that was a new experience. And not one she ever wanted to do again. It made her feel like the bad guy. Like she was the one who was uncaring. Whereas in actual fact she was the only one who cared enough to act like an adult. For half a second she considered retracing her steps, apologising and crawling back into the warmth of his bed. But hey. It wouldn't do either of them any good. And, she had a job to get to.

She should have known her boss would notice something was up as soon as she walked through the door. That was one of the big reasons she had stayed, despite the sociable hours; Bill and Mandy ran the business like one big family. Big warm hugs were the norm. Mandy never forgot to bake a homemade cake for a birthday.

'Come from a funeral this morning?' She heard a voice behind her as she hung up her bag in her locker. Bill stood looking at her, a warm smile on his round face.

Jade shook her head. 'Just don't.' She shut her locker with a bang much harder than she had intended.

Bill's face sobered. 'Come and have a cuppa while you talk about it. Best thing for it. Cleaning can wait. First booking's not until twelve anyways.'

Jade wasn't sure she wanted to talk, but somehow she ended up telling Bill all about the whole thing; how she and Nick had met and what had happened between them. She felt surprisingly calm as she did so. Either that was a good sign, or a very bad one. Bill stroked his carefully trimmed beard as he listened.

When she had finished, he sat back and crossed his arms over the top of his ample belly. 'I had a mate once, we lost him the same way.'

Jade looked at him, surprised. But then, she shouldn't be really. The statistics on suicides were pretty high. Come to think of it, she wouldn't be surprised if everybody probably knew at least one person who had done the same. She didn't know if that comforted her or horrified her. It was comforting, to realise that there were other people in the world who might understand how she felt, and horrifying, to realise that there were lots of people who could maybe have been saved if they'd just got the right help at the right time.

Bill carried on, unaware of her internal thoughts. 'Yeah. We were all pretty shocked when it happened. Always the life and soul of the party, Ron was. Always ready with a joke, or some kind of crazy prank. And then suddenly one day he was just gone.'

He stroked his beard again and gave her a sympathetic nod. 'Let me give you a hug, missus. And then we've got cleaning to do. A business doesn't run itself you know.'

Jade drained the dregs of her tea and gave him a quick hug and a peck on the cheek. Cleaning the toilets. That would take her mind off things.

It was almost automatic for Nick, putting together his kit for the day ahead. He forced down some cereal, knowing he was going to need something to sustain himself. And at the appointed time he was waiting downstairs to be picked up by the boys.

They all had big smiles on their faces as the car pulled up. Sean slapped Nick on the shoulder as he let him into the back. There was a sense of excitement in the car, which just made him feel even more as if he shouldn't be there. Still, he was holding out hope that the walk would drag up his mood.

'Yo!' Pete punched him gently in the shoulder. 'How's tricks?'

Nick mumbled a non-committal reply.

'Just forgive us for all the excitement.' Sean looked at Nick in the rear-view mirror. 'We're all just a bit excited because finally, finally,' he paused for effect, 'Stevie got his new prosthetic!'

'Whoop!' Stevie let out a loud exultation, and Pete followed it with a blood-curdling war cry. Nick put his hands over his ears. The sound in the confines of the small car was almost unbearable. Still, he couldn't help smiling; the enthusiasm of the others was pretty infectious.

'So what's so special about it?'

'Oh man, it's just something else.' Stevie twisted around to face Nick, his arm resting along the back of Sean's seat. 'It's more like, what isn't special about it? Lightweight material, fancy shock absorber, motorised movement. Made specifically for walking up hills. This, my friend, is the Lamborghini of legs.'

'We were going to tell you.' Pete thumped Nick on the arm again. 'But we weren't sure if he'd get in enough practice on it beforehand. He only got it on Wednesday. He's been testing it out everywhere since then.'

Pete gave Nick a celebratory high five. Nick took a deep breath. It was all going to be OK. With friends like these ... and mountains ... who needed professionals?

'Wait up for a minute, guys.' They were about half an hour into the walk when Stevie stopped beside a small boulder. 'I think I need to adjust the settings.' He eased himself down.

'How's it doing?' Sean looked across at him.

Stevie nodded. 'Pretty good. A bit of chafing, but nothing I can't handle. That special moulding foam in the socket works like a dream. But I think the resistance on the knee is just a bit too stiff for what we're doing.' He pulled out his phone and started tapping on it.

'Wait.' Nick couldn't believe it. 'You mean it comes with an app?' He laughed out loud. It all seemed so surreal.

Stevie grinned. 'Yeah. I guess it's got some sort of mini-computer in there. To control the movement and stuff.' He tapped a few more times. 'That should do it.' His phone went back in his pocket.

'How much did that thing cost, if you don't mind me asking?' The words were out before Nick could think better of them.

'Too much.' Stevie grimaced. 'But I was lucky. The bastard that ran me down had to pay out damages – or at least his insurance company did – so there was plenty to go around.'

'Hmm.' Nick pretended to stroke his chin thoughtfully. 'I wonder if I could hack into it. Then we could really have some fun.'

There was a moment's silence, and he wondered if he had gone too far, but then he realised that Stevie was staring at him in horror, while Pete's face showed admiration.

'You are evil.' Pete's face split in a massive grin. 'But please try. I'd love to have him hopping around or something.'

'You do that, and I will never talk to either of you again.' Stevie shook a fist in their faces. Then he looked thoughtful. 'But actually, it might be good to know if it's possible. Just so I know whether to worry about it or not.'

'I would like to remind you that doing that kind of thing is illegal.' Sean was making a valiant effort to keep his voice stern, but Nick knew he was enjoying the conversation as much as any of them.

Sean turned to Nick. 'Anyway, we've been so busy celebrating Stevie's leg, we never asked about you. How's your week been? How's your girlfriend?'

Nick's face fell. 'We split up. Just this morning actually.'

'Ah shit, that sucks.' Stevie clapped him on the shoulder, his face sympathetic.

It did suck, Nick reflected as they resumed their path up the mountain, but having some new friends to take his mind off things made all the difference.

They made good time on their journey, although they still went quite slowly and took lots of breaks. When they all sat down at the top, Stevie pulled his leg off with a sigh of relief. 'I'll just re-tape before we head back down.'

'We're going to have to call you something else from now on,' Pete joked. 'Ironman maybe. Or Little Lamborghini.'

Stevie ducked his head, clearly embarrassed. 'Nah. I like Stumpy just fine. Wouldn't do to get too big for my boots. I mean, too big for my leg and my boot.'

All four of them laughed.

'It is great, though. I'm not worried about our trip to the Alps any more. I can't wait to try out the climbing foot that came with it.'

'You're going to the Alps?' Nick was envious. 'I went there a couple of years ago and it was amazing. I'd love to go back.'

'Yeah.' Pete flashed him a big grin. 'We would have asked you along, but it's been booked, like, forever. I can't wait to see Deem again.' He saw Nick's puzzled expression. 'That's our other friend. The one who moved down to London.'

They sat there in the sunshine for a while, munching away at their sandwiches. White fluffy clouds raced in the sky above them. An amazing vista of green-blue hills spread out in front of them. In the distance they could hear the harsh noise of the commentary on a tour boat passing on the loch below.

'God, I could stay up here, and never come down.' Nick leaned back in the grass.

'Yeah, know what you mean.' Sean looked down at him. 'But you know, winter will come, and it gets pretty brutal up here.'

'Spoilsport.' Stevie scoffed. 'I'd just build an igloo.'

'Oh yeah, an igloo.' Sean's tone betrayed his skepticism. 'And what about supplies?'

'Details, details.' Stevie lay back on the grass too. 'I hear you, big man. Let's stay up here forever. Screw real life and all its problems.'

Nick watched the ever-changing clouds for a few minutes. He suddenly felt much happier. These guys obviously cared a lot about each other. And for some reason, they'd decided to accept him into their close-knit group.

Maybe, just maybe, this was the start of a whole new life. Regardless of whether Jade was in it or not.

Somehow, this feeling of acceptance gave him the courage to ask what he really wanted to know. 'Have you, I mean, any of you, have you ever just felt like life was just too much to handle?'

Stevie snorted, as if it was a stupid question. 'Yeah. Loads of times. But like I said, these guys rescued me. Kept me on the straight and narrow.'

'Any time, man.' Sean ruffled Stevie's hair, clearly embarrassed, and Pete nodded in agreement.

There was a long pause, and then Pete cleared his throat hesitantly, as if he wasn't sure of what he was about to say.

'When Stevie here was struggling, right back in the first few weeks, I had my own problems.'

He pulled back his sleeves, pointing to his arms, and Nick could see fine white lines threading through the tattoos that covered his wrists.

'Oh, fuck, man.' It was Sean who spoke this time, and Nick suddenly realised that the older guy hadn't known about this. 'I can't believe you never told us.' His voice was partly angry, but mainly sad.

'Well.' Pete sounded slightly defensive. 'Stevie here had his own problems to deal with. And you had that thing with your mum going on.'

'True.' Sean made a face. Whatever had happened with his mum must have been pretty serious. 'But still ...' His voice trailed off. 'I mean, shit, man. You still could have told me.'

Pete just shrugged, as if in apology. And Nick suddenly found himself telling the guys the whole story. About everything. While he looked out at that amazing view and tried to keep his voice from cracking.

When he had finished, everyone sat in silence for a long while, as if they weren't sure what to say. Then Sean grasped Nick by the shoulder and turned him until they were looking each other directly in the eyes. 'Look. I'm the last one to tell you what to do with your life. But I'm telling you, don't make the mistake of thinking that it's the best way out. When you need to, call someone. Talk to someone. Hell, call me. You've got my number. Any time. Day or night. If you really need me. If you just want to whine about how your favourite takeaway is shut then forget it.'

He made a dismissive gesture, and Nick knew he was purposely trying to lighten the mood. Sean clasped Nick's hand, as if to seal the deal.

Nick shifted uncomfortably, the casual gesture of friendship making his eyes slightly blurry. This was all too serious. He had to change the topic. 'How's things going with that guy of yours, Pete?' Was that a blush on the Prof's face?

'Ah! I knew it!' Stevie let out a cry. 'They've done it!' He stood up and started singing a striptease theme, wiggling his hips suggestively. Pete leaped up and took a swipe at him. Stevie tried to dodge and overbalanced, but still managed to grab at Pete as he went down and take him with him. They wrestled playfully on the floor for a couple of seconds and then gave up and lay laughing on the wet grass.

'Glad I asked.' Nick couldn't help smiling.

It was a much more subdued group that made their way down the mountainside. Stevie was clearly exhausted from the climb, although he refused to admit it, and Sean seemed to be trying to absorb what Pete had told them. Nick saw him glancing at Pete when he thought no one was looking. But Nick felt the warmth of their friendship settle around him like a comfy blanket. These guys were one in a million, he thought. And they were fast becoming his new friends.

Chapter 18

On Wednesday Nick went to see Archie. Jade wasn't mentioned; presumably the other man had already got the full story through Lily. They spent most of the evening going through Archie's old photo albums. He had done all the Munros, some of them many times, and lots of the mountains in Europe.

'I never got to Canada, though.' Archie sounded a bit regretful. 'It was always on the list, but I never made it.'

Nick paused at a black and white picture, of Archie against the backdrop of yet another mountain range. He looked somewhere around Nick's age. 'What's this one?'

Archie peered at it, and a smile spread across his face. 'Ah. That was one of my proudest days. The day we climbed the Matterhorn. That was before I was old enough to be sensible.'

He looked at the photo for a while longer, and Nick could tell he was remembering the climb. Then he peeled the card carefully off the page. 'You take it. It's a gift. A reminder of what's important.'

Nick took the photo, holding it carefully by the edges. Being gifted with what looked like Archie's only memento of such a special moment was almost too much. 'Are you sure?'

Archie nodded. 'It's for you.' Then he shifted in his chair. 'Could you take me back to my room, lad? I'm feeling a bit tired tonight.'

Nick wheeled him back along the corridor and into the little bed sit that was Archie's home. He was surprised at how bare it was. He had expected that there would be pictures of mountains on the walls or something, but the only personal thing was a family photo on the dresser. That must be his niece.

'Thanks, lad.' Archie shook his hand. 'Come again. Any time.'

When Nick got home he carefully propped up the photo on a shelf. He would frame it. It would look good on his wall. It was a great present and he felt honoured to have it. He hoped that Archie wouldn't miss it.

Jade sat on the sofa, turning her phone around in her hands. She had no idea why she had volunteered to be the one to make the call. But she knew that she just had to do it.

She looked across at Lily and Sandra, both sitting right next to her.

'Are you sure you don't want me to do it, dear?' Lily's tone was gentle. 'I could do it tonight. When he's not at work.'

Jade shook her head. It had to be done. And now, so that it was done as soon as possible.

She pressed the button. The phone rang on the other end.

'Jade?' Nick's voice was hesitant. She hated the hope that was in his voice. Of course, he would be hoping that she'd changed her mind.

'Nick. Hi. Are you somewhere you can talk?'

'Wait. Hang on.' She heard rustling noises. 'I'm just heading out into the corridor. Give me a sec.'

She waited, heart thumping, as the sound of a door opened and closed.

'Right, I'm good. What is it? Is everything OK?'

'Nick, I'm really sorry. It's Archie. He had a heart attack last night.'

There was more rustling. 'Sorry, I'm just sitting down on the stairs.' Nick's voice sounded suddenly tired. 'Is he OK?'

Jade winced. 'No. No. He's not OK. I'm sorry, Nick, but he's gone.'

She felt Lily squeeze her hand and Jade squeezed back, grateful the older woman was there to support her.

'God. That's awful. I only saw him two days ago. And he looked fine.'

'Yeah. I know. It's been a bit of a shock for everyone.'

There was a pause, as if Nick was digesting the news. 'He did have a pretty good run.' His voice was suddenly tight, as if he was struggling to hold back his emotions.

'Yeah.' Jade suddenly wished she was sitting beside him on the stairs. 'Look, the funeral's on Wednesday morning next week. Can you get time off work to go? I know he would have wanted you to be there.'

'Uhm.' There was another pause. 'I'll ask. I don't think it'll be a problem.'

He was silent for a moment. 'Look, I really need to get back to work, OK?'

'I'll call you tonight when I get a break from work,' Jade promised.

'Look, really, thanks, but there's no need.' Nick had switched back into his professional mode, and she knew he was steeling himself to go back into the office. 'I'll see you at the funeral. Can you text me the details of where it's going to be?'

'Sure.' Jade nodded, forgetting he couldn't see her. 'I'll send them as soon as I have them.' She hung up.

'How did he take it?' Lily sounded slightly anxious. It was just like her to be thinking about someone else, even though she had just lost her closest friend.

Jade frowned. 'I don't know. It's always hard to tell over the phone.' She threw it onto the sofa in disgust. 'I hate these things sometimes.'

Lily's arm went around her shoulders, while Sandra rose, heading towards the door. 'I'm going to make a pot of tea.'

Tea, thought Jade gratefully. Everything always looked better from the bottom of a cup of tea.

Nick had thought that the funeral would be held in a church, but it turned out Archie's humanist ceremony was going to be held in a community centre. Nick arrived just a few minutes before it was due to start, hoping to disappear at the back, but Jade was watching out for him and had saved him a seat next to her and her parents, who nodded to him, smiling, as he sat down. Lily was just across the aisle.

Five minutes in Nick knew that Archie had spent quite some time organising his own ceremony. It was just so ... him. Mainly conventional, just a little bit quirky. Lily got up and gave a speech about him. Someone else read a poem. But the adapted song about a Scotsman who went a yodelling, while pictures of Archie climbing mountains flashed up on a big screen, made everyone laugh, and Nick knew the old man had done it on purpose.

He had the photo of Archie in his jacket pocket. Surely the family would want it now. He would give it back to them at the reception.

The family went off to see the body cremated, and the hall was quickly rearranged for the reception. There were sandwiches and amazing scones It was a pretty impressive spread. Jade found him hiding in a corner and dragged him out. 'Come and meet the family. They'll be happy that you're here.'

She introduced him to a middle-aged couple, who shook his hand politely.

'Nick used to take Archie out on our Saturday outings,' Jade explained.

'Oh. How kind of you to come. Uncle Archie really looked forward to those outings.' The woman looked tired, Nick thought. Her voice was remote, as if she was just going through the motions.

'Nick visited Archie not long before he died.' Jade was being helpful again. Nick just wanted to get out of there as fast as he could. All through the funeral he had kept telling himself that he didn't have any right to be upset, that at ninety-two death was only to be expected, but it hadn't done anything to plug his crushing sense of loss. And now his emotions were threatening to overwhelm him.

'Yeah. We were going through some of his old photos. Actually—' Nick reached his hand into his breast pocket.

'Oh, I'm afraid they've all gone now. We just don't have the room for them at home. Not with the two of them still at home.' She nodded to where two lanky young men, who looked maybe just a couple of years younger than himself, sprawled on chairs near the window, clearly bored by the whole thing. 'We had to throw everything out. All his clothes went to the charity shop though.'

Nick froze, then gently placed the photo back into the safety of his pocket. 'Ah. Yes. I can understand.' Inside his mind was racing. They had chucked away all of Archie's photos? All of his personal memories? All his hopes, of being able to continue his connection with the old man through his family, were suddenly in tatters. He had to go before he said something that he would regret later.

He said a polite goodbye to the couple and wandered towards the door. Jade grabbed his arm. 'Where are you going?'

He turned towards her. 'I need to get back to work. Say goodbye to your parents and Lily for me.'

But Jade insisted on dragging him off to see them. They all gave him hugs and told him how glad they were to see him.

Jade came with him to the door, and they stood outside for a few minutes, despite the light drizzle falling.

'Are you OK?'

He looked at her. 'Honestly? I don't know. I think, in the grand scheme of things, then yes. But day to day?' He ran a hand through his hair, which was getting slightly damp. 'I think I'm going to go home for a bit. If I can take some time off work. Just get a bit of perspective on things.'

'That sounds like a good idea.' Jade smiled at him.

On a sudden impulse he pulled her in for a hug. She came willingly into his arms but didn't stay long before she stepped away. 'You take care of yourself, OK?'

'OK.' He took one last look at her before turning off down the street.

Back in work, the usual office banter was somewhat muted, as if the creases of his carefully-pressed suit made them all aware that life was short.

He made his way across to his boss's office, who looked up as he knocked on the open glass door.

'Ah, Nick. My condolences.'

Nick didn't really know what to say in response. 'Erm ...' He hesitated, then gathered himself together. 'I was thinking, I'd really like to take a couple of weeks off sometime fairly soon, if that's possible. I mean, I haven't had a holiday since Christmas. And I'd really like to go home and see my parents.'

The other man nodded sympathetically. 'Let me just pull up the leave spreadsheet.' He fiddled around on his computer for what seemed like an age. 'Actually, if you want to take next week and the week after that, I think we could cover you.'

The response surprised Nick. 'Really?'

Another nod. 'Yes. That means we'll have you back before the school holidays start. When everyone else wants to be off.'

'OK. I mean, that would be great.' Nick brushed aside the idea that he was obviously bottom of the office food chain. He would be home by Saturday night. He'd have to give his parents a call. They'd be thrilled. And Jamie as well. It would be great to see him too.

He felt like skipping back to his desk but restrained himself, anxious not to let his colleagues realise how happy he was at the idea of being away from the office for two whole weeks.

Chapter 19

Saturdays were always tricky now. Jade hadn't realised quite how much she'd enjoyed spending time with Nick until she'd given it up. Even on the days that she hadn't seen him, his messages had buoyed her up.

The weather had been beautiful, and they'd invited a few of their friends over for a barbeque, which had been fun. But now her dad was out at work, and her mum had gone out for a drink with some friends. Jade was sitting on the kitchen doorstep, sipping a cool glass of lemonade, watching the early evening sun filter through next door's tree, and feeling miserable.

She heard the doorbell ring inside the house. That would be next door but one, come to pick up the hat their two-year-old had left behind by accident. She carefully positioned her glass on the step, picked up the hat and went to answer it.

It wasn't who she was expecting. Instead, Carina stood there, looking gorgeous in a pair of pink hot pants and a white t-shirt. Her long brown hair was swept up in its usual effortless style, and a pair of sunglasses rested on the top of her head. Jade took all this in, even as she started to close the door.

'No, wait, please, JJ.'

Something in her friend's tone arrested Jade's movement. Instead she glared at her. 'You've got a nerve. Coming round our house like this.'

'Look. I'm sorry. I'll go. I promise. But I couldn't go a day longer without giving you this.' Carina stepped forward and held out a package, wrapped in a white plastic bag.

Jade took it gingerly and unwrapped it. And as soon as she saw it, she knew what it was. She was looking at Ruby's diary.

'Oh my God. Where did you find it? I looked everywhere for this.'

Carina shifted her weight, as if it was a tale that made uncomfortable telling. 'It's a long story.'

Jade looked at her for one long minute, then nodded. 'You'd better come in.'

Something in Carina's stance shifted, as if she hadn't expected Jade to capitulate. 'Thanks.'

Jade held the door open for her as she passed. 'Go through to the back. There are chairs outside. D'you want a drink?' She was delaying with the social niceties, she realised, to give herself time to regain her mental composure.

'Yeah. Thanks. That'd be great.'

Jade took the lemonade from the fridge and went to pour a large glassful. She found herself trying to do it with the book still clasped in her fingers, and gently put it down on the worktop. It felt almost like a physical wrench to let go of it. She had looked repeatedly for her sister's diary, in those days afterwards, hoping that it might hold some clue as to why she'd done what she had. But when she couldn't find it, she had been forced to conclude that Ruby had tossed it somewhere, wanting to get rid of it. And to think that Carina had been holding onto it all this time! She supposed she should be angry, but she couldn't find it in her. Anyway, it was herself she should be angry at really. She was the one who had fobbed Carina off for so long. And this wasn't the time for anger. It was time for questions.

Carina had dropped her bag and sat down on one of the faded red wooden chairs. Jade set the glass on the table next to her and retired to the step where she had been sitting only a few minutes earlier.

Carina took a long swig from her lemonade. 'Thanks. That's amazing.' She set the glass back on the table. 'First, I want to tell you, I was going to give that back to you at Ruby's funeral.' She grimaced, as if even the memory was painful to her. 'I didn't find it until that morning, just before we were leaving. I was helping Dad put on his cufflinks for his posh shirt, and one of them fell out of my hand and bounced right under the sofa. It was when I was looking for that then I found her diary. She must have just slid it under the sofa and either forgotten it or left it there because she wanted to get rid of it.'

'But how the hell did it get in your house anyway? This is her private diary. She used to keep it locked in her top drawer.' Jade was genuinely puzzled.

Carina shifted in her seat. 'She came, that night.' Her blue eyes seemed to flatten as she spoke, as if the weight of what had happened was dulling their spark. 'It was gone eleven. I was pretty unimpressed, because I had that heavy cold and I was just about to go to bed. But something made me open the door to her. She said she'd tried to call you, but you weren't answering your phone. She thought I might know where you were.'

The thought that her little sister had tried to come and find her that night was like a twist of a knife in Jade's stomach. She leaned back against the doorframe, closing her eyes. It all made so much sense now. Ruby had known that she had three or four favourite places for a night out in town. Had probably gone to check them and found nothing. After all, how was her sister to know that they had gone to try out a new swanky cocktail place in Merchant City? And from town, it was only a ten-minute walk to the bridge.

She opened her eyes. Carina was waiting patiently for her. Was that tears she could see in the other girl's eyes?

'Why didn't you tell me that she had come to see you?' Jade demanded.

Carina sighed. 'Honestly, I had no idea what she was going to do. I mean, she seemed pretty upset, but I never thought she would go that far.'

Another realisation dawned on Jade. 'We never told you about the episode with the pills two weeks before that.'

'Oh God.' Carina put her hands over her mouth. She leaned forward. 'I swear, if I'd known about that I would have never let her go. I would have called your parents. Or the police. Or anyone.'

Jade rubbed her forehead. 'I know. We should have told you. But Mum and Dad were pretty ashamed about the whole thing. They thought they'd failed her in some way.'

She picked up the book from her lap. 'And you were going to give this back to me, and then I acted like an idiot.' She winced as she remembered how she had gone apeshit at her friend, calling her all sorts of names. Shouting that she never wanted to see her again. Going in for a swing at her and having to be restrained by her dad. Now that the anger was finally gone, the memory made her blush.

'But why did you say what you did?' Jade pressed her hands to her still-burning cheeks. Maybe she could blame it on the sunshine. 'It really hurt.'

Carina came to sit beside her on the step. 'I said it because of what she told me that night. My next words after that, if you'd have let me get them out at the time,' she smiled wryly sideways at Jade, 'were that I wasn't surprised, because of all the online abuse she was getting.'

It took Jade a moment to take in what she was saying and then it suddenly registered. 'She was getting trolled?'

Carina nodded. 'And not just trolled. Trolled to the point of harassment. She showed me some of the tweets. They were pretty awful.'

'Shit.' Jade went to take another sip of her own lemonade, but it was suddenly too sweet for her and she set it aside, feeling like she wanted to throw up. 'I mean, there was all that stuff with the bullying at school, but Mum and Dad went in and sorted all that out. That was ages before that. I didn't even know she had a Twitter account.'

Jade wrapped her arms around her knees. 'She used to post a lot of photos on Instagram. And Mum and Dad would check that regularly, after what had happened at school. It was never that bad. Just the odd snarky comment, but never that bad.' She pulled the band out of her hair, letting it fall over her shoulders, massaging her scalp with her fingertips.

Carina pointed at the book. 'I haven't read it. I was really tempted a couple of times, but it seemed rude somehow.' She looked sideways at Jade. 'Really tempted. Especially after that banshee act you pulled.'

Jade's face flamed again. 'I'm sorry about that.' Then she looked at Carina and noticed a tiny upturn at the corner of her mouth and decided to risk some humour. 'I wouldn't really say banshee. More like harpy maybe.'

Carina laughed. A slightly nervous laugh. And Jade realised how hard it must have been for her friend to come here, not knowing how she would react. She reached over and touched her gently on the arm. 'Thanks. For braving the harpy to come here.'

'And your mum.' Carina was unrepentant. 'My dad says he's never been so scared in all his life when your mum called up to tell him to tell me not to contact you anymore.'

'What's this, Make Jade Feel Guilty Day?' Jade grumbled, sweeping her hair back up into its usual messy knot. 'Why, what did she say?'

Carina shrugged. 'I don't know. I gather she was very polite. But very firm. But he did say she scared the shit out of him.'

And Jade was finally able to laugh, something she thought she would never be able to do in the circumstances. 'Sorry about that. She did offer to do it, and to be honest, I was such a mess I was happy to let her. After all, I'd just lost my little sister and my best friend. What was I supposed to do?'

It was Carina's turn to touch Jade on the arm this time, and Jade looked up at her, surprised.

'I'd just lost my little sister and my best friend too. Can you blame me for trying as hard as I could to get one of them back?'

Jade felt her eyes stinging. With Carina being an only child, and her mother gone, she supposed that Ruby and herself had been pretty much like sisters. She just hadn't thought about how much she might mean to her friend.

Carina stood up, brushing down the back of her shorts. 'I've got to get home, or Dad will be wondering where I've got to. I'll leave you to read it.' She picked up her bag and turned, the sunlight winking off her hair as she did so. 'Thanks for seeing me.'

Jade almost went to give her a hug, but the weight of the past year still hung between them. Still, it was slowly fading, she could tell. She settled for a kiss on the cheek. 'I'll text you. I promise.'

Carina smiled briefly, a proper smile this time that transformed her face into a thing of real beauty. 'Do.' And then she was gone.

Jade barely heard the front door slam; instead, all her focus was on the book that she held in her hands. The glittery rainbow unicorn cover she remembered well; she had often seen Ruby slipping it in and out of the drawer when she had been lying in bed of an evening. But she had always respected her sister's privacy, and never tried to take a peek.

She had to steel herself to open it. Her sister had filled in all the details in the contact form; name, address, telephone, year at school, the works. But it was what was at the bottom of the page that made Jade catch her breath. There was the photo that they had taken that day when they had been fooling around in the photo booth together.

It had been so hard getting the three of them in the frame at the same time, mainly because they were laughing so hard, that only one of the photos had come out decent at all. Jade had totally forgotten about it. She had no idea that Ruby had kept it. And not only had she kept it, she had pasted it into the front page of her diary. With a sequined heart frame stuck around it, and the word BESTIES written in marker pen underneath.

Jade shut the book gently. It was too much. There was no way she would be able to read it.

She sat for a long time, until the sun dipped over the edge of the house opposite, and it began to get chilly.

Tea, she decided, straightening up, and rubbing her stiff muscles. She would have a cup of tea, and then work out what to do.

She made the special green tea her mother only kept for certain occasions. Her mum would notice some gone but wouldn't complain. Since Ruby's death she had got much less strict about those kinds of things.

Up on her new double bed, Jade sipped slowly from the tiny cup, feeling the warmth of the liquid warm both her throat and her hands. And when she finally felt ready, she opened the diary and turned the first page.

The first few entries were pretty much what she would expect. Jade was surprised at the formality of the language that was used, but then remembered that Ruby had been a big Jane Austen fan. There was elation on starting a new diary. Worries about homework. Happiness about good things that had happened. And then, the big momentous entry, decorated with heart and diamond stickers:

Today I got my very own Twitter account. Now I'm finally someone! I haven't told anyone at home. I can't tell Mum and Dad, they would look at it and it would just be too embarrassing. And I can't tell JJ either. I'm sure she was the one who told them about my Instagram.

Jade winced; she was indeed the culprit. Although to be fair, she hadn't known that Ruby wanted to keep it a secret. She had actually been proudly showing off some of her sister's photos to her parents.

The Twitter handle was written in bold letters underneath. Jade almost reached for her phone to look it up but found her hand gravitating back to the book. She would have a look later.

All went well for the next few weeks. There was a boy at school she had a crush on, but she seemed to realise that it wasn't serious, that it would pass. She seemed more concerned with the pressures of school work, and very aware that in her final year at school there was everything to play for.

Then, suddenly, in December, there it was.

Someone sent me an awful message on Twitter today. And I don't even know him.

She had reproduced it in full, and the language in it made Jade's blood boil. Basically, it was somehow both an invitation to have sex, and an intimation that she was worthless. At least, that was the polite way of saying it. Her own mouth wasn't entirely a shining example of purity, but this was far beyond any words she would ever use.

Jade tried to think back. The entry was just a few days before Christmas. She couldn't remember Ruby acting any different. But then, how was she supposed to remember things from that long ago?

No, wait. Christmas. Not last year, but the one before. It had been a difficult time. Granny Wilson had died on Christmas Eve the year before that. Ruby had also been very close to her and had taken it very hard. So when Jade had come across her sister crying up in their bedroom, she had assumed it was something to do with the anniversary. She counted on her fingers, her memory sharper now. That would coincide exactly with the date in the diary. She swore, guilt running through her. Because it was after that point, now she remembered it, that Ruby's mood swings had really got serious. If only she hadn't put it down to the usual teenage growing pains. If only she had asked what was really going on.

If only you were perfect, she reminded herself. You can't be all things to all people.

But had their grandmother's death been the start of Ruby's downhill struggle? Losing someone she really felt she could talk to?

Heart beating faster now, she read on.

It was almost as if the incident had never happened in the next few entries. Ruby seemed back to her slightly-concerned-about-study-but-generally-happy persona. But as Jade read on through the weeks, she began to notice a worrying negative trend in what Ruby was writing. Comments about her weight. About her skin. Was she too clever for boys to like her? Was that why she had never been kissed by one? This was almost too personal. Too painful. And she remembered that some of these questions had come up from time to time, as they lay in bed in the evenings. Jade had been very dismissive, trying to bolster Ruby's confidence. But, reading through the diary, it was obvious that many of the issues hadn't been just passing worries. They had wormed through her sister's brain until they had destroyed what little self-confidence she had.

It was partly Jade's fault too. She had been caught up in the stresses of her own final year, chasing a first so that she could be in the running for a graduate scholarship. And in doing so had failed to see the depth of the mess that Ruby was getting herself into.

It was only as she struggled to read the next few entries, written in cramped and hurried writing, that she realised that the light outside was fading. That made it very late indeed. She switched on the light so she could read the page properly. This one was written just the day before Ruby's first attempt.

TBH I don't really see the point. Why bother when even people who say they are my friends are so cruel. FTS.

Fuck This Shit, Jade mentally translated, after a couple of seconds of wondering. She turned the page to the next day. It was blank. And so were all the rest.

If she had thought that leaving Nick was hard, it was nothing compared with her feelings on seeing the unfilled pages in the diary. It was a perfect analogy for what the loss of her sister meant; one blank entry after another, stretching endlessly into the future, where there should be tales of her ups and downs, her loves and hates, her successes and failures.

Jade had thought she was done with crying about all this by now, but this was just too much. She put her head down on the pillow and wept.

Chapter 20

Nick hummed happily to himself as he walked up the hill from the bus station, rucksack on his back. He was finally home. Home! The vast mountains stretched up above him. The sunlight glinted off the wild whipped foam in the sea loch. He took a deep breath of the fresh air and felt his shoulders lose some of their tension. It was two weeks before he had to see the inside of an office again.

His mother had obviously been watching from the window, because soon after the house came into view there she was, waiting on the doorstep. The wind lifted the long curly strands of her brown hair and played them around her face, so she had to hold up a hand to be able to see him.

He willingly opened his arms to her generous hug. 'It's great to see you, Mum.' He held her for just a moment longer, just to make up for all the time she'd been so far away.

His father wasn't that far behind, and Nick made sure to hug him as well, slapping him on the back. It always surprised people that his mother was so tall and his father so short. Nick had inherited the height, but he never laid claim to his mother's level of intelligence. She was the one who kept all the strands of their business woven together. Oh yes, his father was the one who talked to all the guests, but his mother was definitely the one who steered the ship.

'There's dinner waiting.' She looped a hand through his arm and steered him gently towards the side door. Just for a moment, Nick rested his hand against the faded pink paint of the wall of the house, slightly warm from the afternoon sun. If he was fanciful, he could almost imagine it as a living, breathing thing to come back home to.

He smiled. Jade would like that idea very much. Knowing her she would invent some wild futuristic story about a house that was actually a living, breathing organism. He would have to remember to message her after dinner.

Both his parents were looking at him expectantly, and he realised he was lost in his own thoughts. He grinned at them. 'Lead the way. I'm starving.'

Dinner was spent catching up on news. Nick told them all about Sean and the gang, and the walks they'd been on. His parents got him up to speed on the latest local gossip. But really, nothing much had changed, and for that Nick was grateful. Home felt like an anchor to which he could always tie his line. It was the one constant in his life.

Afterwards, his dad went out to dabble in the garden, while Nick sat with his mother on the private patio in comfy cushioned chairs, enjoying the rest of the evening sun. The wind was sending the clouds running across the tops of the mountains, but in the shelter of the walled garden it was very pleasant.

The garden was really at its best in June and July. Nick didn't know much about garden plants, but he didn't need to know their names to admire their beauty. The borders were covered in an array of colours, from bright cheerful yellows to deep dusky purples.

'It's so good to see you, my darling.' His mother cradled the curve of her wine glass in her right palm. 'We've missed you so much.'

'I've missed you too.' Nick suddenly wanted to share everything he had been going through, but instead just took a swig from his bottle of beer. He couldn't tell her absolutely everything. It would break her heart.

'Yeah.' He steadied his voice before he continued, trying to make it sound casual. 'I've not been in a very good place these last few months.'

'What, Glasgow? I've never really liked it myself.' His mother's crack of laughter at her own joke took him by surprise, and he had to smile.

'No, but seriously.' His face became sober again. 'Like a really bad place. I've been pretty depressed.'

She regarded him silently for a few moments as if to check that he was really being serious, and then her shoulders slumped slightly, and she took another sip of her wine. 'To be honest, I'm really not surprised.'

Nick was taken aback by her reply. 'What do you mean?'

She indicated towards the figure kneeling by a flowerbed on the other side of the garden, trowel in hand. 'Your dad has depression. He gets it pretty bad.'

Nick almost dropped the bottle he was holding. 'You're kidding me.'

She shook her head. 'Not at all. I can tell when it's coming on because he'll go all quiet and distant on me.'

It couldn't be true. 'But he's always such a happy person.'

Her hand went up to rub the back of her neck. It was the first time he had ever seen her uncomposed about anything.

'On the surface, yes. He puts on a good front for people. But inside, well, he has some very bad days.'

Nick could identify with that. 'So how long has this been going on?'

She shrugged. 'Hard to tell, really. It just seemed to creep up on us. I guess in some way he'd probably had it most of his life. But there was an awful year a few years after we got married that really brought it all to a head.'

'Will you tell me about it?' Nick reached over and squeezed her hand.

She looked across at him with a small smile and squeezed back. 'I can't believe I've never talked to you about this before really. I suppose I never thought you'd be interested.'

She leaned her head back against the cushioned headrest, staring up at the clouds. 'Let me see. Well. Marrying your dad was where it all started. My family were staunch Catholics, so to marry someone from a non-Catholic background, well, for a while it was like the world had ended. Things are different now, but back then the lines were much more marked between the two camps. I think my father just wanted me to be happy, but my mother refused to speak to me for many years. It was all too much, living so close to them but so far away in spirit. So I applied for a job at Imperial College in London and was really relieved when I got it.'

She took another sip of her wine. 'London was so exciting. So many interesting things going on. I was doing oncology research, and they were just starting to experiment with new technologies in radiotherapy. It was all big news, every time we published something the press was all over it. It really felt like I was making a contribution to society.'

Her gaze fell on his dad again, who caught them both looking and blew them a theatrical kiss. She laughed and returned the gesture, while Nick just rolled his eyes. But he couldn't help smiling. It was so good to be home.

'Your dad got a job in a bank. He's always been good with numbers. That, and his accountancy qualifications, put him in high demand. But I think after a few years the high-pressure environment finally got to him. He was working on these high-profile merger projects, and of course because it was all secret, he couldn't even tell me anything about it.' She frowned. 'Of course, I think he probably kept things a bit too secret. I mean, who would I have told? But I think he got a bit paranoid about it, just thought that it was safest if he didn't mention anything to anyone.'

A deep sigh was the only indication of her feelings on the topic. 'Anyway, to cut a long story short, he started getting bad mood swings, which turned into depression and anxiety. He did get some help and medication, but when it got to the point that he had a panic attack just trying to leave for work I knew we had to do something drastic.'

She drained the rest of her glass in a couple of small swallows, and set it on the wide wooden arm of the chair. 'I left my job and we sold our house. The money we had saved was enough to buy a good portion of this place.' A wave of her hand indicated the house.

'Jeez.' Nick couldn't believe what he was hearing. 'I thought you'd always lived here.'

He suddenly realised how ridiculous that sounded. 'Actually, I guess I'd never really thought about it.' He'd been so busy all his life living in the present and worrying about the future that he'd never taken the time to dig into the past.

That would explain a lot, though. Why his dad's parents had been around but his mum's side of the family hadn't.

He frowned. 'But I don't ever remember Dad being depressed.'

A small smile crept over his mum's face. 'Do you remember your camping trips?'

'Sure.' A few times a year, his dad had taken him off into the mountains. It had been going on for as long as he could remember. 'Yeah. I remember that really crazy one we did in February. The snow was meters deep and we built an igloo. That was pretty cool.'

'Every time he got really depressed, I'd send him off on a trip. A few days in the middle of nowhere would always help. And you were always my insurance policy to make sure he came back to me safely.'

'So is all this why you haven't been down to visit? I was beginning to think that you didn't care about me anymore.' He kept his tone light, so she would know he was joking, but he suddenly realised that the smaller, meaner side of him had started to think that, even though he knew how ridiculous it was.

'Oh, Nick.' The expression on her face chased away lingering doubts he might ever have had. 'Not at all. When we brought you down that time, a couple of hours in the city was as much as your dad could take. He still gets panic attacks in busy places. And I worry when I leave him up here all by himself. I know it's stupid, but I can't help it.' She reached over and touched him gently on the cheek. 'I love you so much. We both do. And we're so proud of you.'

What a lot his mum had been through. Giving up a job she loved, for the sake of the mental health of someone she loved even more. 'Is that why you wanted me to move down to Glasgow?'

She looked at him, puzzled for a few seconds, and then realised what he was referring to. 'I threw away a good career, and while I've never really regretted it, I've often wondered what might have been. I didn't want the same thing to happen to you. Home will always be here for you to come back to. But I just think you're capable of so much more.'

'Sitting in an office all day is killing me, Mum. I stare out the window dreaming of mountains all day.' Nick had been avoiding the truth for so long that even just saying it felt like a relief.

'You only say that because you're not used to it. Give it another year or so and you'll be happy as Larry. Every job is tough at the start. You've only been there, what, just under a year now? Just give it time.'

Everyone was defined by their history, Nick suddenly realised. His mum had given up her high-powered job which she had loved, so naturally she wanted the same opportunities for him. He should consider himself lucky in some ways. So many people were completely unable to find a job at all. Even fewer paid the decent salary that his did. But just because an opportunity was there didn't mean that it had to be taken.

He stood up. 'I'm going to get another beer. Do you want a refill?'

She held out her glass gratefully. 'You'll have to open another bottle, that one's finished.'

By the time he got back his dad had given up on the garden and was sitting in another chair. 'So, what are your plans while you're here?'

'I'm seeing Jamie tomorrow night.' Nick couldn't wait to see his friend again. 'I thought I'd hang around here for a week or so. Maybe go for a few day walks with you if you've got time.' His dad nodded enthusiastically. 'And then probably just head up for a proper few days in the wilderness before heading back to Glasgow.' He couldn't call it home, he realised. For him this would always be home. Would always be where his heart was. Except ... a large bit of his heart was stuck with Jade. And smaller bits with Sean and the boys. And a tiny bit had been buried with Archie. Was this how it went as you got older? Little bits of your heart ripped off and left with other people?

He shook himself mentally. No time for depressing thoughts these next two weeks. There were mountains to be climbed. And, good beer to be drunk. He took a swig from his new bottle and settled back into his chair, enjoying the feel of the sunlight on his face.

The next morning, with it being Sunday, there were lots of beds to be stripped and rooms to be cleaned. Nick relished the feel of the unaccustomed physical activity. But it came with a mental price, because he realised that even what was basically housework was something he enjoyed even more than being in the office. He told himself that it was just because it was good to have a change, but in his heart he knew that it wasn't.

By the time everything was sorted it was late morning. The sheets were fluttering on the line; the good weather was still holding.

'I've booked us Sunday lunch at the fish place.' Nick jumped as his dad appeared behind him on the patio.

'Really?' Nick turned and grinned at him. 'I've been dreaming about their fish and chips.'

The other man regarded him for a long moment. 'You're really not happy in Glasgow, are you?'

Nick blinked; he had never known his dad to be so direct. 'It's complicated, Dad.' He shifted to his other foot. 'I met someone. A girl.'

'Ah.' One word spoke a thousand, and Nick knew that his dad understood exactly what he was trying to say.

'Yeah. And made some friends. And now I don't know. I feel kind of split between the two places.'

'Ah.' There it was again.

'But I do hate my job. I'm thinking of giving it up. But I don't want you and Mum to be disappointed in me.'

There was a long silence, and Nick began to wonder if it was all just a waste of time.

'I think all your mother wants for you is what I want, which is just for you to be happy.'

Tears filled Nick's eyes at his dad's simple statement. He blinked them away defiantly. 'Thanks, Dad.' A brief hug followed.

The older man brushed some imaginary dirt off his trousers. Were his eyes looking slightly shiny too? 'Well, I think we'd better get off down the hill. Reservation's at half twelve.'

Nick was sitting in the garden late that afternoon, when a shadow fell across him. He looked up, squinting against the sun, to see who it was. A tall lanky man with short ginger hair and a massive toothy grin was looking down at him.

'Jamie!' He jumped up and flung himself at his friend, slapping him on the back.

When Nick finally let him go Jamie threw himself down into one of the garden chairs. 'Man, you're white, dude.' His own face and arms were tanned a deep brown. 'You need to get some sun in you.'

'I know.' Nick put his forearm next to Jamie's to compare. 'It's embarrassing.'

'Anyway, tell me. What's been going on?' Jamie held a finger in the air. 'Actually, why don't you hold that thought. Let's walk up to the Inn and have some dinner and a couple of beers? We can talk on the way.'

'Great. Let me just grab my stuff.' Nick went to get a jacket and some shoes.

The pub was maybe a forty-minute walk up Glen Nevis. A popular stop off for people climbing the UK's highest mountain, it was usually mobbed on a weekend. But it wouldn't be too busy on a Sunday evening. And with the weather as it was, they might even get to sit outside.

They turned off the main street and began the walk up the single-track road. 'So, how's business?' Nick wanted to know.

'Yeah, it's alright. Summers are pretty good. And I teach some hours at the ski centre in the winter. It's not bad. Money's a bit tight, but I manage to keep myself afloat. Took some guys out canoeing and mountain biking this weekend. I like the variety. And,' he fished a couple of twenties out of his back pocket, 'they gave me a pretty good tip. So I'm in the mood for a bit of celebration.'

Money would be the reason why Jamie hadn't suggested coming down to see him, Nick suddenly realised. And he instantly felt slightly guilty. He should have known it would be something like that, and not a lack of interest. He should have offered to pay the bus fare. But as soon as he had that thought then he also realised Jamie would be much too proud to take it. Relief and frustration flooded him at the same time. So Jamie did care about him. He would have to work out how to get around his friend's pride. Maybe he could give him the bus fare as an early Christmas present.

'Still, you've got all this.' Nick waved a hand at the scenery. 'That must be something.'

'Yeah.' Jamie grinned. 'Although recently I have been seriously thinking about moving to Canada.'

'Canada?' Nick actually stopped walking, he was so surprised. 'Are you serious?'

'Yeah. They've got special visas for people with outdoor skills. And decent wages too. I thought, maybe better to do it while I'm young, free and single.'

Nick started walking again. At one point Jamie had said he would never leave home. But that was before his dad had died. At one point Nick had said that too, and look where he was now. But Canada? It was a long way away.

'So, what else is new?' Nick looked across at his friend.

Jamie shrugged. 'Nothing much. Same old same old. What about you? How's your fancy pants job going?'

Nick grimaced. 'Let's not talk about that one.' He looked up at the slopes of Ben Nevis rising above them and smiled at a memory that popped into his head. 'Let me tell you about Archie instead.'

And he told Jamie about the old mountaineer. But he had hardly begun to describe him when Jamie interrupted him. 'Archie MacDonald? My God. That guy's a legend. I remember my dad telling me about him.'

'Really?' Nick didn't know why he was surprised.

'Oh, yeah. My dad said he was still volunteering for the mountain rescue when he was well over seventy. He only stopped when the doctors told him he had osteoporosis and shouldn't be lifting heavy weights.' They were at the door of the pub and Jamie held the door open for Nick to pass through. 'I can't believe you met him. How is he doing?'

'He was a great guy. Told me lots of stories about his climbs. And some hairy experiences.'

'I bet.' Jamie laughed. Then he frowned. 'Was? What happened to him?'

'Heart attack. A couple of weeks ago.'

Nick's face must have given away his feelings, because Jamie put an arm around his shoulders. 'Man, I'm sorry, dude. Why don't I buy you a beer and you can drown your sorrows?'

'Yeah.' Nick nodded. 'You do that. Anyway, what's with this dude thing you've picked up? Are you practicing for your North American adventure already?'

Jamie just laughed and steered his way to the bar, leaving Nick to find a seat. He squeezed himself onto the end of a table near the huge window at the end of the room.

This was one of his favourite places for a beer. It had probably originally been a house of some sort, but inside the pub looked like some sort of barn conversion. Split levels, wooden floors, long benches and trestle tables. And the food was great too. The only downside was that it got completely rammed in summer because it was right on the path which led up to the top of Ben Nevis. Since the Three Peaks Challenge had got really popular the tourist traffic was pretty much constant, any time of the day or night. It was good business for the pub though. And good for the local area. Although his parents always liked to complain about the Three Peakers, as they called them, because most of them never stopped in the town or booked any accommodation.

Jamie plonked two glasses onto the table opposite him, disturbing his thoughts. 'I thought you wanted to go outside?'

Nick looked up at him. 'Whatever you want.'

'May as well enjoy it while it lasts. It's supposed to piss it down all week.'

Nick groaned. 'Really? What forecast are you looking at? Mine said just a few showers.'

'Nah.' Jamie retrieved his glass and made his way to the door. 'Mountain report. Always on the money.'

Nick sighed as he picked up his glass. He had so been hoping that the weather would be good. Still, he didn't mind the rain. Good thing he'd brought all his wet weather gear. And it couldn't rain solidly for two weeks. There would have to be some breaks in the cloud.

He couldn't help a smile as he realised that he was ticking off the two last things on Jade's happy list. *Reconnect with an old friend*, the list had read. And the last one was, *Spend some time in nature*. And it was right, he hadn't felt this happy for a long time. He hummed to himself as he followed Jamie out the door.

Chapter 21

When Jade got home from work on Sunday her mind was still buzzing about the journal and she realised she had a dilemma on her hands. Should she show it to her parents, thereby causing them more pain, or keep it from them like a guilty secret?

It only took her a few minutes to decide. They were adults. They could choose to read it or not. She shouldn't hold that information from them. But the thought of her mother's face when she found out about what had been going on took her breath away for a second. Could she really do that to her?

She was still debating what to do when her mum called her for dinner. Sunday night was always a special meal and she was reluctant to spoil it with this kind of news. Why was life so difficult? Why was it left up to her to make these kinds of decisions?

She realised that her first instinct was the right one. They should be able to make their own decision about whether to read it or not. She wrapped the book in a cloth bag and took it downstairs with her.

Her parents were both sitting at the table when she got to the kitchen. It was a full roast dinner tonight; chicken with all the trimmings.

'Thanks Mum, Dad. Looks amazing.' She slid into her seat, placing the book near her plate.

'What's that?' Her mum's sharp eyes never missed anything.

Jade took a breath. 'Carina came over yesterday evening.'

Her mum nodded. 'I take it you two talked?'

'Yeah.' Jade took another deep breath before she spoke. 'And she left me this. It's Ruby's diary.'

The look of pain that crossed her mother's face tugged at Jade's heart. She quickly looked across the table. Her father's face was still as stone, and almost as grey too.

'I'm sorry.' She put up an arm, almost as if to shield herself from the emotions radiating from the other two people in the room. 'Maybe I shouldn't have told you. But I thought you might want to know.'

There was another long silence. Steam slowly lifted from the food on the table, curling into the air like a phantom. As if Ruby's ghost was sitting there in between them.

'Have you read it?' Her mother's voice was quiet.

Jade nodded, not trusting herself to speak.

'And is there anything which might explain why she did what she did?' The voice was still quiet and smooth. If Jade hadn't known the person who was speaking well enough to read beneath the surface, she might have mistaken it for disinterest.

Jade nodded again.

Her mother lifted a hand, as if to touch the package, and then let it fall. 'Put it away, darling. I don't think I could read it now. Maybe ...' She hesitated. 'Maybe later.'

She looked across at her husband, who nodded in agreement. Jade knew instinctively that it would be a lot of laters. She had lost a sister, but how much harder must it be to lose your own child?

It was time to put it away somewhere safe. Pushing back her chair, she ran out of the room and upstairs, to where she kept the shoe box filled with memories of her sister. There was just room to squeeze it in the top. She gave it a quick kiss before she placed it gently in the box. 'There you go, Ruby. I'll see you later.'

It only took a minute, and then she was back downstairs. Her dad was already carving the chicken. Jade decided to pretend she hadn't seen her mum surreptitiously wiping her nose.

'So, how is Carina?' Shirley seated herself back down at the table.

'She's good, I think.' Jade tried to think. They honestly hadn't really discussed much except for Ruby, and that definitely wasn't a topic she wanted to bring up again. 'She looks good anyway. I heard she's started working at that hair and beauty salon in town. You know, the one where her auntie works.'

'And what about Nick? Have you heard from him recently?' Her dad leaned his elbows on the table.

'Oh yeah. He's at home at the moment. He sent me some pictures yesterday.' She reached for her phone, which was charging on the kitchen counter, and found a new photo waiting for her. She scrolled through them, holding them up one by one.

'That's his parents B&B. And that's the view from their house. And that's him with his friend Jamie. He sent that one just now. They're down the pub.' The two of them had their arms slung around each other. Someone else had obviously taken the photo for them.

'He looks pretty happy.' Her mother was already tucking into her plate of food.

'Yeah. I think he likes the mountains. And home is always home, I guess.'

'That's true.' Her mother smiled at the man sitting across the table, who reached over and squeezed his wife's hand.

Jade's phone beeped on the table next to her, almost making her knock over her glass.

She looked at it and smiled. It was a message from Carina.

Brunch tomorrow? Monday's my day off.

Can't tomorrow, promised I'd go in early to help the guys with the maintenance. How about Saturday? Jade sent back a smiley face and a couple of kisses.

'Jade.' Her mother's tone of voice was enough to remind her of the 'no phones at the table' rule.

'Oh come on, Mum. I'm twenty-three.'

Her mum just looked at her. Jade pretended to grumble as she put the phone back on the worktop, but she dropped a kiss on the top of her head as she sat back down. 'Love you, Mum.'

'Love you too.'

After the washing up was done her parents went to watch TV, but Jade retreated to her bedroom. She had too much to think about. And, there was one thing she still had to do, and that was look at Ruby's Twitter account.

But it told her little or nothing. Ruby's tweets were still there, but it was obvious that a lot of the more malicious ones from other people had been deleted. If they were people from her school they had probably panicked when they found out what had happened.

Jade realised she had come a long way in the last few months; being able to think about all of this stuff rationally was definitely progress. She had put aside any idea of going to the police about the harassment either. One look at her parents' faces when they had seen the diary was enough to tell her that stirring things up would only cause them more pain.

She lay back on her bed, arms behind her head. It was strange, how someone could be there one minute and gone the next. No more adding to the pages of their life.

It was then that she knew exactly what she had to do. She got out pen and paper, sat down at her desk, and began to write.

Chapter 22

Nick whistled as he strapped the kit to the trailer. It was disgustingly early for a Saturday morning, but he didn't mind. Jamie was taking a group of American tourists out sea kayaking, and he was going along. Unpaid, of course, but it was just great to get out on the sea. And they would probably forage some cockles for dinner. There was a great beach for them just up the coast which was only accessible from the sea. His dad cooked a mean seafood paella. His mouth watered at the thought.

'Ready?' Jamie appeared from the shed with the last bits of kit in his hands. He chucked them in the bin on the trailer, and started up the engine on the battered old Toyota. 'Jump in. Let's go.'

They swung slowly out of the driveway and onto the main road. First stop was to pick up the family, who were staying about a mile further along.

'Look, man.' Jamie spoke up above the roar of the car. 'Why don't you take over my business when I go to Canada? It would be enough to keep you going. I could give you the car, the equipment, everything. I can't take it with me. I could even give you a decent price for renting the cottage. I'd rather have someone in it who I can trust.'

'Hang on.' Nick braced a hand against the dashboard as they rounded a corner. 'I thought you were just thinking about it?'

'I got an offer from a company yesterday. They want me there in time for the winter season. I'm seriously considering going out for a couple of years. And if I could leave you to take care of things here, then that would make it an even easier decision.' Jamie pulled up outside a beautifully kept farmhouse. 'Anyway, think about it. I'm not going to confirm for a couple of weeks. I told them I'd need some time to consider it and they're OK with that.'

Nick's mind was reeling. To suddenly have his dream dropped in his lap with no warning was really unsettling. But when he had thought about coming home to live, he hadn't imagined a home without Jamie. Be careful what you wish for, he thought.

'Or,' Jamie opened the car door, 'you could just come with me. It would be a blast. The powder in the Rockies is just amazing.'

Canada. Somehow Nick couldn't see the appeal. It would be great for a visit, maybe even for a month or two. But the thought of living out there, so far from home? The mountains around here were like old friends to him. He couldn't just leave them behind. No, he realised. It wasn't that he couldn't, it was that he didn't want to. He loved this place with every bone in his body.

Nick was saved from having to reply by the appearance of the family. Two adults, and four kids, who looked as if they ranged from about eight to eighteen. This would be an interesting day. Hopefully they would all behave themselves.

'Mike.' The man shook their hands. 'And this is my wife Julia.'

The kids were introduced as well and Nick carefully stored their names away for future reference. They all seemed like nice people. They crammed the six skinnier people in the back two rows of seats, while Mike and Jamie sat in the front. The kids were obviously excited.

'Are we going to see any whales?' one of them asked seriously.

'Not many whales around here, but we should see some seals, and if we're really lucky some dolphins.' Nick smiled at him.

'Awesome.' The car filled with excited voices and two of the kids gave each other a high five.

They spent the morning paddling around the rocky coves, watching the bird life. Nick had been worried that the youngest member of the group might get tired, but Jamie had brought two double kayaks, and he and Nick each took one of the smaller kids. In fact, if anything, it was Nick's arms that were tiring by the time they stopped for lunch at their chosen cove.

'Right, in a moment we'll go hunting for cockles, but first it's time for lunch.' Jamie dug the sandwiches out of the cool box that was lying in the back of his kayak.

There was a general cheer about the prospect of food, and everyone sat on the sand, happily munching their sandwiches and fruit. The day wasn't very sunny, but at least it was warm.

This could be your life, Nick thought. But his next thought was, *I miss Jade*.

His life was so messed up and complicated. Jade probably wouldn't have him back unless he got some professional help. And even then, it wasn't certain. He really wanted to come home. But if coming home meant losing Jamie to Canada then he wasn't sure he wanted that either. And anyway, assuming Jade did want him back, he very much doubted that she would want to move up here. She really loved Glasgow, he could tell. Yeah. It was really complicated. Even before you threw his new friends into the mix. He enjoyed spending time with them too.

He thought of Archie, who had seized every opportunity for an adventure his whole life. He wished he could be more like that. Some days he did feel adventurous. But other days he just felt tired. He took another bite of his apple, looking at the calm water slowly lapping against the rocks nearby. Archie would have loved this.

'Who's Archie?' Nick hadn't realised that he'd spoken aloud until Mike asked the question.

'Oh, he was a friend of mine from Glasgow.' He could class him a friend, he thought. It had been brief, but they had shared a lot between the two of them. 'He passed away a couple of weeks ago.' He spoke carefully, trying to hide the depth of the loss he felt. First Jade, then Archie. And now it looked as if Jamie would be leaving him as well. Who would be next?

'I'm sorry for your loss.' The Americans had such a good phrase for condolences, Nick realised. Just the right amount of sorrow, focus on the person they were talking to, and – he realised that Mike might assume it was someone his own age, and hurried to correct his impressions.

'It's OK. I mean, he was old. Ninety-two. It's a pretty good run.'

Mike nodded. 'Gosh. Yeah, I'd say that.'

'He was a mountaineer. He loved the mountains. Until he got stuck in a wheelchair, that is. Well, he still loved the mountains, but it meant he couldn't do stuff anymore.' Nick quickly shut his mouth; he was babbling.

'Shame, that.' Mike said thoughtfully. 'My uncle is the same. He's a pretty keen hiker. Then he fell and broke his back some years ago. We all thought he'd have to give it up, but he found this wheelchair, and what d'you know, it can climb up mountains.'

'Really?' Nick had never heard of such a thing.

Mike grinned widely, adjusting his cap as he did so. 'Oh yeah. Wait a minute. I think I might have a photo.'

He reached into his pocket and extracted his phone from its plastic dry case. 'Let me see.' A few flicks of his thumb, and he passed the device across to Nick. 'Take a look at that.'

Nick looked at the photo. It was pretty much like an electric wheelchair, but with massive tyres that looked almost like the ones you'd get on mountain bikes. If he had to describe it, he would have said that it looked like a cross between a wheelchair and a quad bike.

'And it's electric?' He passed back the phone to Mike.

Mike nodded. 'But a bigger battery than your average scooter, and more torque. These can go a good hundred miles up and down hills without needing a recharge.'

Nick considered. That was a good week's walking for an average walker. Pretty amazing.

'They're not cheap though.' Mike stowed his phone carefully back into his pocket. 'I don't know how much they'd cost over here, but I'm telling you, that thing cost more than my car.'

They would, thought Nick. Not your average walking kit. But still, it was pretty exciting.

They were distracted by a cheer from the kids. Jamie had suggested that it was time to go cockle hunting.

'They're really easy to find.' Jamie led them out onto the lower reaches of the beach, which was uncovering itself slowly as the tide receded. 'You just run your fingers through the sand. But just watch out for the crabs, they can get a bit nippy.' He went to pull a tub from his kayak, leaving them to root about for a few minutes.

It wasn't long before a shout came from one of the kids who held up two cockles, one in each hand.

'Brilliant! Give them a quick rinse in the sea, and dump them in the bucket.' Jamie gave him a congratulatory pat on the back.

Mike and Julia found a few more, and then there was a squeal from the youngest kid who got a nip on his finger. They all crowded round to see him hold up his find. It was a skinny grey crab about half the size of his hand, perfectly camouflaged to fit in with the colour of the sand.

'Let him go. He's too small to make good eating.' Jamie crouched down. 'We've got more cockles to find.'

It didn't take them long to fill their bucket, and Jamie stopped them when they were nearing the top. 'That's enough. We've got to leave some, or there won't be any next year.'

Given how many they'd found in such a small patch of beach, Nick doubted that there was any danger of this happening, but he kept his peace. Knowing Jamie, he was probably here doing the same thing every few weeks in the summer. It was always good for the punters if there was actually something there.

The kids went off to climb on the rocks, while the adults sat back on the beach. It was the sort of place you could stay the whole day and never get bored, Nick thought. Or your whole life. A whole life on a beach? He stopped to consider the idea for a couple of minutes. It would be great in some ways, but it might get a bit lonely all by yourself.

The paddle back took longer, as everyone seemed unwilling to rush after a lazy lunch. It was after four by the time they dropped the family off at their accommodation. The parents made sure that the children chorused their thank yous, and they all disappeared gratefully into the house.

Jamie turned to Nick. 'I'm taking them out mountain biking tomorrow if you want to come.'

Nick considered for a moment, then shook his head. 'I think I'm going to head up into the mountains tomorrow. Just head out for a few days. I've got a lot of things I need to think about. I'll catch you on the way back.'

Jamie nodded, nonchalant as usual. 'Sure. And don't forget to think about what I said.'

Nick nodded. 'I won't.'

Jamie hugged him when he dropped him off. 'You take care of yourself, dude. See you in a few days. Enjoy the peace and quiet.'

'Will do.'

Chapter 23

Jade woke feeling happy on Saturday morning, and then remembered why. She and Carina were going to have brunch today. She checked her phone. Loads of time. But when she opened the curtains she had to groan. It was tipping it down. So much for the summer weather. Where had it gone?

A quick shower was all she needed, and then she opened her cupboard door to pull out some clothes. Maybe the black jeans. She may as well go back to winter clothes at this rate.

She shook off her grumpy mood. She was going to see Carina and hopefully things wouldn't be too awkward between them. Besides, what was the point in worrying about clothes when whatever she wore would look frumpy beside her glamourous friend? It was a good thing that Carina liked her, not for her looks, but for her brain. She cheered at the thought. And with that she pulled on her black jeans and green fleece and went downstairs.

The last time she had worn this combination was when she and Nick had done the abseil together. He seemed to be pretty happy at home, if the pictures he had sent her were anything to go by. A small part of her – well, actually quite a big part of her if she was honest with herself – worried that he wouldn't come back. If that happened, she would miss him.

An ache tugged at her that she couldn't quite place, fuelled by the thought of never seeing Nick again. Idiot, she told herself firmly. You were the one who split up with him. Anyway, Fort William isn't that far away. You could always go up and visit him.

Her mother was waiting with a pot of tea in the kitchen, and there was an amazing smell of toast in the air. 'How's my girl this morning?'

Jade gave her a warm hug. 'I'm good. You?'

She followed her mother's pointing finger to where a big shiny metal box stood by the sink. Jade frowned. It seemed to have a cable coming out of it. But it was like no kitchen appliance she'd ever seen. 'What the hell is that? Is it a slow cooker?'

Shirley laughed. 'Not quite. I saw it on my way home yesterday. Reduced in the sale. It's a bread cooker.'

'Ohhh. So that's what the smell is. So does that mean fresh bread every morning?' Jade couldn't keep the excitement out of her voice.

'Sure does. And if that timer on the front is correct, it's going to be done about ...' There was a ding. 'Now.'

'Wow. That's so cool. Can I try some?' Jade made as if to open the cooker.

'Just be patient a few minutes longer! It will have to cool down. Have some tea while you wait.'

Jade sat down at the table, drumming her fingers on the wood surface as a joke.

'That's not going to make it come any quicker,' her mum teased.

'I can't *believe* I have to wait when you said it was ready. I'm going to *starve*,' Jade teased back in a mock-exasperated voice.

But when the bread came out, Jade had to admit that it was delicious. 'I could get used to this.' She licked the remains of the jam off her fingers. 'Is it very hard to do?'

Shirley shook her head. 'I'll show you tonight when I put the next batch in, if you want.'

'Yeah. That'd be great.'

Jade gave her mum another hug, surprising her. 'What was that for?'

Jade shrugged. If her mum had time to think about bread makers, maybe that meant that finally, finally, her brain wasn't completely taken over by what had happened to Ruby. She had felt kind of side-lined, she realised. As if her sister had taken all the attention and there had been none left for her. She felt selfish and petty admitting that to herself, given what all of them had been through. She knew how much her parents loved her, and she knew they had done their best to make things feel as if there was at least some semblance of normality carrying on in their lives, but she had still felt that way. It was weird how the actions of a person could influence things even when they were no longer around. But now, looking at the bread maker, she was just glad that there was finally something that obviously made her mum happy.

She rinsed her plate in the kitchen sink. 'I've got to go, Mum. I'll see you later.' And she escaped from the kitchen and went to collect her stuff.

Later that night as Jade lay in her bed, she relived her day with a smile on her face. But one thing that Carina had said had surprised her. Jade had been trying to explain why she had broken up with Nick.

Carina leaned forward, pushing her plate out of the way. 'Yeah, but he's an adult. Shouldn't it be his decision how he decides to deal with it?'

Jade shook her head. 'In theory, yeah, but he's clearly not dealing with it. Look where I met him. He's clearly not.'

Carina pursed her lips, considering. 'Maybe, but would you really throw away happiness now, just to avoid a potential pain in the future which might never happen?'

This was so close to what Nick had said that it made Jade hesitate for a moment. 'It's not that. It's just I'd be worried about him constantly. I'd always be watching, waiting for any signs that he might do it again.'

Carina leaned across the table and grasped one of Jade's hands, as if to emphasise the importance of what she was going to say. 'But seriously, if you're really honest with yourself, don't you worry about him anyway? And, accepting that fact, wouldn't you be in a better position to influence things if you were actually with him?'

Jade blew out her cheeks. She couldn't deny the logic of the argument. But it all made things so much more complicated. Just when she thought she had got it all sorted out in her head.

'Look, I'm not going to tell you what to do, because I know you wouldn't listen to me anyway.' Carina spread out her hands,

palms upwards. 'But from the way you talk about this guy, it sounds as if you really like him. And, apart from all this extra stuff, he seems to make you happy.'

Thinking about this exchange made Jade shed a few tears over the fact that her life was so complex. But then, she thought, supposing she had met Nick without ever having gone through what she had done with Ruby? Wouldn't she be struggling even more, trying to process what was happening without some understanding of what was going on?

The thought that something good might have come out of Ruby's death was so shocking that she sat straight upright, clutching the bedcovers to herself. But wasn't that the best way to run your life, to see the best in every situation? Even though that thought seemed almost sacrilegious, then just because something terrible had happened, didn't mean that it couldn't have at least some positive after-effects.

She lay back down again, curling herself up on her side. She would talk to Nick when he got back. Maybe they could sort something out. And she was increasingly aware of just how much she missed him.

She wouldn't commit to anything. But she would think about what Carina had said.

Her phone rang, startling her. Her heart jumped when she saw the name on the screen.

'Nick?' Her voice didn't quite work on the first try, and she cleared her throat before she spoke again. 'Are you OK? It's pretty late.'

'Yeah. I'm good. I've been out with Jamie today, that's why I didn't call earlier.' His words were cheerful, but there was something in his voice that she couldn't quite read.

The phone call had been so unexpected that she didn't know what to say. 'So ... what's it like being at home?'

'It's good. It's great up here. And the weather's been amazing the past few days.'

There was another pause. 'Look, Jade, I just wanted to let you know I talked to my parents. About what's been going on. I didn't tell them everything – you know – about the bridge and stuff, they'd be too worried about me. But apparently the reason they haven't been down to visit is because my dad has problems with his mental health too.' She could hear the relief in his voice.

'Oh Nick, that's great. I mean, it's not great about your dad, but great that —' She stopped, aware that she was wittering on. 'Well. You know what I mean.'

'Well, it's not great, but at least I know now. And I've talked to my dad a lot about it. Which has helped. I think. Well, kind of. Just things seem to be different up here, now that Jamie's off to Canada.'

'Canada? What?' Jade sat up suddenly and had to grab at one of the pillows as it tried to slide off the bed.

'Yeah. It's a bit shit, but I'm happy for him, I guess, if that's what he really wants to do. Anyway. I'll tell you all about everything when I get back. I'm heading up into the mountains for a few days tomorrow. I've been feeling pretty down the last couple of days. I miss Archie, and Jamie leaving has thrown a spanner in the works too. He's offered me his business, but I just don't know. It won't be the same without him. I really need to get away by myself for a few days, get my head straightened out.'

There was silence on the other end of the phone for a minute, then he spoke again. 'I just wanted to say that I might not get reliable phone signal up there, so if you don't hear from me for a couple of days then you're not to worry, OK?'

Jade found her heart was hammering in her throat. *Tell him. How much you care about him. Carina was right.* But all she found herself saying was, 'Thanks for letting me know. You take care of yourself, OK? And stay safe.' And then she mentally kicked herself.

'Thanks. I will. I'll be back soon, so I'll see you around. I'm going to carry on coming to take the oldies out, if you still want me.'

'Sure. We always need people.' Jade smiled. That meant she would be seeing him again. That meant they still had a chance.

'OK, I'll let you go. You're right, it's late. I'll send some pictures from my trip. See ya.' Nick sounded more cheerful now.

'Look, Nick —' But it was too late. He was already gone.

Jade curled up on her side again. She briefly considered calling him back, but decided against it. There would be time enough to talk when he got back. To tell him how she really felt. To try and work things out between them. She hugged herself. The thought of having Nick back in her life was both scary and exciting.

It took her a long time to fall asleep.

Chapter 24

Nick hummed to himself as he double-checked his kit. First aid kit. Check. Emergency shelter. Check. Torch. Check. He'd also packed enough freeze-dried food to last for a week, just in case, and his mini stove burner. His pack must have weighed somewhere around fifteen kilos, but probably a good third of that was food, and it would disappear slowly over the course of the next few days.

He propped his bag by the front door and went to find his parents. His father was washing dishes in the kitchen.

'I'm off, Dad. Bus leaves soon. If I'm not back by Friday then send out a search party.'

He received a soapy hug in return. 'You have a great time, son. It's been great having you here. See you in a few days.'

'Yeah. Cheers, Dad. Where's Mum?'

His dad pointed upwards. 'Stripping beds, I think. That family from Kent is leaving this morning.'

Nick found her on the landing, gathering up a double armful of bedding. She dropped it as soon as she saw him and gathered him into her arms instead. 'Is that you off?'

'Yeah. Bus leaves soon, and I don't want to miss it.'

She ruffled his hair. 'Well, you take care of yourself. And if you need anything just call me, OK? We can always come and rescue you in the car.'

'Thanks, Mum.' Nick gave her another quick squeeze, and a kiss on the cheek. 'See you in a few days.'

It wasn't long before he was on the bus, his bag safely stowed in the bay beneath him. It was only about an hour up the coast, but it would take him right into the heart of what he loved best, countryside unspoiled by roads, and away from the overcrowded tourist trails. But by the time he got dropped off at the village which was his starting point, it was raining. He looked up in displeasure at the sky. There were some blue patches across the way. Maybe he would just go to the pub for a quick drink before he set off. There was no rush, anyway.

The pub was totally empty, which surprised Nick, although it was only eleven o'clock on a Sunday. When he walked in it looked as if the place had just opened; the bartender was stacking glasses behind the bar. There would be plenty of punters in for Sunday lunch, at a guess.

It proved to be a wise decision to take a break, because while he was enjoying a half of a delicious local ale then what had been a gentle shower turned into a fierce downpour. He thanked the lucky weather fairy. Starting a walk with damp equipment would just be miserable.

The bartender leaned over the bar. 'Off for a walking trip, are we?'

'Yeah.' Nick didn't mind talking. Besides, it was good to let as many people as possible know what you were doing, especially if you were going on your own. That way, if something happened to you, hopefully at least someone would remember seeing you and where you'd gone. 'I'm going up over the hills to Ratagan and then on to Skye. I think four days walk probably.'

The other man nodded. From the depth of the tan he was sporting, Nick guessed that he spent most of his free time out on the hills too. 'Wild camping? There're some good spots up there. The top of the ridges can be pretty flat. A bit windy sometimes, but then that's good for keeping the midges away.'

Nick nodded. 'Yeah, that was my plan. I'm just going to see how far I get. I'm a bit out of shape unfortunately.'

'Are you from round here?' The man's eyes sharpened a little, obviously trying to place his accent.

'Kind of. Fort William originally, but I'm living in Glasgow now.'

The other man walked over and picked up Nick's empty glass. 'Having another?'

Nick stood up and stretched. 'Nah. I'd better get off now that the rain has passed over. Thanks anyway.'

'No problem. Have a great walk.' The guy shook his hand. 'See you next time.'

Nick lifted his pack onto his back and walked out of the door. His heart lifted as he saw the green rise of the mountain above him. He was finally back where he belonged. He set up off the hill.

It only took him a couple of hours to get to the top, although the last bit of the route was a pretty hard slog, what with the heavy pack on his back. What a great place to have lunch. He unpacked the sandwiches he had made for himself that morning. From here on in it would be mostly instant food, but at least today he still had fresh bread. A swig of water was enough to wash it down. Maybe when he stopped for the night he would make a pot of tea.

His happy mood continued all the way through the afternoon, as he made his way down the other side of the mountain, and up to the top of the next. It was pretty good progress for his first day. No point in pushing it too much. He put up his tent, cooked himself the promised pot of tea, and rehydrated some spaghetti Bolognese. It was amazing what they could do with freeze-dried food. It almost tasted as good at the real thing. There was a bit of a breeze which kept the worst of the midges off, although he had still smeared himself in plenty of repellent, just in case. He sent a couple of photos to Jamie and Jade, and one to Sean and the other guys. He didn't have any internet, but they would be bound to go through at some point when he was walking tomorrow.

He spent the rest of the evening just looking at the view and thinking about what Jamie had said. Surely this was the future he wanted? Mountains all around him. But then, what were the mountains without the people he loved? The tiredness seemed to seep through his bones just thinking about it. He had been honest with Jade when he said that he was pretty depressed at the moment. But the beautiful scenery, and the beautiful weather, was helping him keep things at bay. Just like it always did. It was possible to be happy and sad at the same time. Up and down. Light and dark. Wasn't that just normal?

Talking to his dad had made him realise that the phases he had written off as 'downers' in the past were actually something more serious. Maybe he should talk to someone when he got back. Someone professional. But until he did, he was going to enjoy this amazing scenery.

The sun was still pretty high in the sky by the time he found himself yawning. Of course, it was June, he reminded himself. It probably wouldn't get dark until around midnight. So he crawled into his sleeping bag and closed his eyes. It wasn't long before he fell asleep, a smile still on his face.

But the next morning when he woke up it was raining.

Nick sighed as he listened to the drumming of the rain on the roof of his tent. The forecast had said there would be rain at some point, but it was a pain packing up in the wet. It meant that his tent would still be wet when he got to his destination, and then that dampness would probably slowly creep into everything else. Unless he got a couple of hours sunshine to help dry things out at some point during the day. That could happen. Positive thinking. That was important.

It took a bit of manoeuvring to have breakfast and get everything packed up in the tiny tent, but it was the only way to keep everything from getting wet. He skipped a cup of tea. If it stopped raining, he could make one later. His dry bags would protect everything while he was walking, and his waterproofs were the best. And he always loved the outdoors in the rain. Everything smelled so fresh and green.

The tent was the last thing to take apart. It only took him a couple of minutes to roll it up and push it into its waterproof bag. Then he set off, feet squishing as he walked across the wet moss.

It must have rained quite a bit in the night, because the ground was pretty boggy in places, and the streams were filled with rushing water. But sometime around mid-morning the rain stopped, and by the time he sat down for lunch the sun had come out. He boiled some water and used it to make a cup of tea and rehydrate another meal.

There was still no mobile signal, but he must have got one at some point, because there was a thumbs up from Jamie, and a strong arm from Jade. But no reply from Sean. They had obviously forgotten about him. This Deem seemed like a far closer friend than he would ever be. For one moment his words to Jade about it being impossible to lose all the people in his life came back to haunt him. He had lost Archie, he was losing Jamie, and Jade only felt sorry for him. And now, it looked as if his new friends didn't care about him either. For one moment he felt irrationally jealous, and then immediately guilty for being so small-minded. Thoughts like that were just his depression talking. They were probably just busy. Or out of mobile range. Or something else. He stuffed his phone quickly back into his pocket.

Mountains. He looked at the quiet valley where he sat, breathing in deep breaths of the fresh air, trying to regain his composure. They had always been enough for him. Had always settled his mood. But today his mind was not in the right place. It was too far away. It felt split into too many places. Part of it was away in the Alps, with his new friends, wishing he was there in body. Part of it was with Jade, wondering how she was doing without him. If he was completely honest with himself, the small uncharitable part of him was hoping that she was sad without him. And he felt guilty about that too. But a big part of his mind was trying to process the offer that Jamie had given him. To feel like his dream was out of his reach for so long, and then to suddenly have it handed to him on a plate? It had knocked him off balance. Because, if he was really honest about that too, then he wasn't sure that it was what he wanted any more.

An annoyed sound escaped him as he pushed himself up onto his feet. He didn't know what he wanted, he realised. Which unsettled him too. His dream had always been so fixed in his mind, and now a year in Glasgow had changed all that.

'I hate Glasgow.' He picked up a stone and hurled it into the stream. The loud splash didn't make him feel any better. 'I wish I'd never gone there.'

But if he hadn't gone there he wouldn't have met Jade. And if he hadn't met Jade, he wouldn't have met Sean. Or Pete. Or Stevie. And come to rely on them for keeping him going.

'Yeah, and life would be much more simple. I'd be off to Canada with Jamie probably.' He muttered to himself as he hoisted his rucksack onto his back, knowing as he said the words that they were a lie. Did it make him a coward, not wanting to leave home? Then he mentally kicked himself. His problems could wait. He was supposed to be here to have a good time. And that's what he would do. Whistling a tune to raise his spirits, he set off.

Nick looked at his watch. Just after six-thirty. He was almost at the place where he had planned to camp that night. He was making pretty good time. After that it was only about eight miles to the village, which made for an easy day tomorrow. He would have proper beer and some proper food. And the chance of a hot shower.

He was pretty tired though. Really out of shape after sitting at a desk for so long. He could feel his feet really dragging these last couple of miles. At least the last bit was downhill all the way.

He had been walking along a fast-flowing stream for a few hundred metres now. The water rushed busily over tumbles of dark brown stones. There was supposed to be a bridge somewhere to cross. It was marked on the map just about ...

Ah. He gazed for a minute at the scene. There had obviously once been three planks laid across the stream, fixed together with a twist of metal wire. But now one plank was broken, the second was sticking up from the shallows downstream, and the other was nowhere else to be seen. That was poor maintenance. He would have to report it to someone.

He looked at the map, considering his options. The spot he had chosen to camp was just a short walk away on the other side of the stream. But if he didn't cross here, then the nearest other option was about three miles downstream. Which made for a six-mile detour.

He could camp on this side of the river. The ground was a bit uneven, but it would be OK. He could decide what to do in the morning. He scratched his head, looking at the river. There was something that looked like it might be a set of stepping stones in drier weather, but with all the rain the water had risen so they were well-submerged. It wasn't even five metres from one side to another. Maybe if he took off his boots he could try to walk across. It would be a bit risky, but all of his stuff was well-packed in dry bags, so even if he fell in then it wouldn't be a disaster. It was time to have a bit of an adventure.

He took his boots off, stuffing his socks into the toes. With careful aim he flung them across the river to land on the other side. At least they would be dry. It would be great to be able to do the same with his pack, but it was just too heavy. It would have to come with him.

Trousers also came off, and with the help of a stone to weigh them down a bit they went the same way as his boots. No one was around to see him in his underwear, so it really didn't matter. He sat down carefully on the back and placed his feet in the water.

Jeez, it was cold. The middle of June and the water was still bloody freezing. He set his first foot on the first stone, and placed his other firmly on the second. The stones felt firm, and he took courage from that.

It made hard going though. The current was strong, and tugged at him, constantly trying to pull him off-balance. The weight of the rucksack was an added complication. And by the time he was half-way across he could barely feel his feet.

Just one step at a time. Take it easy. We're almost there.

As soon as he felt the large stone roll under his feet, he knew what was going to happen and that there was no way of stopping it. He didn't try to save himself, but concentrated on holding his breath as he fell sideways and the water closed over his head. He still managed to swallow a mouthful, but it was better than being half-drowned. He kicked out to find the bottom, and discovered that the water was only at waist height. Still, it took all of his strength to fight against the pull of the current and slowly make his way towards the edge of the river. He collapsed on the bank just to get his breath back, and realised that he was shivering uncontrollably.

Dry clothes. He had to get into some dry clothes. Numb fingers fumbled with the clasps on his pack. The rucksack itself was dripping, but as he had predicted, the stuff inside his dry bags was fine. He stripped down to nothing. After all, who was going to see? He towelled himself dry, and with dry clothes on was soon feeling a lot better, although he still felt freezing. The wet clothes went in a plastic bag. He would try to hang them up tonight to dry, if the weather was still fine.

His jacket was still hanging on a bush where he had placed it. He would just check his phone. Maybe send a message to his parents if he had signal. And send a couple more photos to Jade. That one of the buzzard he had managed to snap just before lunch was pretty amazing.

But when his hand dipped into his pocket, what he came up with was not his mini dry bag, with his phone safely inside, but his phone, by itself, now completely waterlogged and dripping. Too late he remembered that when he had stuffed it away in a fit of pique at lunchtime then he hadn't bothered to put it back in the dry bag. And now it was as useless as a piece of stone.

He stared at it for a few seconds, then cursed aloud at his stupidity. This was where worrying about stuff got you. Out in the middle of nowhere, with no means of communication. Oh sure, his watch could send off a signal, if he really got into trouble, but that was for emergencies only. He had just cut off his only connection to the outside world.

He flung himself down on a rocky outcrop, trying to think. Did it really matter? It wasn't the cost of the phone, although he was slightly annoyed with himself for being so careless with something that expensive. It was that now he was truly alone. Out here with only his thoughts and the mountains for company. And that slightly scared him. For so long he'd been trying to push everything away. He had made an art of avoiding reality. But he had a feeling that everything was just about to hit him.

'Let's get a campsite set up.' He spoke aloud, as if there was someone with him to tell his thoughts to. Placing his dead phone back into his jacket pocket, he gathered his stuff and set off to take the final steps towards his resting place for the night.

It didn't take him long to set up camp, and, exhausted, he crawled thankfully into his sleeping bag. A couple of energy bars did him for dinner. There was no way he could even muster up the energy to boil some water.

But sleep was a long time coming. For one thing, it took him a long time to finally get warm, despite his thermal sleeping bag. And, for some reason, he couldn't get Jade out of his mind. Until now he had been angry at her for leaving him, but now he realised that in some way he had been the one who had let her down. She had given him nothing but honesty about her feelings and what she had been going through, while he had been hanging back, worried about what she would think of him if he showed her the true depths of his depression and exactly what it did to his mind. And that made him feel pretty bad.

He tried to keep himself positive, but by the time he awoke the next morning the black fog of depression had already settled deep into his bones. He knew the feeling all too well. It was almost as if they felt too heavy to lift. And his brain felt too muddled for any real thinking. There was no way it was going to shift away any time soon. So when he heard the rain dripping off his tent again, he made the decision that he wasn't going anywhere. He would stay in his tent until the clouds lifted, both actually and metaphorically. There was no hurry. He was on his own time. No one was expecting him. Not today. He could rest without any sense of guilt.

It was strange how quickly depression could settle in. One day he could be fine, the next feel like this. A bit of a mystery really. Brains were weird. But if he was really honest with himself, this had been building for a while. Ever since Jamie had told him he was thinking of going to Canada. No, before that. Ever since Archie's funeral. He sighed. OK then. Ever since Jade had left him. How his happiness had come to be so tied up with her he didn't know. Surely it couldn't be good to be that dependent on one person.

Food was the last thing his stomach wanted, but he forced down another energy bar just so he wouldn't starve, and lay back down, pulling his sleeping bag over his head again. It was actually a relief to know that he didn't have to be anywhere. Didn't have to pretend to anyone that he was OK. No need to turn up to work as if everything was normal.

It wasn't that he was dependent on one person, he realised. He was dependent on lots of other people. He needed a support network to get him through the bad times. He always had. And his life recently just seemed to be like that big stone that had chucked him in the river. Whenever he seemed to be on a sure footing, something would twist and he would end up going under.

Meeting Jade had been one of the best things that had happened to him. But then she had rejected him because he had been too stubborn to admit he needed help. Meeting Archie had been like rediscovering a long-lost uncle. But then the old man had died just as they were getting to know each other. OK, he could forgive his parents for not coming down to see him, now that he knew the whole story. But Jamie just ditching everything to go off to Canada? That had side swiped his feet from under him. He had thought that Jamie loved it here, but obviously not enough to stop him jumping for a new adventure. And now his new friends seemed not to care about him either. *Call me any time*, Sean had said. And in his heart Nick knew that Sean had meant it. But now, when he really needed a friend, he had no way of getting through to him. And that was all Nick's fault for drowning his phone.

He spent the day alternating between sleep and staring at the wall of his tent, desperately hoping for the feeling of lethargy and the self-destructive thoughts to pass. It was only when his water ran out that he was faced with a decision. He should boil some more up to make sure it wasn't contaminated. But even the thought of getting everything he needed out of his bag, and in the rain too, made him close his eyes in despair. Anyway, why bother? It wasn't as if there was really a need to carry on. No one would really miss him. Jamie was going off to Canada. His parents would do perfectly well by themselves. And Jade ... well, she didn't want to be with him anyway.

Depression lies. He could almost hear Jade's voice in his head, and he clung onto the words like a lifeline. All this wasn't him. Not the real him. The real him was confident. And capable. A nearby stream would do well enough to refill his water bottle. He knew that he should boil his water, but really, this high up in the mountains the risk of contamination was low. And some part of him was past caring what happened to him. It was strange, how his depression just took over everything. A part of him, somewhere, was shouting at him not to be so stupid, but it was just too much effort to listen. Especially when he had to muster all the energy he had just to get up off the ground.

He pushed away the voices in his head. If he could manage a yoga class when he was feeling like this then he could go and get some damn water. He forced himself to get up and out. Another energy bar made up his dinner. He would try to muster up the energy for proper food tomorrow.

When he started to retch just after midnight, he cursed his mistake. Cursed the fact that he hadn't bothered to follow the proper procedure. And cursed himself that the way he was had led to him doing something so stupid. He emptied the meagre contents of his stomach into the nearby heather, and crawled back into his sleeping bag, feeling even lower than before. Maybe this was it. Maybe it was his time. Stuck out here without anyone to talk to. It seemed quite fitting. Why bother to jump off a bridge when you could just die from bacterial poisoning?

He listened to the sounds all around him. The soft patter of the rain on his tent. The quiet gurgle of the small traitorous stream nearby. There were worse ways to die. He closed his eyes.

Chapter 25

Jade sat on her bed, turning her phone over and over in one hand. She had been planning to wait until Nick got back, but she found she just couldn't. She had to apologise to him. For trying to press him into a mould that was defined by the way her sister had acted. He had been totally right. He needed to live his own life and solve his problems in his own way. The problem was, what to write?

I'm sorry, you were right. She typed the words into her phone, considered the message for a minute, then deleted it. A few more tries, and she was no closer to anything she wanted to send.

She was going to be late for work at this rate.

Need to talk to you. I miss you. Call me when you get this. She typed the words in and hit the button before she had time to regret it, and then scrambled for her clothes.

She dived for her phone after her shift was over, desperate to see if he had replied. But there was nothing. Was he angry at her? She mulled it over as she walked home.

What to do? Up in her bedroom she drummed her fingers on the pillow, trying to think. No. The way he had called her ruled that out. He wasn't the type to hold a grudge; he would call her as soon as he received a message like that. Now that she looked more carefully, she could see that he hadn't even received it. Which meant that something was wrong with his phone, or he was out of mobile signal. She bit her lip. Give it one more day. But, just to be sure, she sent him an ordinary text message too.

The message still hadn't got through to him the next morning, and when she came back from work that evening the single tick was still staring accusingly at her to show that he hadn't been in mobile range. Or was it really that? Could it be that he was in trouble? Or was she just being paranoid?

He wasn't Ruby, she reminded herself. He was a grownup, perfectly able to take care of himself. He was probably out somewhere in the back of beyond with no mobile signal. But then, what if he really was in trouble? Could she really live with herself if that turned out to be true?

She considered her options. Number one, call his parents. She was reasonably sure she could manage to find the number for their B&B, even though Nick hadn't given her the name. His parents would have the same surname as him, and by the power of the internet she would find them. But then, she didn't want to worry them needlessly. How would her parents feel getting a weird call from a total stranger who was worried that she was in trouble?

She tapped a finger against her lips as she thought some more. Wait. This friend of his, Jamie, wasn't it? Nick had said that he ran his own business. Surely she'd be able to find him.

It didn't take her long. Jamie McCulloch, outdoor adventures, his website said proudly. She compared the picture with the one that Nick had sent of the two of them. Yes, that was definitely him. Nervously she dialled the number, hoping he wouldn't shout at her for calling him so late in the evening.

'Yo.' Jamie had an unconventional greeting for someone he didn't know, but then, it was definitely out of office hours.

'Hi.' Jade firmed up her voice. 'Is that Jamie? It's Jade.'

She could tell he was trying to place her name, but it didn't take him long. 'Oh yeah, Jade. Great to hear from you. But Nick's not here. He headed up into the mountains on Sunday. Won't be back for another couple of days.'

'Yeah. I guessed it was something like that. But that's why I'm calling you. I sent him a really important message and I haven't heard anything from him for a couple of days, and I'm a bit worried about him.'

'Reception's a bit patchy up there, so I'm not surprised.' Jamie's voice was cheerful. 'Anyway, Nick can take care of himself. He knows these mountains like the back of his hand.'

He doesn't know. The realisation hit Jade with a force that took her breath away. *He doesn't know.* And then anger washed over her, followed immediately by sadness. How could Nick not have told his best friend about his mental health issues? At least he had told his parents though. That was a start.

'Patchy enough that he wouldn't get a message for two days?' She tried to keep her voice level. 'I've sent him an old-fashioned text as well as a message.'

'That is a bit weird, but he's probably just turned his phone off to save battery.' She could tell from Jamie's voice that he thought she was perhaps a bit weird too. 'That's one of the great things about being up there. Getting away from everything.'

So what were her options now? She wouldn't be able to convince Jamie without telling him the whole story, and why would he believe her when he didn't even know her?

'Can you at least tell me which way he went?' At least she could get that from him.

'Sure.' She could almost feel him shrugging as he wondered what this crazy woman was doing, calling him at ten o'clock at night. 'He was going to do Glenfinnan to Ratagan, and then maybe on to Skye depending on how he got on.'

Jade quickly wrote down the unfamiliar names before she forgot them. 'Thanks. Really appreciate it. Sorry to bother you.'

She rang off and sat back against the pillows, chewing on a nail. Nick wasn't really her responsibility. She should trust in his promise that he would be back. But then was it her fault that she cared?

Yes, she cared about him. She would admit that. Oh hell, why didn't she just be honest with herself. She loved him. And she would do anything for him.

'OK. I said it. Are you happy now?' She spoke to the empty room.

Two days without hearing anything. That wasn't like him. Sure, she hadn't expected an immediate response, but two days without turning on his phone? Surely something was wrong.

So what was she to do? Admit that she was probably over-reacting, just because of what had happened with her sister, or stick on the safe side and try to do something about it?

With a twist of her heart, she realised there was no help for it. She would just have to go up there and find him, otherwise she would never be able to live with herself if something was wrong. He was probably fine, but at least then she would know. And if he was fine, then she could at least tell him how she felt.

The next morning she packed a bag. Practical clothes only. There was no knowing where she might have to go. She didn't have any walking gear, but she put on her most comfy pair of sturdy trainers and grabbed her waterproof jacket. They would have to do.

She left a note for her parents. She'd call them later and explain.

Next stop was work. Luckily Bill would be in early this morning; Thursday was maintenance day.

'Bill, I need some time off.' The words tumbled out of her mouth as soon as she burst through the door. 'Nick could be in trouble, and I need to go and find him.'

'Woah, woah, woah.' Bill held up a hand. 'You've got yourself all in a tizz. Sit down and explain to me what's going on.'

'It's Nick.' Jade stubbornly remained standing. 'He's up in the mountains, and I've not heard from him for days.'

Bill's face creased into a worried frown as Jade filled him in. 'Hmm,' he said when she'd finished. 'Sounds serious. How long are you going to need?'

'I really hope I'll be back by Sunday. Could you do without me until then?'

Bill nodded. 'I'll ask young Alfie to come in. He's been saying he wants a few more hours.' He patted her shoulder. 'I would offer to drive you up there myself, but with things the way they are ...' His voice trailed off.

'Don't be silly. I'm going to get the bus and then rent a car when I get up there. It's all arranged.'

Bill's chin lifted. 'You were very sure of me, weren't you?' He cracked a grin when he saw her worried expression. 'Go on, get on with you. I'll see you Sunday. You deserve a break with the hours you've been putting in these last few months.'

Three hours on the bus did nothing to lessen Jade's worries and she barely registered the beautiful scenery that they drove through. Her messages still hadn't been delivered to Nick's phone.

By the time she got to Fort William it was after three. The salty smell that greeted her as she climbed down from the bus took her back to the day that they had been up the crane, and she swallowed a lump in her throat. She would find him.

He had to be somewhere. And she refused to even think about the idea that something might have happened to him.

The car hire office was just a short walk from the bus station.

'Ah yes.' The woman behind the counter was polite and efficient. 'Three days rental, is that correct?'

'Yes.' Jade carefully produced her credit card, and her driving licence.

The was tapping on the computer. 'Ah. I'm really sorry, madam, but because you're under twenty-five there will be an extra charge of thirty pounds a day to cover the insurance. Is that OK?'

Jade sucked in a breath. Ninety pounds! She had carefully calculated, and the meagre limit on her credit card was only just enough to cover the deposit and the cost of the rental. She was regretting splashing out on posh sheets for her new bed now. And the abseil had been pretty expensive.

She clutched the edge of the desk. 'That's not possible. I don't have that kind of money. And I really need to get to Glenfinnan today.'

'I really shouldn't be saying this as it's bad for our business, but if that's where you're going, there's a train leaving for

Glenfinnan in,' she checked her watch, 'just over forty minutes. It will be a lot cheaper and probably just as quick.'

Jade considered, biting her lip. The train would undoubtedly be cheaper. But when she got there, what then? She didn't want to get stuck there if it turned out that she needed to be somewhere else. She really needed that car.

'Would you mind?' She tried to speak politely, knowing that it wasn't the other woman's fault that she was tired and worried. 'Would you mind if I just took the car for twenty-four hours instead of the three days that I originally booked? I'll have it back to you by this time tomorrow.'

The assistant nodded. 'Certainly, madam. And I have to apologise that it wasn't made clearer at the time of booking.'

Jade took the keys, heart racing. Time was really against her now. But she would manage. She would find him.

She drove slowly, taking time to get used to the unfamiliar car. It wasn't far to Glenfinnan. But where to start?

She had been expecting at least a village shop, but a quick walk around proved fruitless. There was a small tourist office selling souvenirs, but the young man in there hadn't seen Nick. He did however confirm that the route Nick had taken was off the usual popular tourist trails, which made Jade even more anxious. She thanked him and left. Her stomach was rumbling by now. She hadn't thought about food. She would just have to spend some of her meagre budget on some food. And probably sleep in the car. It was one of the advantages of being short; the back seat would do her very well.

There were two pubs in the village. Jade made her way to the one that looked less upmarket, hoping that would translate into cheaper prices. It was pretty cosy inside, buzzing with sweaty walkers relaxing over their drinks. She ordered something filling. She would need it.

She was almost done with her steak pie when a sudden thought struck her and she went up to the bar, waving to get the attention of one of the serving staff. 'You haven't seen this guy, have you?'

Jade held out her phone, where she had brought up the picture of Nick with Jamie. 'This guy.' She pointed. 'He would have come through some time on Sunday.'

He girl nodded across to where an older guy was leaning on the bar, chatting to a customer. 'You'll have to ask the boss. I don't work on Sundays.'

Jade went over and repeated her question. The guy scratched his head. 'Sunday. God. I can barely remember what I did this morning.' He frowned. 'Wait. I do remember him. He came in here early, I was just open. Big pack. Looked like he was going for a long trip. But he only stayed for a quick drink. Headed out soon after.' He frowned again. 'What's it to you?'

'He's a friend.' Jade didn't want to tell the whole story, so she kept it simple. 'I haven't heard from him since Monday. I'm worried about him.'

When he heard her words it looked like the lines on the man's face were going to score right through his forehead. 'Hmm. That's not good. Not good at all. I always say it's risky to go walking alone. But really, young lady, if you're that worried about him you should call the police in Fort William.' The other man beside him nodded in agreement.

'Oh no, I don't want to trouble them. Surely they've got enough to do.' Jade didn't know why she was so reluctant to get the police involved. Maybe because part of her still thought that Nick would be just fine.

'Rubbish.' The bartender pulled out his phone. 'I'm going to call Mhairi myself. She'll be able to advise us what to do.'

Jade didn't miss the use of the word us, and it warmed her heart. She waited as the man spoke to someone on the other end of the phone, feeding him information as he asked for it. At one point he scribbled something on a piece of paper. Finally he rang off and turned to her.

'Good news and bad news. Apparently there's been a big accident up on Ben Nevis, and she won't be able to get the mountain rescue out until first thing tomorrow morning if they're needed. But you're to go up to Ratagan tonight. She's told her colleagues up at Kyle and they're coming down to make enquiries locally, see if anyone knows anything. She said to send her his picture to this number.' He handed her the scrap of paper. 'You can use our Wi-Fi to do that if you need to.'

'Thank you so much.' Jade grabbed the man's hand and shook it heartily, but he waved her away.

'You just get going.' He pulled a card off the bar and handed it to her. 'Here's our number. Just make sure you call me when you find him so I know that he's safe.'

Jade nodded, took half a minute to send the picture, then grabbed her things and fled. She had no idea how long it would take to get to Ratagan, but her phone told her almost two hours. She had better get going. Hopefully the police would still be waiting when she got there.

By the time she got to her destination she was exhausted. But she couldn't miss the brightly marked police car parked outside the hostel, with two uniformed men sitting in it. She eased herself out of the driving seat, rubbing her tired eyes. Thank goodness for the long summer evenings. At least she hadn't been forced to drive in the dark.

'Ms Wilson?' The younger of the men got out of the car.

'Just call me Jade, please.'

The man nodded. He had kind eyes. He couldn't have been much older than herself. 'We've had a good ask around, but no one's seen anything of him. The lady who runs the hostel knows him well, and she said he wouldn't have passed through without saying hello. Which should mean he's somewhere between here and Glenfinnan.'

'So he could be perfectly fine then?' Jade felt a flush of relief. 'I'm sorry to waste your time.'

Just then the door to the hostel opened. 'Oh Duncan, I'm so glad to catch you!' A woman of about fifty stepped out, her hair scraped back into a pony tail, wellies on her feet. 'I was away down to my daughter's on Sunday, and my neighbour came in to take care of things. He's just told me that young Nick called him on Sunday morning to say he'd be through here yesterday evening, and could we save him a room? He wrote it down for me on a scrap of paper, and left it on the kitchen table, but it must have got lost somewhere. Bloody cats, you know what they're like.'

Jade nodded mutely, unsure of what to say to that.

'I'm so sorry.' The woman continued. 'If I'd known I would have called it in when he didn't turn up.'

The meaning of the words slowly sank in. So that meant Nick *was* in trouble. Jade would have been elated that her hunch was right, if she hadn't been gripped with fear at the realisation that something had actually happened to him. She found she had been desperately hoping all this time that nothing was wrong.

The policeman reached out and squeezed her shoulder. 'Don't worry. We'll find him. Mountain rescue will be out first thing in the morning.'

'In the meantime,' the woman interjected, 'you must stay here tonight. And don't even think about paying.'

Jade slumped against the car, and found tears flowing down her face. Everyone was being so kind. It had been just the same when they had lost Ruby. Neighbours showing up with random meals for the family. People offering to do their garden. Back then she had felt rather overwhelmed by the kindness, but now she realised that it was just people trying to help in any way they could.

She felt another squeeze of her shoulder. 'Don't worry. I'm sure we'll find him. Now you just get some rest and we'll see you in the morning.'

'Thank you.' Jade did her best to smile at him. 'Thank you so much.'

Chapter 26

Nick drifted in a haze. A body could go three days without water. He remembered hearing that statistic somewhere when he was very small. He must be getting pretty close to that now. His lips were dry and cracked, and his body burned as if he was in the heat of the midday sun. If he slept now then maybe he wouldn't wake up again.

Jade was with him. He could feel the touch of her skin on his, the delicious feeling as she lay on top of him, moving her body in time with his. He reached up, arms around her, enjoying the sounds of pleasure she made. Then, out of nowhere, she slapped him. One cheek, and then the other. Hard.

All thoughts of pleasure fled his mind as he glared up at her. 'What was that for?'

She looked down at him, rage mingling with tears on her face. 'What the fuck are you doing? Are you crazy?' Her shouting hurt his head.

He frowned at her. 'What do you mean?'

'How can you do this? Your parents will be devastated. I'll be devastated. And Jamie, Sean, Pete and Stevie will never forgive you.'

His eyes flipped open and he found himself staring at the roof of his tent. The dream had been so real that he found himself turning his head, just to check that Jade wasn't there. But she was right. What was he doing when he had so many people who loved him?

He wanted to give life a second chance, he realised. He wanted to talk to Jade again, to try and work things out between them. He wanted to take a risk on his new friends, to see what he could make of his life. And he had to start asking for what he really needed. And have the courage to walk his own path through the ups and downs that were always going to be part of his life.

He unzipped the flap of his tent with a shaking hand and pushed himself up to a standing position. Black dots danced in front of his eyes, and he had to sit down on a rock for a couple of minutes just to catch his breath.

He left everything and started walking. Didn't even stop to put on his boots, because the effort of pulling them on would have exhausted what little mental strength he had.

Jade spent an hour waiting outside the hostel in the morning, anxious not to miss the mountain rescue. Eight o'clock sharp three cars pulled up outside. One was her police friends from yesterday, and the other two had mountain rescue stickers on the outside.

The leader of the group was an older man with a weathered face that showed he'd been doing this a while. He didn't bother with any niceties, but Jade didn't mind. She knew his type. Gruff on the outside, heart of gold on the inside. 'Helicopter's been over already this morning, we found his tent. Let a man down to it, but there was no one there.'

Oh shit. Jade didn't know whether to be relieved that they hadn't found Nick dead, or worried because he had left his tent. But couldn't he have just gone off for a walk? She clung onto that possibility.

'Anyway, it's about eight miles in that way.' He pointed up the valley. 'Plan is now to go in as far as we can by vehicle. Then continue on foot until we get to his tent and do a sweep with the dog, try to see which way he might have gone.' He looked at her again. 'But I have to warn you, it's not looking good. They found his mobile phone and GPS watch in his tent. And he'd even left his boots.'

Jade swore mentally, her hope almost evaporating. Nick would never leave his precious watch. 'I'm coming with you.'

He looked her up and down, gaze coming to rest on her grubby trainers, then his gaze softened. 'We'll be pretty fast. Are you sure you'll be able to keep up?'

She must look very young to him, Jade realised. She squared her shoulders, accepting the challenge. 'Just you watch me.'

He looked at her for another few seconds, as if assessing something, then nodded decisively. 'Fine. But you do exactly what you're told, you hear? I don't want you becoming another casualty we have to deal with.' He turned away, ready to issue orders to the others in the group, but Jade touched him gently on the shoulder.

'I want to thank you all, for giving up your time to do this.' She was proud of how strong and firm her voice sounded. 'It means a lot to me.'

The man looked at her wordlessly for a few seconds. Was that embarrassment she saw on his face, or just simple modesty? Then he patted her shoulder gently. 'Don't you worry. We'll find him.'

Nick rested in a patch of heather, taking deep breaths to slow the pounding of his heart. Two minutes. Just two minutes rest. Then he would carry on. He counted out the seconds aloud, anxious not to lose track of time. He had no idea how far he'd come. It felt like miles, but in his current state it could be much less. Still, he could no longer see his tent, which meant he had come quite a way. He had heard a helicopter fly over a while ago while he was taking another rest, buried in the heather to try and shelter from the wind. Maybe they were looking for him? He was so terribly thirsty, but he didn't dare drink from the stream again.

He forced himself up, though every inch of his body protested at the movement and he felt like retching again. He had to go. Find Jade. And tell her how much he loved her.

Thank goodness Glasgow was so hilly. Walking around the city had definitely made her fit. But without her recent running stints Jade knew she would never have managed it. The group set a pace which had her tiring after barely a mile. She pushed herself to the limit, knowing that she had to do this. She couldn't just wait around for news.

She lost track of the time they spent walking. Didn't even dare to pull out her phone to check the time in case she fell behind. And then, in the distance, she saw a figure stumbling down the mountainside opposite.

'That's him.' She pointed.

'Don't get your hopes up.' The woman who was walking next to her kept her tone even. 'It could be anyone.'

Jade knew the comment was well-meaning, but she was sure of herself. She would have quickened her pace, but they were already walking as fast as she could manage without running.

She knew as soon as Nick caught sight of them, because he stopped, swaying slightly, shading his eyes with his hand. Or was he rubbing his forehead? She couldn't tell at this distance. They quickly descended to meet him.

When she was just twenty paces from him he looked at her, and cracked a smile that was more of a grimace. 'Jade. You came. I love you.'

And then he dropped to the ground at her feet.

Jade knelt down on the muddy track, lifting Nick's head onto her lap, and watched while the professionals did what they were trained to do. She stroked a finger gently down his cheek and whispered quietly in his ear. 'I love you too.'

Was that a flicker of his eyelids? She looked again, but there was nothing, and for one moment she thought she had imagined it. Then she saw his mouth curve into a faint smile, and her heart leaped. He was going to be OK. He had to be. Because she wasn't ready to lose another person she loved so soon.

Epilogue: Three Weeks Later

Jade held Nick's hand firmly as they walked along the country track.

'So what do you think of the little eco pods? Pretty cool right?' He flashed a grin at her.

She nodded. 'Yeah. A bit crowded with four of us in there, but they're great. Better than camping.'

Nick rolled his eyes. 'One day I'll get you enthusiastic about camping.'

She squeezed his hand. 'I would have thought you'd go off camping after your latest adventures.'

'Never.' Nick squeezed back, then dropped her hand to drape an arm around her shoulders. 'Thanks for coming to find me.'

'Yeah, like you haven't said that a hundred times. A million, maybe. It was nothing.' Jade leaned her head into his shoulder briefly. 'Anyway, I'm keeping an eye on you now.'

'You don't have to, honestly. Sean gave me a right talking to. I don't think I've ever seen someone so angry.' Nick had the grace to blush.

'How's the CBT going?' Jade asked.

Nick took a deep breath, then let it out. 'OK, I guess. It still feels a bit weird talking to a complete stranger about things, but I'll try anything if it has a chance of helping. I'll keep you posted.' He gave her a look that revealed just how hard it was for him to open himself up like that.

She pulled him down towards her so she could give him a light kiss on the cheek, just to show that she understood. Then she motioned with her head towards where Jamie walked about twenty metres in front of them, discussing something with Carina animatedly. 'Have you talked your plans over with Jamie?'

'Weren't you listening when we were talking about it in bed last night?' Nick suddenly stopped walking and turned to her.

It was Jade's turn to blush. 'Must have fallen asleep. All that fresh mountain air from yesterday.'

Nick just looked at her with a big grin and said nothing.

'Come on, spit it out.' Jade took a pretend swipe at him. 'A girl could waste away here while you get to the point.'

He laughed and pulled her to him, crushing her against his chest while he kissed the top of her head. 'God, Jade, I love you. Never change.'

Jade tapped her foot in mock impatience, although she couldn't help laughing too. 'Still waiting.'

'It's all sorted. The money Archie's family promised us should be enough to buy two of those fancy wheelchairs, and we're going to apply somewhere for funding for a minibus. The plan is to try and get up and running to do trips on the weekends. Jamie's going to use his business to take bookings. Stevie also offered to help up both out. He's well excited. And, it means I can fit it in around my day job for the time being.'

'So you don't have any plans to ditch Awesome Andy and the gang just yet?' Jade teased.

Nick sighed. 'Not yet. I'd love to though. Maybe if this becomes a success.'

'One step at a time.' Jade kissed him, properly this time. 'Anyway, I've got some good news of my own. I think I might have found someone who is interested in my book proposal. If it's true, then all I have to do is actually finish the thing.'

'Your book?' Nick took her shoulders and looked at her. 'Jeez, you kept that quiet. Why didn't you tell me? When did you hear about it?'

Jade just smiled. 'I wanted to wait until they sent me a proper contract. You know, not to jinx it. But I realised just now that it's too big a piece of news to keep to myself. Let's catch up to the others first, then I can tell all of you all the details at the same time.'

She nodded to where the other two could be seen some way off, still too engrossed in their conversation to notice that there was no one behind them. 'Looks like Jamie has yet another reason not to go to Canada now.'

Nick just laughed, pulling her to her feet, and they walked off hand in hand down the grassy path.

THE END

Author Note

This book grew out of a wish to write about ordinary people who are struggling with their mental health but just getting on with their lives as best as they can. You'll find a diverse range of characters in this book, which represents the Glasgow I know and love. If you liked the book please tell a friend, or leave a review, so that other people can enjoy it as much as you did.

I am aware that this book contains subjects which some people may find emotional or triggering. If this is the case then I really recommend that you talk to someone, whether that be a trusted friend, or a qualified professional. There are lots of organisations which can provide information and assistance, and an internet search will help you find them, or you can always talk to your local doctor.

Stevie's app for his prosthetic is a work of fiction, although with the pace of current technology advancements I can't imagine that it will be too long before it becomes a reality. The Necropolis is real though, and the view from the top is as stunning as I have described. If you have never visited Glasgow then I would invite you to make a trip and experience all that the city has to offer.

Acknowledgements

As with any project, there are lots of people who have contributed to making this book a reality, and thanks need to go to them.

My family, for always encouraging me to follow my dreams and telling me I can do anything.

The writer Kate Walker, for her brilliant teaching on a number of romance writing courses, and for introducing me to the Romantic Novelists' Association.

The RNA, for their excellent New Writers' Scheme, the sole purpose of which is to encourage aspiring writers, and all the other supportive and friendly people who I've met through the organisation.

The Walkers' Stalkers writing group, for all their encouragement when I was starting out, and their ongoing support.

Christina Petrie, for casting her professional eye over early versions of my manuscripts.

My wonderful neighbours, for making me laugh and supplying me with plenty of food when things get tough.

Cliff, for making a shepherd's pie so good it just had to go in a book.

I also want to thank all the people, both in real life and on the internet, who have been so open about their struggles with mental health. There are too many to list here, and some of them wouldn't want to be named, but I have found Matt Haig and @Liv1204 particularly inspiring.

And last but by no means least, I owe a big thanks to my editor at Harper Impulse, Charlotte Ledger, for seeing the potential in my writing, and working with me to make this book what it is. Plus all the rest of the Harper Impulse team who have helped put this book together.

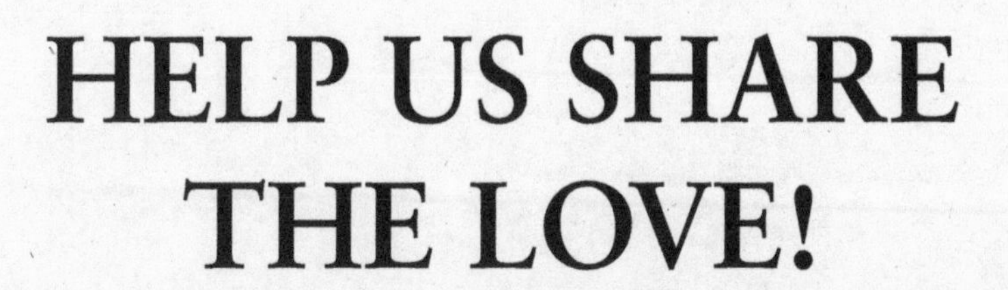

HELP US SHARE THE LOVE!

If you love this wonderful book as much as we do then please share your reviews online.

Leaving reviews makes a huge difference and helps our books reach even more readers.

So get reviewing and sharing, we want to hear what you think!

Love, HarperImpulse x

Please leave your reviews online!

amazon.co.uk kobo goodreads Lovereading  iBooks

And on social!

/HarperImpulse @harperimpulse

@HarperImpulse

